CHOKE

Chuck Palahniuk's novels include the bestselling *Haunted*, *Fight Club*, *Diary*, *Survivor*, *Invisible Monsters*, *Lullaby* and *Rant*. He is also the author of two non-fiction books, *Fugitives and Refugees*, a profile of Portland, Oregon, and *Non-Fiction*. He lives in the Pacific Northwest.

ALSO BY CHUCK PALAHNIUK

CHUCK PALAHNIUK

Choke

VINTAGE BOOKS
London

Published by Vintage 2008

2 4 6 8 10 9 7 5 3 1

Portions of this book have appeared in *Playboy*

First published in Great Britain in 2001 by Jonathan Cape
First published by Vintage in 2002

Vintage
Random House, 20 Vauxhall Bridge Road,
London SW1V 2SA

www.vintage-books.co.uk

Addresses for companies within The Random House Group Limited
can be found at: www.randomhouse.co.uk/offices.htm

The Random House Group Limited Reg. No. 954009

A CIP catalogue record for this book
is available from the British Library

ISBN 9780099535256

The Random House Group Limited supports The Forest
Stewardship Council (FSC), the leading international forest
certification organisation. All our titles that are printed on
Greenpeace approved FSC certified paper carry the FSC logo.
Our paper procurement policy can be found at:
www.rbooks.co.uk/environment

Printed in the UK by CPI Bookmarque, Croydon, CR0 4TD

For Lump.

Forever.

Choke

Chapter 1

If you're going to read this, don't bother.

After a couple pages, you won't want to be here. So forget it. Go away. Get out while you're still in one piece.

Save yourself.

There has to be something better on television. Or since you have so much time on your hands, maybe you could take a night course. Become a doctor. You could make something out of yourself. Treat yourself to a dinner out. Color your hair.

You're not getting any younger.

What happens here is first going to piss you off. After that it just gets worse and worse.

What you're getting here is a stupid story about a stupid little boy. A stupid true life story about nobody you'd ever want to meet. Picture this little spaz being about waist high with a handful of blond hair, combed and parted on one side. Picture the icky little shit smiling in old school photos with some of his baby teeth missing and his first adult teeth coming in crooked. Picture him wearing a stupid sweater striped blue and yellow, a birthday sweater that used to be his favorite. Even that young, picture him biting his dickhead fingernails. His favorite shoes are Keds. His favorite food, fucking corn dogs.

Imagine some dweeby little boy wearing no seat belt and riding in a stolen school bus with his mommy after dinner. Only there's a police car parked at their motel so the Mommy just blows on past at sixty or seventy miles an hour.

This is about a stupid little weasel who, for sure, used to be about the stupidest little rat fink crybaby twerp that ever lived.

The little cooz.

The Mommy says, "We'll have to hurry," and they drive uphill on a narrow road, their back wheels wagging from side to side on the ice. In their headlights the snow looks blue, spreading from the edge of the road out into the dark forest.

Picture this all being his fault. The little peckerwood.

The Mommy stops the bus a little ways back from the base of a rock cliff, so the headlights glare against its white face, and she says, "Here's as far as we're going to get," and the words come boiling out as white clouds that show how big inside her lungs are.

The Mommy sets the parking brake and says, "You can get out, but leave your coat in the bus."

Picture this stupid runt letting the Mommy stand him right

2

in front of the school bus. This bogus little Benedict Arnold just stands looking into the glare of the headlights, and lets the Mommy pull the favorite sweater off over his head. This wimpy little squealer just stands there in the snow, half naked, while the bus's motor races, and the roar echoes off the cliff, and the Mommy disappears to somewhere behind him in the night and the cold. The headlights blind him, and the motor noise covers any sound of the trees scraping together in wind. The air is too cold to breathe more than a mouthful at a time so this little mucous membrane tries to breathe twice as fast.

He doesn't run away. He doesn't do anything.

From somewhere behind him, the Mommy says, "Now whatever you do, don't turn around."

The Mommy tells him how there used to be a beautiful girl in ancient Greece, the daughter of a potter.

Like every time she gets out of jail and comes back to claim him, the kid and the Mommy have been in a different motel every night. They'll eat fast food for every meal, and just drive all day, every day. At lunch today, the kid tried to eat his corn dog while it was still too hot and almost swallowed it whole, but it got stuck and he couldn't breathe or talk until the Mommy charged around from her side of the table.

Then two arms were hugging him from behind, lifting him off his feet, and the Mommy whispered, "Breathe! Breathe, damn it!"

After that, the kid was crying, and the entire restaurant crowded around.

At that moment, it seemed the whole world cared what happened to him. All those people were hugging him and petting his hair. Everybody asked if he was okay.

It seemed that moment would last forever. That you had to risk your life to get love. You had to get right to the edge of death to ever be saved.

"Okay. There," the Mommy said as she wiped his mouth, "now I've given you life."

The next moment, a waitress recognized him from a photograph on an old milk carton, and then the Mommy was driving the evil little squealer back to their motel room at seventy miles an hour.

On the way back, they'd got off the highway and bought a can of black spray paint.

Even after all their rushing around, where they've arrived is the middle of nowhere in the middle of the night.

Now from behind him, this stupid kid hears the rattle of the Mommy shaking the spray paint, the marble inside the can knocking from end to end, and the Mommy says how the ancient Greek girl was in love with a young man.

"But the young man was from another country and had to go back," the Mommy says.

There's a hissing sound, and the kid smells spray paint. The bus motor changes sounds, clunks, running faster now and louder, and the bus rocks a little from tire to tire.

So the last night the girl and her lover would be together, the Mommy says, the girl brought a lamp and set it so it threw the lover's shadow on the wall.

The hiss of spray paint stops and starts. There's a short hiss, after that a longer hiss.

And the Mommy says how the girl traced the outline of her lover's shadow so she would always have a record of how he looked, a document of this exact moment, the last moment they would be together.

Our little crybaby just keeps looking straight into the headlights. His eyes water, and when he shuts them he can see the light shining, red, right through his eyelids, his own flesh and blood.

And the Mommy says how the next day, the girl's lover was gone, but his shadow was still there.

Just for a second, the kid looks back to where the Mommy is tracing the outline of his stupid shadow against the cliff face, only the boy's so far away that his shadow falls a head taller than the mother. His skinny arms look big around. His stubby legs stretch long. His pinched shoulders spread wide.

And the Mommy tells him, "Don't look. Don't move a muscle or you'll ruin all my work."

And the doofus little tattletale turns to stare into the headlights.

The can of spray paint hisses, and the Mommy says that before the Greeks, nobody had any art. This was how painting pictures was invented. She tells the story of how the girl's father used the outline on the wall to model a clay version of the young man, and that's the way sculpture was invented.

For serious, the Mommy told him, "Art never comes from happiness."

Here is where symbols were born.

The kid stands, shivering now in the glare, trying to not move, and the Mommy keeps working, telling the huge shadow how someday it will teach people everything that she's taught it. Someday it will be a doctor saving people. Returning them to happiness. Or something better than happiness: peace.

It'll be respected.

Someday.

This is even after the Easter Bunny turned out to be a lie. Even after Santa Claus and the Tooth Fairy and Saint Christopher and Newtonian physics and the Niels Bohr model of the atom, this stupid, stupid kid still believed the Mommy.

Someday, when he's grown up, the Mommy tells the shadow,

the kid will come back here and see how he's grown into the exact outline she'd planned for him this night.

The kid's bare arms shake with the cold.

And the Mommy said, "Control yourself, damn it. Hold still or you'll ruin everything."

And the kid tried to feel warmer, but no matter how bright they were, the headlights didn't give off any heat.

"I need to make a clear outline," the Mommy said. "If you tremble, you'll turn out all blurred."

It wasn't until years later, until this stupid little loser was through college with honors and he'd busted his hump to get into the University of Southern California School of Medicine—until he was twenty-four years old and in his second year of medical school, when his mother was diagnosed and he was named as her guardian—it wasn't until then that it dawned on this little stooge that growing strong and rich and smart was only the first half of your life story.

Now the kid's ears ache with the cold. He feels dizzy and hyperventilated. His little stool-pigeon chest is all dimpled chicken skin. His nipples are pinched up by the cold into hard red pimples, and the little ejaculate tells himself: *For real, I deserve this.*

And the Mommy says, "Try to at least stand up straight."

The kid rolls his shoulders back and imagines the headlights are a firing squad. He deserves pneumonia. He deserves tuberculosis.

See also: Hypothermia.

See also: Typhoid fever.

And the Mommy says, "After tonight, I'm not going to be around to nag you."

The bus motor idles, putting out a long tornado of blue smoke.

And the Mommy says, "So hold still, and don't make me spank you."

And sure as hell, this little brat deserved to get spanked. He deserved whatever he got. This is the deluded little rube who really thought the future would be any better. If you just worked hard enough. If you just learned enough. Ran fast enough. Everything would turn out right, and your life would amount to something.

The wind gusts and dry grains of snow scatter down from the trees, each flake stinging against his ears and cheeks. More snow melts between the laces of his shoes.

"You'll see," the Mommy says. "This will be worth a little suffering."

This would be a story he could tell his own son. Someday.

The ancient girl, the Mommy tells him, she never saw her lover ever again.

And the kid is stupid enough to think a picture or a sculpture or a story could somehow replace anybody you love.

And the Mommy says, "You have so much to look forward to."

It's hard to swallow, but this is the stupid, lazy, ridiculous little kid who just stood shaking, squinting into the glare and the roar, and who thought the future would be so bright. Picture anybody growing up so stupid he didn't know that hope is just another phase you'll grow out of. Who thought you could make something, anything, that would last forever.

It feels stupid even to remember this stuff. It's a wonder he's lived this long.

So, again, if you're going to read this, don't.

This isn't about somebody brave and kind and dedicated. He isn't anybody you're going to fall in love with.

Just so you know, what you're reading is the complete and re-lentless story of an addict. Because in most twelve-step recovery programs, the fourth step makes you take inventory of your life. Every lame, suck-ass moment of your life, you have to get a note-book and write it down. A complete inventory of your crimes. That way, every sin is right at your fingertips. Then you have to fix it all. This goes for alcoholics, drug abusers, and overeaters, as well as sex addicts.

This way you can go back and review the worst of your life any time you want.

Because supposedly, those who forget the past are condemned to repeat it.

So if you're reading this, to tell the truth, it's really none of your business.

That stupid little boy, that cold night, all of this will just be-come more of the stupid shit to think about during sex, to keep from shooting your load. If you're a guy.

This is the weak little suck-ass whose mommy said, "Just hold on a little while longer, just try a little harder and everything will be all right."

Hah.

The Mommy who said, "Someday, this will be worth all our effort, I promise."

And this little dickwad, this stupid stupid little sucker, he stood there this whole time shaking, half naked in the snow, and really believed somebody could even promise something so im-possible.

So if you think this is going to save you . . .

If you think anything is going to save you . . .

Please consider this your final warning.

Chapter 2

It's dark and starting to rain when I get to the church, and Nico's waiting for somebody to unlock the side door, hugging herself in the cold.

"Hold on to these for me," she says and hands me a warm fistful of silk.

"Just for a couple hours," she says. "I don't have any pockets." She's wearing a jacket made of some fake orange suede with a bright orange fur collar. The skirt of her flower-print dress shows hanging out. No pantyhose. She climbs up the steps to the church door, her feet careful and turned sideways in black spike heels.

What she hands me is warm and damp.

It's her panties. And she smiles.

Inside the glass doors, a woman pushes a mop around. Nico knocks on the glass, then points at her wristwatch. The woman dunks the mop back in a bucket. She lifts the mop and squeezes it. She leans the mop handle near the doorway and then fishes a ring of keys out of her smock pocket. While she's unlocking the door, the woman shouts through the glass.

"You people are in Room 234 tonight," the woman says. "The Sunday school room."

By now, more people are in the parking lot. People walk up the steps, saying hi, and I stash Nico's panties in my pocket. Behind me, other people hustle the last few steps to catch the door before it swings shut. Believe it or not, you know everybody here.

These people are legends. Every single one of these men and women you've heard about for years.

In the 1950s a leading vacuum cleaner tried a little design improvement. It added a spinning propeller, a razor-sharp blade mounted a few inches inside the end of the vacuum hose. Inrushing air would spin the blade, and the blade would chop up any lint or string or pet hair that might clog the hose.

At least that was the plan.

What happened is a lot of these men raced to the hospital emergency room with their dicks mangled.

At least that's the myth.

That old urban legend about the surprise party for the pretty housewife, how all her friends and family hid in one room, and when they burst out and yelled "Happy birthday" they found her stretched out on the sofa with the family dog licking peanut butter from between her legs . . .

Well, she's real.

The legendary woman who gives head to guys who are driving, only the guy loses control of his car and hits the brakes so hard the woman bites him in half, I know them.

Those men and women, they're all here.

These people are the reason every emergency room has a diamond-tipped drill. For tapping a hole through the thick bottoms of champagne and soda bottles. To relieve the suction.

These are the people who come waddling in from the night, saying they tripped and fell on the zucchini, the lightbulb, the Barbie doll, the billiard balls, the struggling gerbil.

See also: The pool cue.

See also: The teddy bear hamster.

They slipped in the shower and fell, bull's-eye, on a greased shampoo bottle. They're always being attacked by a person or persons unknown and assaulted with candles, with baseballs, with hard-boiled eggs, flashlights, and screwdrivers that now need removing. Here are the guys who get stuck in the water inlet port of their whirlpool hot tub.

Halfway down the hallway to Room 234, Nico pulls me against the wall. She waits until some people have walked past us and says, "I know a place we can go."

Everybody else is going into the pastel Sunday school room, and Nico smiles after them. She twirls one finger next to her ear, the international sign language for crazy, and she says, "Losers." She pulls me the other way, toward a sign that says *Women*.

Among the folks in Room 234 is the bogus county health official who calls to quiz fourteen-year-old girls about the appearance of their vagina.

Here's the cheerleader who gets her stomach pumped and they find a pound of sperm. Her name is LouAnn.

The guy in the movie theater with his dick stuck through the bottom of a box of popcorn, you can call him Steve, and tonight his sorry ass is sitting around a paint-stained table, squeezed into a child's plastic Sunday school chair.

All these people you think are a big joke. Go ahead and frigging laugh your frigging head off.

These are sexual compulsives.

All these people you thought were urban legends, well, they're human. Complete with names and faces. Jobs and families. College degrees and arrest records.

In the women's room, Nico pulls me down onto the cold tile and squats over my hips, digging me out of my pants. With her other hand, Nico cups the back of my neck and pulls my face, my open mouth, into hers. Her tongue wrestling against my tongue, she's wetting the head of my dog with the pad of her thumb. She's pushing my jeans down off my hips. She lifts the hem of her dress in a curtsey with her eyes closed and her head tilted a little back. She settles her pubes hard against my pubes and says something against the side of my neck.

I say, "God, you're so beautiful," because for the next few minutes I can.

And Nico pulls back to look at me and says, "What's that supposed to mean?"

And I say, "I don't know." I say, "Nothing, I guess." I say, "Never mind."

The tile smells disinfected and feels gritty under my butt. The walls go up to an acoustical tile ceiling and air vents furry with dust and crud. There's that blood smell from the rusty metal box for used napkins.

"Your release form," I say. I snap my fingers. "Did you bring it?"

Nico lifts her hips a little and then drops, lifts and settles herself. Her head still back, her eyes still closed, she fishes inside the neckline of her dress and brings out a folded square of blue paper and drops it on my chest.

I say, "Good girl," and take the pen clipped on my shirt pocket.

A little higher each time, Nico lifts her hips and sits down hard. Grinding a little front to back. With a hand planted on the top of each thigh, she pushes herself up, then drops.

"Round the world," I say. "Round the world, Nico."

She opens her eyes maybe halfway and looks down at me, and I make a stirring motion with the pen, the way you'd stir a cup of coffee. Even through my clothes, I'm getting the grid of the tile engraved in my back.

"Round the world, now," I say. "Do it for me, baby."

And Nico closes her eyes and gathers her skirt around her waist with both hands. She settles all her weight on my hips and swings one foot over my belly. She swings the other foot around so she's still on me, but facing my feet.

"Good," I say and unfold the blue paper. I spread it flat against her round humped back and sign my name at the bottom, on the blank that says *sponsor*. Through her dress, you can feel the thick back of her bra, elastic with five or six little wire hooks. You can feel her rib bones under a thick layer of muscle.

Right now, down the hall in Room 234 is the girlfriend of your best friend's cousin, the girl who almost died banging herself on the stick shift of a Ford Pinto after she ate Spanish fly. Her name is Mandy.

There's the guy who snuck into a clinic in a white coat and gave pelvic exams.

There's the guy who always lies in his motel room, naked on top of the covers with his morning boner, pretending to sleep until the maid walks in.

All those rumored friends of friends of friends of friends . . . they're all here.

The man crippled by the automatic milking machine, his name is Howard.

The girl hanging naked from the shower curtain rod, half dead from autoerotic asphyxiation, she's Paula and she's a sexaholic.

Hello, Paula.

Give me your subway feelers. Your trench coat flashers.

The men mounting cameras inside the lip of some women's room toilet bowl.

The guy rubbing his semen on the flaps of deposit envelopes at automatic tellers.

All the peeping toms. The nymphos. The dirty old men. The restroom lurkers. The handballers.

All these sexual bogeymen and -women your mom warned you about. All those scary cautionary tales.

We're all here. Alive and unwell.

This is the twelve-step world of sexual addiction. Compulsive sexual behavior. Every night of the week, they meet in the back room of some church. In some community center conference room. Every night, in every city. You even have virtual meetings on the Internet.

My best friend, Denny, I met him at a sexaholics meeting. Denny had got up to the point where he needed to masturbate fifteen times a day just to break even. Anymore, he could barely make a fist, and he was worried about what all that petroleum jelly might do to him, long term.

He'd considered changing to some lotion, but anything made to soften skin seemed to be counterproductive.

Denny and all these men and women you think are so horrible or funny or pathetic, here's where they all let their hair down. This is where we all go to open up.

Here are prostitutes and sex criminals out on a three-hour release from their minimum-security jail, elbow to elbow with women who love gang bangs and men who give head in adult bookstores. The hooker reunites with the john here. The molester faces the molested.

Nico brings her big white ass almost to the top of my dog and bangs herself down. Up and then down. Riding her guts tight around the length of me. Pistoning up and then slamming down. Pushing off against my thighs, the muscles in her arms get bigger and bigger. My thighs under each of her hands go numb and white.

"Now that we know each other," I say, "Nico? Would you say you liked me?"

She turns to look back over her shoulder at me, "When you're a doctor, you'll be able to write prescriptions for anything, right?"

That's if I ever go back to school. Never underestimate the power of a medical degree for getting you laid. I bring my hands up, each hand open against the stretched smooth underside of each thigh. To help lift her, I figure, and she twines her cool soft fingers through mine.

Sleeved tight around my dog, without looking back, she says, "My friends bet me money that you're already married."

I hold her smooth white ass in my hands.

"How much?" I say.

I tell Nico that her friends might be right.

The truth is, every son raised by a single mom is pretty much born married. I don't know, but until your mom dies it seems like all the other women in your life can never be more than just your mistress.

In the modern Oedipal story, it's the mother who kills the father and then takes the son.

And it's not as if you can divorce your mother.

Or kill her.

And Nico says, "What do you mean *all the other women?* Jeez, how many are we talking about?" She says, "I'm glad we used a rubber."

For a complete list of sexual partners, I'd have to check my fourth step. My moral inventory notebook. The complete and relentless history of my addiction.

That's if I ever go back and complete the damn step.

For all those people in Room 234, working on their twelve steps in a sexaholics meeting is a valuable important tool for understanding and recovering from . . . well, you get the idea.

For me, it's a terrific how-to seminar. Tips. Techniques. Strategies for getting laid you never dreamed of. Personal contacts. When they tell their stories, these addict people are frigging brilliant. Plus there's the jail girls out for their three hours of sex addict talk therapy.

Nico included.

Wednesday nights mean Nico. Friday nights mean Tanya. Sundays mean Leeza. Leeza sweats yellow with nicotine. You can almost put your hands around her waist since her abs are rockhard from coughing. Tanya always smuggles in some rubber sex toy, usually a dildo or a string of latex beads. Some sexual equivalent of the prize in a box of cereal.

The old rule about how a thing of beauty is a joy forever, in my experience, even the most beauteous thing is only a joy for about three hours, tops. After that, she'll want to tell you all about her childhood traumas. Part of meeting these jail girls is it's so sweet to look at your watch and know she'll be behind bars in half an hour.

It's a Cinderella story, only at midnight she turns back into a fugitive.

It's not that I don't love these women. I love them just as much as you'd love a magazine centerfold, a fuck video, an adult website, and for sure, for a sexaholic that can be buckets of love. And it's not that Nico loves me much, either.

This isn't so much romance as it is opportunity. You put twenty sexaholics around a table, night after night, and don't be surprised.

Plus the sexaholic recovery books they sell here, it's every way you always wanted to get laid but didn't know how. Of course, all this is to help you realize you're a sex junkie. It's delivered in a kind of "if you do any of the following things, you may be an alcoholic" checklist. Their helpful hints include:

Do you cut the lining out of your bathing suit so your genitals show through?

Do you leave your fly or blouse open and pretend to hold conversations in glass telephone booths, standing so your clothes gap open with no underwear inside?

Do you jog without a bra or athletic supporter in order to attract sexual partners?

My answer to all the above is, *Well, I do now!*

Plus, being a pervert here is not your fault. Compulsive sexual behavior is not about always getting your dick sucked. It's a disease. It's a physical addiction just waiting for the *Diagnostic Statistical Manual* to give it a code of its own so treatment can be billed to medical insurance.

The story is even Bill Wilson, a founder of Alcoholics Anonymous, couldn't overcome the sex monkey on his back, and spent his sober life cheating on his wife and filled with guilt.

The story is that sex addicts become dependent on a body chemistry created by constant sex. Orgasms flood the body

17

with endorphins that kill pain and tranquilize you. Sex addicts are really addicted to the endorphins, not the sex. Sex addicts have lower natural levels of monoamine oxidase. Sex addicts really crave the peptide phenylethylamine that might be triggered by danger, by infatuation, by risk and fear.

For a sex addict, your tits, your dick, your clit or tongue or asshole is a shot of heroin, always there, always ready to use. Nico and I love each other as much as any junkie loves his fix.

Nico bears down hard, bucking my dog against the front wall of her insides, using two wet fingers on herself.

I say, "What if that cleaning woman walks in?"

And Nico stirs me around inside herself, saying, "Oh yeah. That would be so hot."

Me, I can't help imagining what kind of a big shining butt print we're going to polish into the waxed tile. A row of sinks look down. Fluorescent lights flicker, and reflected in the chrome pipes under each sink you can see Nico's throat is one long straight tube, her head thrown back, eyes closed, her breath panting out at the ceiling. Her big flower-print breasts. Her tongue hangs off to one side. The juice coming off her is scalding hot.

To keep from triggering I say, "What all did you tell your folks about us?"

And Nico says, "They want to meet you."

I think about the perfect thing to say next, but it doesn't really matter. You can say anything here. Enemas, orgies, animals, admit to any obscenity, and nobody is ever surprised.

In Room 234, everybody compares war stories. Everybody takes their turn. That's the first part of the meeting, the check-in part.

After that they'll read the readings, the prayer things, they'll discuss the topic for the night. They'll each work on one of the twelve steps. The first step is to admit you're powerless. You have an addiction, and you can't stop. The first step is to tell your story, all the worst parts. Your lowest lows.

The problem with sex is the same as with any addiction. You're always recovering. You're always backsliding. Acting out. Until you find something to fight for, you settle for something to fight against. All these people who say they want a life free from sexual compulsion, I mean forget it. I mean, what could ever be better than sex?

For sure, even the worst blow job is better than, say, sniffing the best rose . . . watching the greatest sunset. Hearing children laugh.

I think that I shall never see a poem as lovely as a hot-gushing, butt-cramping, gut-hosing orgasm.

Painting a picture, composing an opera, that's just something you do until you find the next willing piece of ass.

The minute something better than sex comes along, you call me. Have me paged.

None of these people in Room 234 are Romeos or Casanovas or Don Juans. These aren't Mata Haris or Salomes. These are people you shake hands with every day. Not ugly, not beautiful. You stand next to these legends on the elevator. They serve you coffee. These mythological creatures tear your ticket stub. They cash your paycheck. They put the Communion wafer on your tongue.

In the women's room, inside Nico, I cross my arms behind my head.

For the next I don't know how long, I've got no problems in the world. No mother. No medical bills. No shitty museum job. No jerk-off best friend. Nothing.

I feel nothing.

To make it last, to keep from triggering, I tell Nico's flowered backside how beautiful she is, how sweet she is and how much I need her. Her skin and hair. To make it last. Because this is the only time I can say it. Because the moment this is over, we'll hate each other. The moment we find ourselves cold and sweating on the bathroom floor, the moment after we both come, we won't want to even look at each other.

The only person we'll hate more than each other is ourselves.

These are the only few minutes I can be human.

Just for these minutes, I don't feel lonely.

And riding me up and down, Nico says, "So when do I get to meet your mom?"

And, "Never," I say. "That's impossible, I mean."

And Nico, her whole body clenched and jacking me with her boiling wet insides, she says, "She in prison or a loony bin or something?"

Yeah, for a lot of her life.

Ask any guy about his mom during sex, and you can delay the big blast forever.

And Nico says, "So is she dead now?"

And I say, "Sort of."

Chapter 3

Anymore, when I go to visit my mom, I don't even pretend to be myself.

Hell, I don't even pretend to know myself very well.

Not anymore.

My mom, it's like her sole occupation at this point is losing weight. What's left of her is so thin, she has to be a puppet. Some kind of special effect. There's just not enough of her yellow skin left to fit a real person inside. Her thin puppet arms hover around on the blankets, always picking at bits of lint. Her shrunken head will collapse around the drinking straw in her mouth. When I used to come as myself, as Victor, her son Victor Mancini, none of those visits lasted ten minutes before she'd ring for the nurse and tell me she was just too tired.

Then one week, my mom thinks I'm some court-appointed public defender who represented her a couple times, Fred Hastings. Her face opens up when she sees me and she lies back into her stack of pillows and shakes her head a little, saying, "Oh, Fred." She says, "My fingerprints were all over those boxes of hair dye. It was reckless endangerment, open and shut, but it was still a brilliant sociopolitical action."

I tell her that's not how it looked on the store's security camera.

Plus, there was the kidnapping charge. It was all on videotape.

And she laughs, she actually laughs and says, "Fred, you were such a fool to try and save me."

She talks that way a half hour, mostly about that misguided incident with the hair dye. Then she asks me to bring her a newspaper from the dayroom.

In the hall outside her room is some doctor, a woman in a white coat holding a clipboard. She has, it looks like, long dark hair twisted into the shape of a little black brain on the back of her head. She's not wearing makeup so her face just looks like skin. A pair of black-framed glasses are folded and sticking out of her chest pocket.

Is she in charge of Mrs. Mancini, I ask.

The doctor looks at the clipboard. She unfolds the glasses and slips them on and looks again, the whole time saying, "Mrs. Mancini, Mrs. Mancini, Mrs. Mancini . . ."

She keeps clicking and unclicking a ballpoint pen in one hand.

I ask, "Why is she still losing weight?"

The skin along the parts in her hair, the skin above and behind the doctor's ears, is as clear and white as the skin inside her other tan lines must look. If women knew how their ears come across, the firm fleshy edge, the little dark hood at the top, all the smooth contours coiled and channeling you to the tight darkness inside, well, more women would wear their hair down.

"Mrs. Mancini," she says, "needs a feeding tube. She feels hunger, but she's forgotten what the feeling means. Consequently, she doesn't eat."

I say, "How much is this tube going to cost?"

A nurse down the hall calls, "Paige?"

This doctor looks at me in my britches and waistcoat, my powdered wig and buckle shoes, and she says, "What are you supposed to be?"

The nurse calls, "Miss Marshall?"

My job, it's too hard to explain here. "I just happen to be the backbone of early colonial America."

"Which is?" she says.

"An Irish indentured servant."

She just looks at me, nodding her head. Then she looks down at the chart. "It's either we put a tube into her stomach," the doctor says. "Or she'll starve to death."

I look into the dark secret insides of her ear and ask if we could maybe explore some other options.

Down the hall, the nurse stands with her fists planted on her hips and shouts, "Miss Marshall!"

And the doctor winces. She holds up an index finger to stop me talking, and she says, "Listen." She says, "I really do have to finish rounds. Let's talk more on your next visit."

Then she turns and walks the ten or twelve steps to where the nurse is waiting and says, "*Nurse* Gilman." She says, her voice

23

rushed and the words crushed together, "You can at least pay me the respect of calling me *Dr. Marshall.*" She says, "Especially in front of a *visitor.*" She says, "*Especially* if you're going to shout down the length of a hallway. It's a small courtesy, *Nurse* Gilman, but I think I've earned that, and I think if you start behaving like a professional yourself, you'll find everyone around you will be a great deal more cooperative. . . ."

By the time I get the newspaper from the dayroom, my mom's asleep. Her terrible yellow hands are crossed on her chest, a plastic hospital bracelet heat-sealed around one wrist.

Chapter 4

The moment Denny bends over, his wig falls off and lands in the mud and horse poop and about two hundred Japanese tourists giggle and crowd forward to get his shaved head on videotape.

I go, "Sorry," and go to pick up the wig. It's not very white anymore, and it smells bad since, for sure, about a million dogs and chickens take a leak here every day.

Since he's bent over, his cravat hangs in his face, blinding him. "Dude," Denny says, "tell me what's happening."

Here I am, the backbone of early colonial America.

The stupid shit we do for money.

From the edge of the town square, His Lord High Charlie, the colonial governor, is watching us, standing with his arms crossed, his feet planted about ten feet apart. Milkmaids carry around buckets of milk. Cobblers hammer on shoes. The blacksmith bangs away on the same piece of metal, pretending the same as everybody else not to be watching Denny bent over in the middle of the town square, getting locked in the stocks again.

"They caught me chewing gum, dude," Denny says to my feet.

Being bent over, his nose starts to run, and he sniffs. "For sure," he says and sniffs, "His Highness is going to blab to the town council this time."

The wooden top half of the stocks swings closed to hold him around the neck, and I snug it down, careful not to pinch his skin. I say, "Sorry, dude, that's got to be way cold." Then I do the padlock. Then I fish a rag out of my waistcoat pocket.

A clear little drop of snot dangles off the tip of Denny's nose, so I hold the rag against it and say, "Blow, dude."

Denny blows a long rattling goob I feel slam into the rag.

The rag's pretty nasty and full already, but all I'd have to do is offer him a nice clean facial tissue and I'd be next in line for a disciplinary action. There's about countless ways you can screw up around here.

On the back of his head, somebody's felt-penned "Eat me" in bright red, so I shake out his shitty wig and try to cover the writing, except the wig's soaked full of nasty brown water that trickles around the shaved sides of his head and drips off the tip of his nose.

"I'm banished for sure," he says and sniffs.

Cold and starting to shake, Denny says, "Dude, I feel air. . . . I think my shirt's pulled out of my breeches in back."

He's right, and tourists are shooting his butt crack from every angle. The colonial governor is eyeballing this, and the tourists keep right on taping as I grab Denny's waistband in both hands and tug it back up.

Denny says, "The good part about being in the stocks is I've racked up three weeks of sobriety." He says, "At least this way I can't go in the privy every half hour and, you know, beat off."

And I say, "Careful with that recovery stuff, dude. You're liable to explode."

I take his left hand and lock it in place, then his right hand. Denny's spent so much of this past summer in the stocks he has white rings around his wrists and neck where he never gets any sun.

"Monday," he says, "I forgot and wore my wristwatch."

The wig slides off again, landing smack wet in the mud. His cravat, soaked in snot and crap, flaps in his face. The Japanese all giggle as if this is a gag we'd rehearsed.

The colonial governor keeps staring at Denny and me for signs of us being historically inappropriate so he can lobby the town council to banish us to the wilderness, just boot us out the town gate and let the savages shoot arrows and massacre our unemployed butts.

"Tuesday," Denny tells my shoes, "His Highness saw I had Chap Stick on my lips."

Every time I pick up the stupid wig, it weighs more. This time I slap it against the side of my boot before spreading it over the "Eat me" words.

"This morning," Denny says and sniffs. He spits some brown gunk that got in his mouth. "Before lunch, Goodwife Landson caught me smoking a cigarette behind the meetinghouse. Then, while I'm bent over here, somebody's little shitface fourth-grader grabs my wig off and writes that shit on my head."

With my snot rag I wipe the worst of the mess away from his eyes and mouth.

Some black-and-white chickens, chickens with no eyes or only one leg, these deformed chickens wander over to peck at the shiny buckles on my boots. The blacksmith keeps beating his metal, two fast and then three slow beats, again and again, that you know is the bass line to an old Radiohead song he likes. Of course, he's ripped out of his mind on ecstasy.

A little milkmaid I know named Ursula catches my eye, and I shake my fist in front of my crotch, giving her the universal sign language for hand job. Blushing under her starchy white hat, Ursula slips a dainty pale hand out of her apron pocket and gives me the finger. Then she goes to jerk off some lucky cow all afternoon. That, and I know she lets the king's constable feel her up because one time he let me sniff his fingers.

Even from here, even over the horse shit, you can smell the reefer coming off her in a fog.

Milking cows, churning butter, for sure you know milkmaids must give great hand jobs.

"Goodwife Landson's a bitch," I tell Denny. "The minister guy says she gave him a scorching case of herpes."

Yeah, she's a Yankee blue blood from nine to five, but behind her back everybody knows she went to high school in Springburg where the whole football team knew her as Douche Lamprini.

This time the nasty wig stays in place. The colonial governor gives up glowering at us and goes inside the Customs House. The tourists wander on to other photo opportunities. It starts to rain.

"It's okay, dude," Denny says. "You don't have to stand out here with me."

This is just, for sure, another shitty day in the eighteenth century.

You wear an earring, you go to jail. Color your hair. Pierce your nose. Put on deodorant. Go directly to jail. Do not pass Go. Do not collect jack shit.

The Lord High Governor bends Denny over at least twice a week, for chewing tobacco, for wearing cologne, shaving his head.

Nobody in the 1730s had a goatee, His Governess will lecture Denny.

And Denny will sass him back, "Maybe the real cool colonists did."

And it's back to the stocks for Denny.

Our joke is Denny and me have been codependent since 1734. That's how far back we go. Since we met in a sexaholics meeting. Denny showed me an ad in the classifieds, and we both came to the same job interview.

Just being curious, at the interview, I asked if they'd hired a village whore yet.

The town council just looks at me. The hiring committee, even where nobody can see them, all six old guys wear those fake colonial wigs. They write everything with feathers, from birds, dipped in ink. The one in the middle, the colonial governor, sighs. He leans back so he can look at me through his wire-framed glasses. "Colonial Dunsboro," he says, "doesn't have a village whore."

Then I say, "Then how about the village idiot?"

The governor shakes his head, no.

"Pickpocket?"

No.

"Hangman?"

Certainly not.

This is the worst problem with living history museums. They always leave the best parts out. Like typhus. And opium. And scarlet letters. Shunning. Witch-burning.

"You've been warned," the governor says, "that all aspects of your behavior and appearance must coincide with our official period in history."

My job is I'm supposed to be some Irish indentured servant. For six dollars an hour, it's incredibly realistic.

The first week I was here, a girl got canned for humming an Erasure song while she was churning butter. It's like, yeah, Erasure is historic, but not historic enough. Even somebody as ancient as the Beach Boys can get you in trouble. It's like they don't even think of their stupid powdered wigs and breeches and buckle shoes as *retro*.

His Highness, he forbids tattoos. Nose rings have to stay in your locker while you're at work. You can't chew gum. You can't whistle any songs by the Beatles.

"Any violation of character," he says, "and you will be punished."

Punished?

"You'll be let go," he says. "Or you can spend two hours in the stocks."

Stocks?

"In the village square," he says.

He means bondage. Sadism. Role playing and public humiliation. The governor himself, he makes you wear clocked stockings and tight wool breeches with no underwear and calls this authentic. This is who wants women bent over in the stocks for just wearing nail polish. Either that or you're fired with no unemployment checks, nothing. And a bad job reference to boot. And for sure, nobody wants it on their résumé that they were a shitty candlemaker.

Being unmarried twenty-five-year-old guys in the eighteenth century, our options were pretty limited. Footman. Apprentice. Gravedigger. Cooper, whatever that is. Bootblack, whatever that is. Chimneysweep. Farmer. The minute they say town crier, Denny said, "Yeah. Okay. I can do that. Really, I spend half my life crying."

His Highness looks at Denny and says, "Those glasses you're wearing, do you need them?"

"Only to see with," Denny says.

I took the job because there are worse things than working with your best friend.

Sort-of best friend.

Still, you'd think this would be more fun, a fun job with a bunch of Drama Club types and community theater folks. Not this chain gang of throwbacks. These Puritan hypocrites.

If the Ye Old Town Council only knew Mistress Plain, the seamstress, is a needle freak. The miller is cooking crystal meth. The innkeeper deals acid to the busloads of bored teenagers who get dragged here on school field trips. These kids sit in rapt attention watching while Mistress Halloway cards wool and spins it into yarn, the whole time she's lecturing them on sheep reproduction and eating hashish johnnycake. These people, the potter on methadone, the glassblower on Percodans, and the silversmith popping Vicodins, they've found their niche. The stableboy, hiding his headphones under a tricorner hat, plugged in on Special K and twitching to his own private rave, they're all a bunch of hippie burnouts peddling their agrarian bullshit, but okay, that's just my opinion.

Even Farmer Reldon has his plot of primo weed out behind the corn and the pole beans and junk. Only he calls it hemp.

The only funny part about Colonial Dunsboro is maybe it's too authentic, but for all the wrong reasons. This whole crowd of losers and nutcases who hide out here because they can't make it in the real world, in real jobs—isn't this why we left England in the first place? To establish our own alternate reality. Weren't the

Pilgrims pretty much the crackpots of their time? For sure, instead of just wanting to believe something different about God's love, the losers I work with want to find salvation through compulsive behaviors.

Or through little power and humiliation games. Witness His Lord High Charlie behind lace curtains, just some failed drama major. Here, he's the law, watching whoever gets bent over, yanking his dog with one white-gloved hand. For sure, they don't teach you this in history class, but in colonial times, the person who got left in the stocks overnight was nothing less than fair game for everybody to nail. Men or women, anybody bent over had no way of knowing who was doing the ram job, and this was the real reason you never wanted to end up here unless you had a family member or a friend who'd stand with you the whole time. To protect you. To watch your ass, for real.

"Dude," Denny says. "It's my pants, again."

So I pull them back up.

The rain's wet Denny's shirt flat to his skinny back so the bones of his shoulders and the trail of his spine show through, even whiter than the unbleached cotton material. The mud's up around the tops of his wooden clogs and spilling in. Even with my hat on, my coat's getting soaked, and the damp makes my dog and dice all wadded up in the crotch of my wool breeches start to itch. Even the crippled chickens have clucked off to find somewhere dry.

"Dude," Denny says, and sniffs. "For serious, you don't have to stay."

From what I remember about physical diagnosis, Denny's pallor could mean liver tumors.

See also: Leukemia.

See also: Pulmonary edema.

It starts raining harder, from clouds so dark that people start lighting lamps inside. Smoke settles down on us from chimneys. The tourists will all be in the tavern drinking Australian ale out of pewter mugs made in Indonesia. In the woodwright's shop, the cabinetmaker will be huffing glue out of a paper bag with the blacksmith and the midwife while she talks about fronting the band they dream of putting together but never will.

We're all trapped. It's always 1734. All of us, we're stuck in the same time capsule, the same as those television shows where the same people are marooned on the same desert island for thirty seasons and never age or escape. They just wear more makeup. In a creepy way, those shows are maybe too authentic.

In a creepy way, I can see myself standing here for the rest of my life. It's a comfort, me and Denny complaining about the same shit, forever. In recovery, forever. Sure, I'm standing guard, but if you want to get really authentic about it, I'd rather see Denny locked in the stocks than let him get banished and leave me behind.

I'm not so much a good friend as I'm the doctor who wants to adjust your spine every week.

Or the dealer who sells you heroin.

"Parasite" isn't the right word, but it's the first word that comes to mind.

Denny's wig flops to the ground, again. The words "Eat me" bleeding red in the rain, running pink down behind his cold, blue ears, trickling pink around his eyes and down his cheeks, dripping pink into the mud.

All you can hear is the rain, water falling against puddles, against thatched roofs, against us, erosion.

I'm not so much a good friend as I'm the savior who wants you to worship him forever.

Denny sneezes, again, a long hank of yellowy goob that snakes out of his nose and lands on the wig in the mud, and he says, "Dude, do not put that nasty rug back on my head, okay?" And he sniffs. Then coughs, and his glasses drop off his face into the mess.

Nasal discharge means Rubella.

See also: Whooping cough.

See also: Pneumonia.

His glasses remind me of Dr. Marshall, and I say how there's this new girl in my life, a real doctor, and for serious, worth the effort to bag.

And Denny says, "You still stuck on doing your fourth step? You need any help remembering stuff to write in your note-book?"

The complete and relentless story of my sexual addiction. Oh, yeah, that. Every lame, suck-ass moment.

And I say, "Everything in moderation, dude. Even recovery."

I'm not so much a good friend as I'm the parent who never wants you to really grow up.

And facedown, Denny says, "It helps to remember the first time for everything." He says, "My first time I jacked off, I thought I'd invented it. I looked down at my sloppy handful of junk and thought, *This is going to make me rich.*"

The first time for everything. The incomplete inventory of my crimes. Just another incomplete in my life full of incompletes.

And still facedown, blind to everything in the world except the mud, Denny says, "Dude, you still there?"

And I put the rag back around his nose and tell him, "Blow."

Chapter 5

Whatever lighting the photographer used was harsh and made bad shadows on the cement-block wall behind them. Just a painted wall in somebody's basement. The monkey looked tired and patchy with mange. The guy was in lousy shape, pale with rolls around his middle, but there he was, relaxed and bent over with his hands braced against his knees and his poochy gut hanging down, his face looking back over his shoulder at the camera, smiling away.

"Beatific" isn't the right word, but it's the first word that comes to mind.

What the little boy first loved about pornography wasn't the sex part. It wasn't the pictures of beautiful people dorking each other, their heads thrown back, making those fake orgasm faces. Not at first. He'd found all those pictures on the Internet even before he knew what sex was. They had the Internet in every library. They had it at all the schools.

The way you can move from city to city and always find a Catholic church, the same Mass said everywhere, no matter what foster place the kid was sent, he could always find the Internet. The truth was, if Christ had laughed on the cross, or spat on the Romans, if he'd done anything more than just suffer, the kid would've liked church a lot more.

As it was, his favorite website was pretty much not sexy, at least not to him. You could just go there, and there would be about a dozen photographs of this one dumpy guy dressed as Tarzan with a goofy orangutan trained to poke what looked like roasted chestnuts up the guy's ass.

The guy's leopard-print loincloth is tossed to one side, the elastic waistband sunk into his tubby waist.

The monkey's crouched there, ready with the next chestnut.

There's nothing sexy about it. Still, the counter showed more than a half million people had been to see it.

"Pilgrimage" isn't the right word, but it's the first word that comes to mind.

The monkey and the chestnuts wasn't anything the kid could understand, but he sort of admired the guy. The kid was stupid, but he knew this was something way beyond him. The truth was, most people wouldn't even want a monkey to see them naked. They'd be terrified about how their asshole might look, if it might look too red or baggy. There's no way most people would ever have the nerve to bend over in front of a monkey, much less a monkey and a camera and lights, and even then they'd have to do about a zillion sit-ups first and go to a tanning booth and get their hair cut. After that, they'd spend hours bent over in front of a mirror, trying to determine their best profile.

And then, even with just chestnuts, you'd have to stay somewhat relaxed.

Just the thought of auditioning monkeys was terrifying, the possibility of being rejected by monkey after monkey. Sure, you can pay a person enough money and they'll stick stuff into you or they'll take pictures. But a monkey. A monkey's going to be honest.

Your only hope would be to book this same orangutan, since it obviously didn't look too picky. Either that or it was exceptionally well trained.

The point was, there'd be nothing to this if you were beautiful and sexy.

The point was, in a world where everybody had to look so pretty all the time, this guy wasn't. The monkey wasn't. What they were doing wasn't.

The point was, it's not the sex part of pornography that hooked the stupid little boy. It was the confidence. The courage. The complete lack of shame. The comfort and genuine honesty. The up-front-ness of being able to just stand there and tell the world: *Yeah, this is how I chose to spend a free afternoon. Posing here with a monkey putting chestnuts up my ass.*

And I really don't care how I look. Or what you think.

So deal with it.

He was assaulting the world by assaulting himself.

And even if the guy wasn't loving every moment, the ability to smile, to fake your way through this, that would be even more admirable.

The same way every porno movie implies a score of people standing just off camera, knitting, eating sandwiches, looking at their wristwatches, while other people do naked sex only a few feet away . . .

To the stupid little boy, that was enlightenment. To be that comfortable and confident in the world, that would be Nirvana.

"Freedom" isn't the right word, but it's the first word that comes to mind.

That's the kind of pride and self-assurance the little boy wanted to have. Someday.

If it was him in those pictures with the monkey, he could look at them every day and think: *If I could do this, I could do anything.* No matter what else you came up against, if you could smile and laugh while a monkey did you with chestnuts in a dank concrete basement and somebody took pictures, well, any other situation would be a piece of cake.

Even hell.

More and more, for the stupid little kid, that was the idea . . .

That if enough people looked at you, you'd never need anybody's attention ever again.

That if someday you were caught, exposed, and revealed enough, then you'd never be able to hide again. There'd be no difference between your public and your private lives.

That if you could acquire enough, accomplish enough, you'd never want to own or do another thing.

That if you could eat or sleep enough, you'd never need more.

That if enough people loved you, you'd stop needing love.

That you could ever be smart enough.

That you could someday get enough sex.

These all became the little boy's new goals. The illusions he'd have for the rest of his life. These were all the promises he saw in the fat man's smile.

So after that, every time he was scared or sad or alone, every night he woke up panicked in a new foster home, his heart racing, his bed wet, every day he started school in a different neighborhood, every time the Mommy came back to claim him, in every damp motel room, in every rented car, the kid would think of those same twelve photos of the fat man bent over. The monkey and the chestnuts. And it calmed the stupid little shit right down. It showed him how brave and strong and happy a person could become.

How torture is torture and humiliation is humiliation only when you choose to suffer.

"Savior" isn't the right word, but it's the first word that comes to mind.

And it's funny how when somebody saves you, the first thing you want to do is save other people. All other people. Everybody.

The kid never knew the man's name. But he never forgot that smile.

"Hero" isn't the right word, but it's the first word that comes to mind.

Chapter 6

The next time I go visit my mom I'm still Fred Hastings, her old public defender, and she keeps me yakking all afternoon. Until I tell her I'm still not married, and she says that's a shame. Then she turns on the television, some soap opera, you know, real people pretending to be fake people with made-up problems being watched by real people to forget their real problems.

The next visit, I'm still Fred but married and with three children. That's better, but three children . . . Three is too many. People should stop at two, she says.

The next visit, I have two.

Every visit there's less and less of her under the blanket.

In another way, there's less and less of Victor Mancini sitting in the chair next to her bed.

The next day, I'm myself again, and it's only a few minutes before my mom rings for the nurse to escort me back to the lobby. We sit not talking until I pick up my coat, then she says, "Victor?"

She says, "I need to tell you something."

She's rolling a ball of lint between her fingers, rolling it smaller and tighter, and when she finally looks up at me, she says, "Fred Hastings was here. You remember Fred, don't you?"

Yeah, I remember.

These days, he has a wife and two perfect children. It was such a pleasure, my mom says, to see life work out for such a good person.

"I told him to buy land," my mom says, "they're not making it anymore."

I ask her who she means by "they," and she presses the nurse button again.

On my way out, I find Dr. Marshall waiting in the hallway. She's standing just outside my mom's door, leafing through notes on her clipboard, and she looks up at me, her eyes beady behind her thick glasses. Her one hand is clicking and unclicking a ballpoint pen, fast.

"Mr. Mancini?" she says. She folds her glasses and puts them in the chest pocket of her lab coat and says, "It's important that we discuss your mother's case."

The stomach tube.

"You asked about other options," she says.

From the nurse's station down the hallway, three staffers watch us, their heads tilted together. One named Dina calls, "Do we need to chaperon the two of you?"

And Dr. Marshall says, "Mind your own business, please."

To me, she whispers, "These small operations, the staff acts as if they're still in high school."

Dina, I've had.

See also: Clare, RN.

See also: Pearl, CNA.

The magic of sex is it's acquisition without the burden of possessions. No matter how many women you take home, there's never a storage problem.

To Dr. Marshall, her ears and nervous hands, I say, "I don't want her force-fed."

The nurses still watching, Dr. Marshall cups a hand behind my arm and walks me farther away from them, saying, "I've been talking to your mother. She's quite a woman. Her political actions. All her demonstrations. You must love her very much."

And I say, "Well, I wouldn't go as far as that."

We stop, and Dr. Marshall whispers something so I have to step closer to hear. Too close. The nurses still watching. And breathing against my chest, she says, "What if we could completely restore your mother's mind?" Clicking and unclicking her pen, she says, "What if we could make her the intelligent, strong, vibrant woman she used to be?"

My mother, the way she used to be.

"It may be possible," says Dr. Marshall.

And not thinking how it sounds, I say, "God forbid."

Then real fast, I say that's probably not such a great idea.

And down the hall, the nurses are laughing, their hands cupped over their mouths. And from even that far away, you can hear Dina say, "It would serve him right."

On my next visit, I'm still Fred Hastings and my kids both get straight A's in school. That week, Mrs. Hastings is painting our dining room green.

"Blue is better," my mom says, "for a room you're going to put any sort of food in."

After that, the dining room is blue. We live on East Pine Street. We're Catholics. We save our money at City First Federal. We drive a Chrysler.

All at my mom's suggestion.

The next week, I start writing things down, the details, so I won't forget who I'm supposed to be from one week to the next. The Hastings always drive to Robson Lake for our vacation, I write. We fish for steelhead. We want the Packers to win. We never eat oysters. We were buying land. Each Saturday, I first sit in the dayroom and study my notes while the nurse goes to see if my mom is awake.

Whenever I step into her room and introduce myself as Fred Hastings, she points the remote control to turn the television off.

Boxwoods around a house are fine, she tells me, but privets would be better.

And I write it down.

The best kind of people drink scotch, she says. Clean your gutters in October, then again in November, she says. Wrap your car's air filter in toilet paper for longer service life. Prune evergreens only after the first frost. And ash makes the best firewood.

I write it all down. I inventory what's left of her, the spots and wrinkles and her swollen or empty skin and flakes and rashes, and I write reminders to myself.

Every day: Wear sunblock.

Cover your gray.

Don't go insane.

Eat less fats and sugars.

Do more sit-ups.

Don't start forgetting stuff.

Trim the hair in your ears.

Take calcium.

Moisturize. Every day.

Freeze time to stay in one place forever.

Do not get frigging old.

She says, "Do you hear anything from my son, Victor? Do you remember him?"

I stop. I feel my heart ache, but I've forgotten what that feeling means.

Victor, my mom says, never comes to visit, and if he does, he never listens. Victor's busy and distracted and doesn't care. He's dropped out of medical school and is making a big mess out of his life.

She picks at the lint on her blanket. "He's got some minimum-wage kind of job as a tour guide or something," she says. She sighs, and her terrible yellow hands find the remote control.

I ask, wasn't Victor looking after her? Didn't he have a right to live his own life? I say, maybe Victor is so busy because he's out every night, literally killing himself to pay her bills for constant care. That's three grand each month just to break even. Maybe that's why Victor left school. I say, just for the sake of argument, that maybe Victor's doing his frigging best.

I say, it could be that Victor does more than anybody gives him credit for.

And my mom smiles and says, "Oh Fred, you're still the defender of the hopelessly guilty."

My mom turns on the television, and a beautiful woman in a glittering evening dress hits another beautiful young woman over the head with a bottle. The bottle doesn't even mess her hair, but it gives her amnesia.

Maybe Victor's struggling with problems of his own, I say.

The one beautiful woman reprograms the amnesia woman into thinking she's a killer robot that must do the beautiful

44

woman's bidding. The killer robot accepts her new identity so easy you have to wonder if she's just faking the amnesia and was always looking for a good reason to go on a killing spree.

Me talking to my mom, my anger and resentment just sort of piddles out as we sit and watch.

My mother used to serve eggs scrambled with dark flakes of the nonstick coating from the frying pan. She cooked with aluminum pots, and we drank lemonade out of spun aluminum cups while we chewed on their soft cold lips. We used underarm deodorants made with aluminum salts. For sure, there's about a million ways we could've got to this point.

During a commercial, my mom asks for just one good thing about Victor's personal life. What did he do for fun? Where did he see himself in another year? Another month? Another week?

By now, I have no idea.

"And just what the hell do you mean," she says, "about Victor killing himself every night?"

Chapter 7

After the waiter's gone, I fork up half my sirloin steak and go to cram it all in my mouth, and Denny says, "Dude." He says, "Don't do it, here."

The people all around us, eating in their dressy clothes. With the candles and the crystal. With all the extra specialty forks. Nobody suspects a thing.

My lips crack, trying to get around the chunk of steak, the meat salty and juicy with fat and crushed pepper. My tongue pulls back to make more room, and the drool in my mouth wells up. Hot juice and drool slop out on my chin.

People who say red meat will kill you, they don't know the half of it.

Denny looks around quick, and says, through his teeth says, "You're getting greedy, my friend." He shakes his head and says, "Dude, you can't fool people into loving you."

Next to us, a married couple with wedding rings, gray hair, they eat without looking up, each of them head down, reading a program from the same play or concert. When the woman's wine is gone, she reaches for the bottle to fill her own glass. She doesn't fill his. The husband's wearing a thick gold wristwatch.

Denny sees me watching the old couple and says, "I'll warn them. I swear."

He watches for waiters who might know about us. He's glaring at me with his bottom teeth stuck out.

The bite of steak is so big my jaws can't come together. My cheeks bulge. My lips pucker tight to close, and I have to breathe through my nose while I try to chew.

The waiters in black jackets, each with a nice towel folded over one arm. The violin music. The silver and china. This isn't the normal kind of place we'd do this, but we're running out of restaurants. There are only so many places to eat in any town, and this is for sure the kind of stunt you never repeat in the same place.

I drink a little wine.

At another table near us, a young couple hold hands while they eat.

Maybe it will be them, tonight.

At another table, a man in a suit eats staring off into space.

Maybe he'll be tonight's hero.

I drink some wine and try to swallow, but the steak's too much. It sits in the back of my throat. I don't breathe.

In the next instant, my legs snap straight so fast my chair flies over behind me. My hands go to gripping around my throat. I'm on my feet and gaping at the painted ceiling, my eyes rolled back. My chin stretches out away from my face.

With his fork, Denny reaches over the table to steal my broccoli and goes, "Dude, you are way overacting."

Maybe it will be the eighteen-year-old busboy or the corduroy guy in the turtleneck sweater, but one of these people will treasure me for the rest of their life.

Already people are half out of their seats.

Maybe the woman with the wrist corsage.

Maybe the man with the long neck and wire-framed glasses.

This month, I got three birthday cards, and it's not even the fifteenth. Last month, I got four. The month before, I got six birthday cards. Most of these people I can't remember. God bless them, but they'll never forget me.

From not breathing, the veins in my neck swell. My face gets red, gets hot. Sweat springs up on my forehead. Sweat blots through the back of my shirt. With my hands, I hold tight around my neck, the universal sign language for someone choking to death. Even now, I get birthday cards from people who don't speak English.

The first few seconds, everybody is looking for someone else to step in and be the hero.

Denny reaches over to steal the other half of my steak.

With my hands still tight around my throat, I stagger over and kick him in the leg.

With my hands, I yank at my tie.

I rip open my collar button.

And Denny says, "Hey, dude, that hurt."

The busboy hangs back. No heroics for him.

The violinist and the wine steward are neck and neck, headed my way.

From another direction, a woman in a short black dress is pushing through the crowd. Coming to my rescue.

From another direction, a man strips off his dinner jacket and charges forward. Somewhere else, a woman screams.

This never takes very long. The whole adventure lasts one, two minutes, tops. That's good, since that's about how long I can hold my breath with a mouthful of food.

My first choice would be the older man with the thick gold wristwatch, somebody who will save the day and pick up our check for dinner. My personal choice is the little black dress for the reason she has nice tits.

Even if we have to pay for our own meal, I figure you have to spend money to make money.

Shoveling food into his face, Denny says, "Why you do this is so infantile."

I stagger over and kick him, again.

Why I do this is to put adventure back into people's lives.

Why I do this is to create heroes. Put people to the test.

Like mother, like son.

Why I do this is to make money.

Somebody saves your life, and they'll love you forever. It's that old Chinese custom where if somebody saves your life, they're responsible for you forever. It's as if now you're their child. For the rest of their lives, these people will write me. Send me cards on the anniversary. Birthday cards. It's depressing how many people get this same idea. They call you on the phone. To find out if you're feeling okay. To see if you maybe need cheering up. Or cash.

It's not as if I spend the money phoning up escort girls. Keeping my mom in St. Anthony's Care Center costs around three grand each month. These Good Samaritans keep me alive. I keep her. It's that simple.

You gain power by pretending to be weak. By contrast, you make people feel so strong. You save people by letting them save you.

All you have to do is be fragile and grateful. So stay the underdog.

People really need somebody they feel superior to. So stay downtrodden.

People need somebody they can send a check at Christmas. So stay poor.

"Charity" isn't the right word, but it's the first word that comes to mind.

You're the proof of their courage. The proof they were a hero. Evidence of their success. I do this because everybody wants to save a human life with a hundred people watching.

With the sharp tip of his steak knife, Denny's sketching on the white tablecloth, sketching the architecture of the room, the cornices and paneling, the broken pediments above each doorway, all this while still chewing. He lifts his plate to his mouth and just shovels in the food.

To perform a tracheotomy, you'd find the dent just below the Adam's apple, but just above the cricoid cartilage. With a steak knife, make a half-inch horizontal incision, then pinch the incision and insert your finger to open it. Insert a "trache" tube; a drinking straw or half a ballpoint pen works best.

If I can't be a great doctor saving hundreds of patients, this way I'm a great patient creating hundreds of would-be doctors.

Closing in fast is a man in a tuxedo, dodging between the onlookers, running with his steak knife and his ballpoint pen.

By choking, you become a legend about themselves that these

people will cherish and repeat until they die. They'll think they gave you life. You might be the one good deed, the deathbed memory that justifies their whole existence.

So be the aggressive victim, the big loser. A professional failure.

People will jump through hoops if you just make them feel like a god.

It's the martyrdom of Saint Me.

Denny scrapes my plate onto his and keeps forking food into his mouth.

The wine steward is here. The little black dress is up against me. The man with the thick gold watch.

In another minute, the arms will come around me from behind. Some stranger will be hugging me tight, double-fisting me under the rib cage and breathing into my ear, "You're okay."

Breathing into your ear, "You're going to be fine."

Two arms will hug you, maybe even lift you off your feet, and a stranger will whisper, "Breathe! Breathe, damn it!"

Somebody will pound you on the back the way a doctor pounds a newborn baby, and you'll let fly with your mouthful of chewed steak. In the next second, you'll both be collapsed on the floor. You'll be sobbing while someone tells you how everything is all right. You're alive. They saved you. You almost died. They'll hold your head to their chest and rock you, saying, "Everybody get back. Make some room, here. The show's over."

Already, you're their child. You belong to them.

They'll put a glass of water to your lips and say, "Just relax. Hush. It's all over."

Hush.

For years to come, this person will call and write. You'll get cards and maybe checks.

Whoever it is, this person will love you.

Whoever will be so proud. Even if maybe your real folks aren't. This person will be proud of you because you make them so proud of themselves.

You'll sip the water and cough just so the hero can wipe your chin with a napkin.

Do anything to cement this new bond. This adoption. Remember to add details. Stain their clothes with snot so they can laugh and forgive you. Cling and clutch. Really cry so they can wipe your eyes.

It's okay to cry as long as you're faking it.

Just don't hold anything back. This is going to be the best story of somebody's life.

What's most important is unless you want a nasty trache scar, you'd better be breathing before anybody gets near you with a steak knife, a pocketknife, a box cutter.

Another detail to remember is when you blast out your mouthful of wet crud, your ground wad of dead meat and drool, you'll need to be facing straight at Denny. He's got parents and grandparents, aunts and uncles and cousins up the ass, a thousand people who have to save him from every mess-up. That's why Denny will never understand me.

The rest of the people, everyone else in the restaurant, sometimes they'll stand there and applaud. People will cry with relief. People just pour out of the kitchen. Within minutes, they'll be telling the story to each other. Everybody will buy drinks for the hero. Their eyes all shining with eye juice.

They'll all shake the hero's hand.

They'll pat the hero on the back.

It's so much more their birth than it is yours, but for years to come this person will send you a birthday card on this day and month. They'll become another member of your own very very extended family.

And Denny will just shake his head and ask for a dessert menu.

That's why I do all this. Go to all this trouble. To showcase just one brave stranger. To save just one more person from boredom. It's not *just* for the money. It's not *just* for the adoration.

But neither one hurts.

It's all so easy. It's not about looking good, at least not on the surface—but you still win. Just let yourself be broken and humiliated. Just your whole life, keep telling people, *I'm sorry. I'm sorry. I'm sorry. I'm sorry. I'm sorry.* . . .

Chapter 8

Eva follows me down the hallway with her pockets full of roast turkey. There's chewed-up Salisbury steak in her shoes. Her face, the powdery crushed velvet mess of her skin, is a hundred wrinkles that all run into her mouth, and she wheels along after me, saying, "You. Don't you run away from me."

Her hands woven with lumpy veins, she wheels herself along. Hunched in her wheelchair, pregnant with her own huge swollen spleen, she keeps after me, saying, "You hurt me."

Saying, "You can't deny it."

Wearing a bib the color of food, she says, "You hurt me, and I'm telling Mother."

Where they have my mom, she has to wear a bracelet. Not a jewelry kind of bracelet, it's a strip of thick plastic that's heat-sealed around her wrist so she can never take it off. You can't cut it. You can't melt it apart with a cigarette. People have tried all these ways to get out.

Wearing the bracelet, every time you walk around the hall-ways, you hear locks snapping shut. A magnetic strip or some-thing sealed inside the plastic gives off a signal. It stops the elevator doors from opening for you to get on. It locks almost every door if you get within four feet. You can't leave the floor you're assigned. You can't get to the street. You can go into the garden or the dayroom or the chapel or the dining room, but nowhere else in the world.

If somehow you do get past an exterior door, for sure the bracelet sets off an alarm.

This is St. Anthony's. The rugs, the drapes, the beds, pretty much everything is flameproof. It's all stain-resistant. You could do just about anything anywhere, and they could wipe it up. It's what they call a care center. It feels bad, telling you all this. Spoiling the surprise, I mean. You'll see it all yourself, soon enough. That is, if you live too long.

Or if you just give up and go nuts ahead of schedule.

My mom, Eva, even you, eventually everybody gets a bracelet.

This isn't one of those snake pit places. You don't smell urine the minute you step in the door. Not for three grand every month. It used to be a convent a century ago, and the nuns planted a beautiful old rose garden, beautiful and walled and fully escape-proof.

Video security cameras watch you from every angle.

From the minute you get in the front door, there's a slow scary migration of the residents edging toward you. Every wheelchair, all the people with walkers and canes, they all see a visitor and come creeping.

Tall, glaring Mrs. Novak is an undresser.

The woman in the room next to my mom is a squirrel.

With an undresser, they take their clothes off at every possible moment. These are the folks who the nurses dress in what look like shirt and pants combinations, but are really jumpsuits. The shirts are sewn into the waistband of the pants. The shirt buttons and the fly are fake. The only way in or out is a long zipper up the back. These are old people with limited range of motion, so an undresser, even what they call an aggressive undresser, is trapped three times over. In her clothes, in her bracelet, in her care center.

A squirrel is someone who chews her food and then forgets what to do next. They forget how to swallow. Instead, she spits each chewed mouthful in her dress pocket. Or in her handbag. This is less cute than it sounds.

Mrs. Novak is Mom's roommate. The squirrel is Eva.

At St. Anthony's, the first floor is for people who forget names and run around naked and put chewed food in their pockets, but who are otherwise pretty undamaged. Here are also some young people fried on drugs and smoked by massive head traumas. They walk and talk, even if it's just word salad, a constant stream of words that seem random.

"Fig people road little dawn singing rope purple veil gone," that's how they talk.

The second floor is for bed patients. The third floor is where people go to die.

Mom's on the first floor for now, but nobody's there forever.

How Eva got here is, people will take their aging parents to some public place and just leave them behind with no identification. These are old Dorothys and Ermas with no idea who or where they are. People think the city or state government or whoever will collect them. Kind of what the government does with litter.

The same as what happens when you ditch your old car and take the license plates and the VIN decal off so the city has to tow it away.

No kidding, but this is called granny dumping, and St. Anthony's has to take a certain number of dumped grannies and ecstasy-fried street kids and suicidal bag ladies. Only they don't call them *bag ladies*, or call the street girls *prosti-tots*. My guess is somebody slowed their car down and just shoved Eva out the door and never shed a tear. Kind of what people do with pets they can't house-train.

Eva still trailing me, I get to my mom's room and she's not there. Instead of Mom, her bed's empty with a big wet dent sunk in the mattress soaked with urine. It's shower time, I figure. A nurse takes you down the hall to a big tiled room where they can hose you clean.

Here at St. Anthony's, they show the movie *The Pajama Game* every Friday night, and every Friday all the same patients crowd in to see it for the first time.

They have bingo, crafts, visiting pets.

They have Dr. Paige Marshall. Wherever she's disappeared to.

They have fireproof bibs that cover you from your neck to your ankles so you don't set fire to yourself while you smoke. They have Norman Rockwell posters. A hair dresser comes twice a week to do your hair. That costs extra. Incontinence costs extra. Dry cleaning costs extra. Monitoring urine output costs extra. Stomach tubes.

They have lessons every day in how to tie your shoe, how to

button a button, snap a snap. Buckle a buckle. Someone will demonstrate Velcro. Someone will teach you how to zip your zipper. Every morning, they tell you your name. Friends who've known each other sixty years get reintroduced. Every morning.

These are doctors, lawyers, captains of industry, who, day to day, can't master a zipper anymore. This is less teaching than it is damage control. You might as well try to paint a house that's on fire.

Here at St. Anthony's, Tuesday means Salisbury steak. Wednesday means mushroom chicken. Thursday is spaghetti. Friday, baked fish. Saturday, corned beef. Sunday, roast turkey.

They have thousand-piece jigsaw puzzles for you to do while you're running out the clock. There isn't a mattress in the place a dozen people haven't already died on.

Eva's wheeled her chair up to my mom's doorway and she's sitting there, looking pale and wilted, as if she's a mummy somebody just unwrapped and then set its thin cruddy hair. Her curly blue head never stops bobbing in slow, tight little prizefighter circles.

"Don't come near me," Eva says every time I look at her. "Dr. Marshall won't let you hurt me," she says.

Until the nurse gets back, I just sit on the edge of my mom's bed and wait.

My mom has one of those clocks where each hour is marked by the call of a different bird. Prerecorded. One o'clock is the American Robin. Six is the Northern Oriole.

Noon is the House Finch.

The Black-capped Chickadee means eight o'clock. The White-breasted Nuthatch means eleven.

You get the idea.

The problem is, associating birds with specific times can get confusing. Especially if you're outside. You turn from a clock watcher to a bird watcher. Every time you hear the lovely trill of the White-throated Sparrow, you think: *Is it ten o'clock already?*

Eva wheels a little bit into my mom's room. "You hurt me," she says to me. "And I never told Mother."

These old people. These human ruins.

It's already half-past the Tufted Titmouse, and I have to catch my bus and be at work by the time the Blue Jay sings.

Eva thinks I'm her big brother who diddled her about a century ago. My mom's roommate, Mrs. Novak with her horrible big hanging breasts and ears, she thinks I'm her bastard business partner who gypped her out of a patent for the cotton gin or the fountain pen or something.

Here I get to be all things to all women.

"You hurt me," Eva says and rolls a little closer. "And I've never forgotten it for a minute."

Every time I visit, some old raisin down the hall with wild eyebrows, she calls me Eichmann. Another woman with a clear plastic tube of piss looping out from under her bathrobe, she accuses me of stealing her dog and wants it back. Anytime I pass this other old woman who sits in her wheelchair, slumped inside a pile of pink sweaters, she hisses at me. "I saw you," she says, and looks at me with one cloudy eye. "The night of the fire, I saw you with them!"

You can't win. Every man who's ever passed through Eva's life has probably been her big brother in some form. Whether she knew it or not, she's spent her whole life waiting and expecting men to diddle her. For serious, even mummied up in her wrinkled skin, she's still eight years old. Stuck. Just the same as Colonial Dunsboro with its granola crew of burnouts, everybody at St. Anthony's is trapped in their past.

I'm no exception, and don't think you are either.

Just as stuck as Denny in the stocks, Eva's arrested in her development.

"You," Eva says, and pokes a trembling finger at me. "You hurt my woo-woo."

These stuck old people.

"Oh, you said it was just our game," she says and rolls her head, her voice getting sing song. "It was just our secret game, but then you put your big man thing inside me." Her bony, carved little finger keeps poking in the air at my crotch.

For serious, just the idea makes my big man thing want to run screaming from the room.

The trouble is, anywhere else at St. Anthony's it's the same deal. Another old skeleton thinks I borrowed five hundred dollars from her. Another baggy old woman calls me the devil.

"And you hurt me," Eva says.

It's tough not to come here and soak up the blame for every crime in history. You want to shout in everybody's old toothless face. Yes, I kidnapped that Lindbergh baby.

The *Titanic* thing, I did that.

That Kennedy assassination deal, yeah, that was me.

The big World War II gizmo, that atom bomb contraption, well guess what? That was my doing.

The AIDS bug? Sorry. Me, again.

The correct way to handle a case like Eva is to redirect her attention. Distract her by mentioning lunch or the weather or how nice her hair looks. Her attention span is about a clock tick long, and you can shove her on to a more pleasant topic.

You can guess this is how men have been handling Eva's hostility for her whole life. Just distract her. Get through the moment. Avoid confrontation. Run away.

That's pretty much how we get through our own lives, watching television. Smoking crap. Self-medicating. Redirecting our own attention. Jacking off. Denial.

Her whole body leaning forward, her little stick finger trembles in the air at me.

Screw it.

She's already pretty much engaged to become Mrs. Death.

"Yeah, Eva," I say. "I boned you." And I yawn. "Yup. Every chance I got, I stuck it in you and humped out a load."

They call this psychodrama. You could call it just another kind of granny dumping.

Her twisted little finger wilts, and she settles back between the arms of her wheelchair. "So you finally admit it," she says.

"Hell yes," I say. "You're a great piece of ass, baby sis."

She looks off at a blank spot on the linoleum floor and says, "After all these years, he admits it."

This is role-playing therapy, only Eva doesn't know it's not for real.

Her head still loops in little circles, but her eyes come back to me. "And you're not sorry?" she says.

Well, I guess if Jesus could die for my sins, I suppose I can soak up a few for other people. We all get our chance to play scapegoat. Take the blame.

The martyrdom of Saint Me.

The sins of every man in history landing square on my back.

"Eva," I say. "Baby, sweetheart, little sister, love of my life, of course I'm sorry. I was a pig," I say and look at my watch. "You were just such a hot tamale that I was out of control."

Like I need this shit to deal with. Eva just stares at me with her big hyperthyroid eyes until a big tear splurts out of one eye and cuts through the powder on her wrinkled cheek.

I roll my eyes at the ceiling and say, "Okay, I hurt your little woo-woo, but that was eighty frigging years ago, so get over it. Move on with your life."

Then her horrible hands come up, wasted and veined as tree roots or old carrots, and they cover her face. "Oh, Colin," she says behind them. "Oh, Colin."

She takes her hands away, and her face is hosed with eye juice. "Oh, Colin," she whispers, "I forgive you." And her face nods toward her chest, bobbing with short breaths and sniffs, and her terrible hands bring the edge of her bib up to wipe at her eyes.

We just sit there. Jeez, I wish I had some chewing gum. My watch says twelve thirty-five.

She wipes her eyes and sniffs and looks up a little. "Colin," she says. "Do you still love me?"

These frigging old people. Jesus H.

And just in case you're wondering, I'm not a monster.

Just like something in a frigging book, for real I say, "Yeah, Eva." I say, "Yeah, for sure, I guess I can probably still love you."

Eva sobs now, her face hanging over her lap, her whole body rocking. "I'm so glad," she says, her tears dropping straight, gray stuff from her nose dripping right into her empty hands.

She says, "I'm so glad," and she's still crying, and you can smell the chewed-up Salisbury steak squirreled away in her shoe, the chewed mushroom chicken in the pocket of her smock. That, and the damn nurse is never going to get my mom back from her shower, and I have to be back at work in the eighteenth century by one o'clock.

It's hard enough remembering my own past so I can do my fourth step. Now it's mixed up with the past of these other people. Which defense attorney I am, today, I can't remember. I look at my fingernails. I ask Eva, "Is Dr. Marshall here, do you think?" I ask, "Do you know if she's married?"

The truth about myself, who I really am, my father and everything, if my mom knows then she's too freaked out with guilt to tell.

I ask Eva, "Could you maybe cry somewhere else?"

Then it's too late. The Blue Jay starts singing.

And Eva, she still won't shut up, crying and rocking, her bib pressed to her face, the plastic bracelet trembling around one wrist, she's saying, "I forgive you, Colin. I forgive you. I forgive you. Oh, Colin, I forgive . . ."

Chapter 9

It was one afternoon when our stupid little boy and his foster mother were in a shopping mall that they heard the announcement. This was summer, and they were shopping for back to school, the year he was going to be in fifth grade. The year you had to wear shirts with stripes to really fit in. This was years and years ago. This was only his first foster mother.

Up-and-down stripes, he was telling her when they heard it.

The announcement:

"Would Dr. Paul Ward," the voice told everybody, "please meet your wife in the cosmetics department of Woolworth's."

This was the first time the Mommy came back to claim him.

"Dr. Ward, please meet your wife in the cosmetics department of Woolworth's."

That was the secret signal.

So the kid lied and said he needed to find the bathroom and instead he went to Woolworth's, and there, opening boxes of hair color, was the Mommy. She had a big yellow wig that made her face look too small and smelled like cigarettes. With her fingernails, she opened each box and took out the dark brown bottle of dye inside. She'd open another box and take out the other bottle. She put the one bottle in the other box and put it back on the shelf. She opened another box.

"This one's pretty," the Mommy said, looking at the picture of a woman smiling on the box. She switched the bottle inside with another bottle. All the bottles the same dark brown glass.

Opening another box, she said, "Do you think she's pretty?"

And the kid's so stupid he says, "Who?"

"You know who," the Mommy said. "She's young, too. I just saw the two of you looking at clothes. You were holding her hand, so don't lie."

And the kid was so stupid he didn't know to just run away. He couldn't begin to even think about the very definite terms of her parole or the restraining order or why she'd been in jail for the past three months.

And switching bottles of blond into boxes for redheads and bottles of black into boxes for blondes, the Mommy said, "So do you like her?"

"You mean Mrs. Jenkins?" the boy said.

Not closing the boxes just perfect, the Mommy was putting

them back on the shelf a little messed up, a little faster, and she said, "Do you like her?"

And like this is going to help, our little stooge said, "She's just a foster mom."

And not looking at the kid, still looking at the woman smiling on the box in her hand, the Mommy said, "I asked you if you liked her."

A shopping cart rattled up next to them in the aisle and a blond lady reached past to take a bottle with a blond picture but a bottle of some other color inside it. This lady put the box in her cart and got away.

"She thinks of herself as a blonde," the Mommy said. "What we have to do is mess with people's little identity paradigms."

What the Mommy used to call "Beauty Industry Terrorism."

The little boy looked after the lady until she was too far away to help.

"You already have me," the Mommy said. "So what do you call this foster one?"

Mrs. Jenkins.

"And do you like her?" the Mommy said, and turned to look at him for the first time.

And the little boy pretended to make up his mind and said, "No?"

"Do you love her?"

"No."

"Do you hate her?"

And this spineless little worm said, "Yes?"

And the Mommy said, "You got that right." She leaned down to look him in the eyes and said, "How much do you hate Mrs. Jenkins?"

And the little cooz said, "Lots and lots?"

"And lots and lots and lots," the Mommy said. She put her

hand for him to take and said, "We have to be fast. We have a train to catch."

Then leading him through the aisles, tugging his boneless little arm toward daylight outside the glass doors, the Mommy said, "You are mine. Mine. Now and forever, and don't you ever forget it."

And pulling him through the doors, she said, "And just in case the police or anybody asks you later on, I'm going to tell you all the dirty, filthy things this so-called foster mother did to you every time she could get you alone."

Chapter 10

Where I live now, in my mom's old house, I sort through my mom's papers, her college report cards, her deeds, statements, accounts. Court transcripts. Her diary, still locked. Her entire life.

The next week, I'm Mr. Benning, who defended her on the little charge of kidnapping after the school bus incident. The week after, I'm public defender Thomas Welton, who plea-bargained her sentence down to six months after she was charged with assaulting the animals in the zoo. After him, I'm the American civil liberties attorney who went to bat with her on the malicious mischief charge stemming from the disturbance at the ballet.

There's an opposite to déjà vu. They call it jamais vu. It's when you meet the same people or visit places, again and again, but each time is the first. Everybody is always a stranger. Nothing is ever familiar.

"How is Victor doing?" my mom asks me on my next visit.

Whoever I am. Whatever public defender du jour.

Victor *who?* I want to ask.

"You don't want to know," I say. It would break your heart. I ask her, "What was Victor like as a little boy? What did he want from the world? Did he have any big goal he dreamed about?"

At this point, how my life starts to feel is like I'm acting in a soap opera being watched by people on a soap opera being watched by people on a soap opera being watched by real people, somewhere. Every time I visit, I watch the halls for another chance to talk with the doctor with her little black brain of hair, her ears and glasses.

Dr. Paige Marshall with her clipboard and attitude. Her scary dreams about helping my mom live another ten or twenty years.

Dr. Paige Marshall, another potential dose of sexual anesthetic.

See also: Nico.

See also: Tanya.

See also: Leeza.

More and more, it feels like I'm doing a really bad impersonation of myself.

My life makes about as much sense as a Zen koan.

A House Wren sings, but whether it's a real bird or it's four o'clock I'm not sure.

"My memory isn't any good," my mom says. She's rubbing her temples with the thumb and index finger of one hand, and says, "I worry that I should tell Victor the truth about himself." Propped on her stack of pillows, she says, "Before it's too late, I wonder if Victor has a right to know who he really is."

"So just tell him," I say. I bring food, a bowl of chocolate pudding, and try to sneak the spoon into her mouth. "I can go call," I say, "and Victor can be here in a couple minutes."

The pudding is lighter brown and smelly under a cold dark brown skin.

"Oh, but I can't," she says. "The guilt is so bad, I can't even face him. I don't even know how he'll react."

She says, "Maybe it's better Victor never finds out."

"So tell me," I say. "Get it off your chest," I say, and I promise not to tell Victor, not unless she says it's okay.

She squints at me, her old skin all cinching tight around her eyes. With chocolate pudding smeared in the wrinkles around her mouth, she says, "But how do I know I can trust you? I'm not even sure who you are."

I smile and say, "Of course you can trust me."

And I stick the spoon in her mouth. The black pudding just sits on her tongue. It's better than a stomach tube. Okay, it's cheaper.

I take the remote control out of her reach and tell her, "Swallow."

I tell her, "You have to listen to me. You have to trust me."

I say, "I'm him. I'm Victor's father."

And her milky eyes swell at me while the rest of her face, her wrinkles and skin, seem to slide into the collar of her nightgown. With one terrible yellow hand, she makes the sign of the cross and her mouth hangs open to her chest. "Oh, you're him, and you've come back," she says. "Oh, blessed Father. Holy Father," she says. "Oh, please forgive me."

Chapter 11

This is me talking to Denny, locking him in the stocks again, this time for having a stamp on the back of his hand from some nightclub, and I say, "Dude."

I say, "It's so weird."

Denny's got both hands in place for me to lock them. He's got his shirt tucked in tight. He knows to bend his knees a little to take the stress off his back. He remembers to visit the restroom before he gets locked up. Our Denny's turned into a regular expert at getting punished. In good old Colonial Dunsboro, masochism is a valuable job skill.

It is in most jobs.

Yesterday at St. Anthony's, I tell him, it was the same as that old movie where there's a guy and a painting, and the guy gets to party and live to be about a hundred years old, and he never looks any different. The painting of him, it keeps getting uglier and trashed with alcohol-related everything and the nose falls off from secondary syphilis and the clap.

All the residents at St. Anthony's, now they're all eyes closed and humming. Everybody's all smiling and righteous.

Except me. I'm their stupid painting.

"Congratulate me, dude," Denny says. "Being in the stocks so much, I put together four weeks of sobriety. For sure, that's like four weeks more than I've had since I was thirteen."

My mom's roommate, I tell him, Mrs. Novak, she's all nodding and satisfied now that I've finally fessed up to stealing her invention for toothpaste.

Another old lady is jabbering and happy as a parrot since I admitted to peeing in her bed every night.

Yeah, I tell them all, I did it. I burned down your house. I bombed your village. I deported your sister. I sold you a shitty blue Nash Rambler in 1968. Then, yeah, I killed your dog.

So get over it!

I tell them, heap it on me. Make me play the big passive bottom in your guilt gang bang. I'll take everybody's load.

And after everybody's humped out their load in my face, they're all smiling and humming. They're laughing at the ceiling, still all crowded around me, patting my hand and saying it's all right, they forgive me. They're gaining fucking weight. The whole hen party's chatting at me, and this real tall nurse walks by, and she says, "Well, aren't you Mister Popular."

Denny sniffs.

"You need a snot rag, dude?" I say.

The weird part is my mom's not getting any better. No matter how much I play Pied Piper and take the blame away from these people. No matter how much fault I sponge up, my mom doesn't believe I'm me anymore, that I'm Victor Mancini. So she won't unload her own big secret. So she's going to need some stomach tube thing.

"Sobriety is okay enough," Denny says, "but someday, I'd like to live a life based on doing good stuff instead of just not doing bad stuff. You know?"

What's even weirder, I tell him, is I'm figuring how I can turn my new popularity into a fast broom closet ram session with this tall nurse, maybe get her to throat my dog. A nurse thinks you're a caring nurturing guy who's patient with hopeless old people, and you're halfway to boning her.

See also: Caren, RN.

See also: Nanette, LPN.

See also: Jolene, LPN.

But no matter who I'm with, my head's inside this other girl. This Dr. Paige Something. Marshall.

So no matter who I'm boning, I have to think about big infected animals, big roadkill raccoons all swollen up with gas and getting hit by fast trucks on the highway on a blistering day in the sun. Either that or I trigger right away, that's how hot this Dr. Marshall is in my head.

It's funny how you never think about the women you've had. It's always the ones who get away that you can't forget.

"It's just that my internal addict is so strong," Denny says, "that I'm afraid to not be locked up. My life needs to be about more than just *not* jerking off."

Other women, I say, no matter who, you can imagine them

getting rammed. You know, straddling the driver's seat in some car, her G-spot, the back of her urethral sponge, getting hammered on by your fat hot slider. Or you can see her bent over the edge of a hot tub getting plugged. You know, her, in her private life.

But with this Dr. Paige Marshall, she seems to be above getting boned.

Some kind of vultury birds are circling overhead. According to bird time, that makes it around two o'clock. A gust of wind throws the tails of Denny's waistcoat up over his shoulders, and I pull them back down.

"Sometimes," Denny says and sniffs, "it's like I want to be beaten and punished. It's okay if there isn't a God anymore, but I still want to respect something. I don't want to be the center of my own universe."

With Denny in the stocks all afternoon, I have to split all the firewood. By myself, I have to grind the corn. Salt the pork. Candle the eggs. The cream needs to be dipped. The hogs, slopped. You wouldn't think the eighteenth century would be so hectic. With me picking up all the slack for him, I tell Denny's hunched back, the least he could do is come visit my mom and pretend to be me. To hear her confession.

Denny sighs at the ground. From two hundred feet up, one of the vulture birds drops a nasty white dump on his back.

Denny says, "Dude, what I need is a mission."

I say, "So do this one good thing. Help out an old lady."

And Denny says, "How's your number four step coming along?" He says, "Dude, I have an itch on my side, can you help me out?"

And careful of the bird crap, I start scratching him.

Chapter 12

In the phone book, there's more and more red ink. More and more restaurants are crossed out in red felt-tipped pen. These are all places where I almost died. Italian. Mexican. Chinese places. For real, every night I have fewer options for where to eat out if I want to make any money. If I want to trick anybody into loving me.

The question is always: *So what do you feel like choking on tonight?*

There's French food. Mayan food. East Indian.

For where I live, in my mom's old house, picture a really dirty antique store. The kind where you have to walk sideways, the way you'd walk in Egyptian hieroglyphics, it's that kind of crowded. All the furniture carved out of wood, the long dining-room table, the chairs and chests and cabinets with faces carved on everything, the furniture's all oozed over with some thick syrup kind of varnish that turned black and crackled about a million years before Christ. Covering the bulgy sofas is that bullet-proof kind of tapesty you'd never want to sit on naked.

Every night after work, first there's the birthday cards to go through. The checks to total. This is spread out across the black acre of dining-room table, my base of operations. Here's the next day's deposit slip to fill out. Tonight, it's one lousy card. One crapmo card comes in the mail with a check for fifty bucks. That's still a thank-you note I have to write. There's still the groveling next generation of underdog letters to send out.

It's not that I'm an ingrate, but if all you can cut me is fifty bucks, next time just let me die. Okay? Or better yet, stand aside and let some rich person be the hero.

For sure, I can't write that in any thank-you note, but still.

For my mom's house, picture all this castle furniture crammed into a two-bedroom newlywed house. These sofas and paintings and clocks are all supposed to be her dowry from the Old Country. From Italy. My mom came here for college and never went back after she had me.

She's not Italian in any way you'd notice. No garlic smell or big armpit hair. She came here to attend medical school. Frigging medical school. In Iowa. The truth is, immigrants tend to be more American than people born here.

The truth is, I'm more or less her green card.

Looking through the phone book, what I need to do is take my act to a classier audience. You have to go where the money is and bring it home. Don't be choking to death on chicken nuggets in some deep-fried joint.

Rich people eating French food want to be the hero as much as anybody else.

My point is, discriminate.

My advice to you is: identify your target market.

In the phone book, there's still fish houses to try. Mongolian grills.

The name on today's check is some woman who saved my life in a smorgasbord last April. One of those all-you-can-eat buffets. *What was I thinking?* Choking in cheap restaurants is for sure a false economy. It's all worked out, all the details, in the big book I keep. Here's everything from who saved me where and when, to how much have they spent so far. Today's donor is Brenda Munroe signed at the bottom of the birthday card, with love.

"I hope this little bit helps," she's written across the bottom of the check.

Brenda Munroe, Brenda Munroe. I try, but I don't get a face. Nothing. Nobody can expect you to remember every near-death experience. For sure, I should keep better notes, hair and eye color at least, but for real, look at me here. As it is, I'm already drowning in paperwork.

Last month's thank-you letter was all about my struggle to pay for I forget what.

It was rent I told people I needed, or dental work. It was to pay for milk or counseling. By the time I send out a couple hundred of the same letter, I never want to read it again.

It's a homegrown version of those overseas children's charities. These are the ones where for the price of a cup of coffee, you could save a child's life. Be a sponsor. The hook is you can't just save somebody's life one time. People are having to save me again and again. The same as real life, there is no happily ever after.

The same as in medical school, you can only save somebody so many times before you can't. It's the Peter Principle of Medicine.

These people sending money, they're paying for heroism in installments.

There's Moroccan food to choke on. There's Sicilian. Every night.

After I was born, my mom just stayed put in the States. Not in this house. She didn't live here until her last release, after the school bus theft charge. Auto theft and kidnapping. This isn't any house I remember from childhood, or this furniture. This is everything her parents sent from Italy. I guess. She could've won it on a game show for all I really know.

Just once, I asked her about her family, my grandparents back in Italy.

And she said, this I remember, she said:

"They don't know about you so don't make any trouble."

And if they don't know about her bastard child, it's a safe bet they don't know about her obscenity conviction, her attempted murder conviction, her reckless endangerment, her animal harassment. It's a safe bet they're insane, too. Just look at their furniture. They're probably insane and dead.

I flip back and forth through the phone book.

The truth is it costs three thousand bucks a month to keep my mom in St. Anthony's Care Center. At St. Anthony's, fifty bucks gets you about one diaper change.

God only knows how many deaths I'll have to almost die to pay for a stomach tube.

The truth is, so far the big book of heroes has just over three hundred names recorded in it, and I still don't pull in three grand every month. Plus there's the waiter every night with a bill. Plus there's the tip. The damn overhead is killing me.

The same as any good pyramid scheme, you always have to be enrolling people at the bottom. The same as Social Security, it's a mass of good people all paying for somebody else. Nickel-and-diming these Good Samaritans is just my own personal social safety net.

"Ponzi scheme" isn't the right phrase, but it's the first that comes to mind.

The miserable truth is, every night I still have to pick through the telephone directory and find a good place to almost die.

What I'm running is the Victor Mancini Telethon.

It's no worse than the government. Only in the Victor Mancini welfare state, the people who foot the bill don't complain. They're proud. They actually brag about it to their friends.

It's a gifting scam with just me at the top and new members lined up to buy in by hugging me from behind. Bleeding these good generous people is.

Still, it's not like I'm spending the money on drugs and gambling. It's not like I even get to finish a meal anymore. Halfway through every main course, I have to go to work. Do my gagging and thrashing. Even then, some people never come across with any money. Some never seem to give it another thought. After long enough even the most generous people will stop sending a check.

The crying part, where I'm hugged in somebody's arms, gasping and crying, that part just gets easier and easier. More and more, the hardest part of crying is when I can't stop.

Not crossed out in the phone book, there's still fondue. There's Thai. Greek. Ethiopian. Cuban. There's still a thousand places I haven't gone to die.

To increase cash flow, you have to create two or three heroes every night. Some nights you have to hit three or four places before you've had a full meal.

I'm a performance artist doing dinner theater, doing three shows a night. Ladies and gentlemen, may I have a volunteer from the audience.

"Thank you, but no thank you," I'd like to tell my dead relatives. "But I can build my own family."

Fish. Meat. Vegan. Tonight, like most nights, the easiest way is to just close your eyes.

Hold your finger over the open phone book.

Step right up and become a hero, ladies and gentlemen. Step right up and save a life.

Just let your hand drop, and let fate decide for you.

Chapter 13

Because of the heat, Denny strips off his coat, then his sweater. Without undoing the buttons, even the cuffs or the collar one, he pulls his shirt off over his head, inside out, so now his head and hands are bagged in red plaid flannel. The T-shirt underneath works up around his armpits while he's fighting the shirt off his head, and his bare stomach looks rashy and caved-in. Some long twisted hairs sprout around his little dot nipples. His nipples look cracked and sore.

"Dude," Denny says, still struggling inside his shirt. "Too many layers. Why's it got to be so hot in here?"

Because it's a kind of a hospital. It's a constant care residence.

Over his jeans and belt, you can see the dead elastic waistband of his bad underpants. Orange rust stains show on the loose elastic. In front, a few coiled hairs poke out. There's yellowy sweat stains on, for real, his underarm skin.

The front desk girl is sitting right here, watching with her face all bunched up tight around her nose.

I try and tug his T-shirt back down, and there's for sure many colors of lint in his navel. At work in the locker room, I've seen Denny pull his pants off inside out with the underpants still on them the way I did when I was little.

And still with his head wrapped up in his shirt, Denny goes, "Dude, can you help me? There's a button somewheres I don't know about."

The front desk girl is giving me her look. She's got the telephone receiver halfway to her ear.

With most of his clothes on the floor next to him, Denny gets skinnier until he's down to just his sour T-shirt and his jeans with dirt on each knee. His tennis shoes are double-knotted with the knots and eye holes glued forever with dirt.

It's somewhere around a hundred degrees here because most of these people don't have any circulation, I tell him. It's a lot of old folks here.

It smells clean, which means you only smell chemicals, cleaning stuff, or perfumes. You have to know the pine smell is covering up shit somewhere. Lemon means somebody vomited. Roses are urine. After an afternoon at St. Anthony's, you never want to smell another rose the rest of your life.

The lobby has stuffed furniture and fake plants and flowers.

This decorator stuff will peter out after you get beyond the locked doors.

To the front desk girl, Denny says, "Will anybody mess with my junk if I just leave it here?" He means the pile of his old clothes. He says, "I'm Victor Mancini." He looks at me. "And I'm here to see my mom?"

To Denny, I go, "Dude, jeez, *she* doesn't have brain damage." To the desk girl, I say, "*I'm* Victor Mancini. I'm here all the time to see my mom, Ida Mancini. She's in Room 158."

The girl presses a phone button and says, "Paging Nurse Remington. Nurse Remington to the front desk, please." Her voice comes out huge through the ceiling.

You have to wonder if Nurse Remington is a real person.

You have to wonder if maybe this girl thinks Denny's just another aggressive chronic undresser.

Denny goes to kick his clothes under a stuffed chair.

A fat man comes jogging down the hall with one hand pressed over a bouncing chest pocket full of pens and another hand on his hip holster of hot pepper spray. Keys jingle on his other hip. To the front desk girl, he says, "So what's the situation here?"

And Denny says, "Is there a bathroom I can use? Like, for civilians?"

The problem is Denny.

So he'll hear her confession, he needs to meet what's left of my mom. My plan is I'll introduce him as Victor Mancini.

This way Denny can find out who I really am. This way my mom can find some peace. Gain some weight. Save me the cost of a tube. Not die.

When Denny's back from the bathroom, the guard is walking us to the living part of St. Anthony's and Denny says, "There's no lock on the bathroom door here. I was settled on the can and some old lady just barged in on me."

I ask if she wanted sex.

And Denny says, "How's that again?"

We go through a set of doors the guard has to unlock, then another set. As we walk, his keys bounce against his hip. Even the back of his neck has a big roll of fat.

"Your mom?" Denny says. "So does she look like you?"

"Maybe," I say, "except, you know . . ."

And Denny says, "Except starved and with no brain left, right?"

And I go, "Stop already." I say, "Okay, she was a shitty mother, but she's the only mom I have."

"Sorry, dude," Denny says, and he goes, "But won't she notice I'm not you?"

Here at St. Anthony's, they have to close the curtains before it gets dark, since if a resident sees themself reflected in a window they'll think somebody's peeping in at them. It's called "sundowning." When all the old folks get crazy at sunset.

You could put most of these folks in front of a mirror and tell them it's a television special about old dying miserable people, and they'd watch for hours.

The problem is my mom won't talk to me when I'm Victor, and she won't talk to me when I'm her attorney. My only hope is to be her public defender while Denny's me. I can goad. He can listen. Maybe then she'll talk.

Think of this as some kind of Gestalt ambush.

Along the way, the guard asks wasn't I the guy who raped Mrs. Field's dog?

No, I tell him. It's a long story, I say. About eighty years long.

We find Mom in the dayroom, sitting at a table with a shattered jigsaw puzzle spread out in front of her. There must be a thousand pieces, but there's no box to show how it's supposed to look. It could be anything.

Denny says, "That's her?" He says, "Dude, she looks nothing like you."

My mom's pushing puzzle pieces around, some of them turned over so the gray cardboard side shows, and she's trying to fit them together.

"Dude," Denny says. He turns a chair around and sits at the table so he can lean forward on the chair back. "In my experience, these puzzles work best if you find all the flat edge pieces first."

My mom's eyes crawl all over Denny, his face, his chapped lips, his shaved head, the holes open in the seams of his T-shirt.

"Good morning, Mrs. Mancini," I say. "Your son, Victor, is here to visit you. This is him." I say, "Don't you have something important to tell him?"

"Yeah," Denny says, nodding. "I'm Victor." He starts picking up pieces with a flat edge. "Is this blue part supposed to be sky or water?" he says.

And my mom's old blue eyes start to fill up with juice.

"Victor?" she says.

She clears her throat. Staring at Denny, she says, "You're here."

And Denny keeps spreading the puzzle pieces with his fingers, picking out the flat ones and getting them off to one side. On the stubble of his shaved head, from his red plaid shirt, there are lumps of red lint.

And my mom's old hand creaks out across the table and closes around Denny's hand. "It's so good to see you," she says. "How are you? It's been so long." A little eye juice tips out the bottom of one eye and follows the wrinkles to the corner of her mouth.

"Jeez," Denny says, and he pulls his hand back. "Mrs. Mancini, your hands are freezing."

My mother says, "I'm sorry."

You can smell some kind of cafeteria food, cabbage or beans, that's being cooked down to mush.

This whole time, I'm still standing here.

Denny pieces together a few inches of the edge. To me, he says, "So when do we meet this perfect lady doctor of yours?"

My mom says, "You're not going already, are you?" She looks at Denny, her eyes swamped and her old eyebrow bushes kissing together in the middle above her nose. "I've missed you so much," she says.

Denny says, "Hey, dude, we lucked out. Here's a corner!"

My mom's shaky, boiled-looking old hand shakes over and picks a clump of red lint off Denny's head.

And I say, "Excuse me, Mrs. Mancini." I say, "But wasn't there something you needed to tell your son?"

My mom just looks at me, then at Denny. "Can you stay, Victor?" she says. "We need to talk. There's so much I need to explain."

"So explain," I say.

Denny says, "Here's an eye, I think." He says, "So is this supposed to be somebody's face?"

My mom holds one shaky old hand open at me, and she says, "Fred, this is between my son and me. This is an important family matter. Go someplace. Go watch the television, and let us visit in private."

And I say, "But."

But my mom says, "Go."

Denny says, "Here's another corner." Denny picks out all the blue pieces and puts them off to one side. All the pieces are the same basic shape, liquid crosses. Melted swastikas.

"Go try to save someone else for a change," my mom says,

not looking at me. Looking at Denny, she says, "Victor will come find you when we're done."

She watches me until I step back as far as the hallway. After that she says something to Denny I can't hear. Her shaky hand reaches to touch Denny's shiny blue scalp, to touch it just behind one ear. Where her pajama sleeve stops, her old wrist shows stringy and thin brown as a boiled turkey neck.

Still nosing around in the puzzle, Denny flinches.

A smell comes around me, a diaper smell, and a broken voice behind me says, "You're the one who threw all my second-grade primers in the mud."

Still watching my mom, trying to see what she's saying, I go, "Yeah, I guess."

"Well, here, at least you're honest" the voice says. A dried little mushroom of a woman slips her skeleton's arm through mine. "Come along with me," she says. "Dr. Marshall would like very much to talk to you. Alone somewhere."

She's wearing Denny's red plaid shirt.

Chapter 14

Leaning her head back, her little black brain, Paige Marshall points up into the vaulted beige ceiling. "There used to be angels," she says. "The story is they were incredibly beautiful, with blue feathery wings and real gilded halos."

The old woman leads me to the big chapel at St. Anthony's, big and empty since it used to be a convent. One whole wall is a window of stained glass in a hundred different colors of gold. The other wall is just a big wood crucifix. Between the two is

Paige Marshall in her white lab coat, golden in the light, under the black brain of her hair. She's wearing her black glasses and looking up. All of her black and gold.

"According to the decrees of Vatican II," she says, "they painted over church murals. The angels and the frescoes. They weeded out most of the statues. All those gorgeous mysteries of faith. All gone."

She looks at me.

The old woman is gone. The chapel door clicks shut behind me.

"It's pathetic," Paige says, "how we can't live with the things we can't understand. How if we can't explain something we'll just deny it."

She says, "I've found a way to save your mother's life." She says, "But you may not approve."

Paige Marshall starts undoing the buttons of her coat, and there's more and more skin showing inside.

"You may find the idea entirely repugnant," she says.

She opens the lab coat.

She's naked inside. Naked and as pale white as the skin under her hair. Naked white and about four steps away. And very doable. And she shrugs the coat off her shoulders so it drapes behind her, still hanging from her elbows. Her arms still in the sleeves.

Here are all those tight furry shadows where you're dying to go.

"We only have this small window of opportunity," she says.

And she steps toward me. Still wearing her glasses. Her feet still in their white deck shoes, only they look gold here.

I was right about her ears. For sure, the resemblance is awesome. Another hole she can't close, hidden and frilled with skin. Framed in her soft hair.

89

"If you love your mother," she says, "if you want her to live, you'll need to do this with me."

Now?

"It's my time," she says. "My mucosa is so thick you could stand a spoon in it."

Here?

"I can't see you outside of here," she says.

Her ring finger is as bare as most of her. I ask, is she married?

"Do you have an issue with that?" she says. Just one reach away is the curve of her waist going down along the outline of her ass. Just that far is the shelf of each breast pushing up a dark button nipple. Just my arm away is the warm hot space where her legs come together.

I say, "No. Nope. No issues here."

Her hands come together around my top shirt button, then the next, and the next. Her hands spread the shirt back off my shoulders so it falls behind me.

"I just need you to know," I say, "since you're a doctor and everything," I say, "I might be a recovering sex addict."

Her hands spring my belt buckle, and she says, "Then just do what comes naturally."

The smell of her isn't roses or pine or lemons. It isn't anything, not even skin.

How she smells is wet.

"You don't understand," I say. "I have almost two whole days of sobriety."

The gold light shows her warm and glowy. Still, the feeling is if I kissed her my lips would stick the way they would on frozen metal. To slow things down, I think of basal cell carcinomas. I picture the bacterial skin infection impetigo. Corneal ulcers.

She pulls my face into her ear. Into my ear she whispers,

"Fine. That's very noble of you. But how about if you start your recovery tomorrow. . . ."

She thumbs my pants off my hips and says, "I need you to put your faith in me."

And her smooth cool hands close around me.

Chapter 15

If you're ever in a big hotel lobby, and they start to play "The Blue Danube Waltz," get the hell out. Don't think. Run.

Anymore, nothing is straightforward.

If you're ever in a hospital and they page Nurse Flamingo to the cancer ward, do not go anywhere near there. There is no Nurse Flamingo. If they page Dr. Blaze, there is no such person.

In a big hotel, that waltz means they need to evacuate the building.

In most hospitals, Nurse Flamingo means a fire. Dr. Blaze

means a fire. Dr. Green means a suicide. Dr. Blue means somebody stopped breathing.

This is stuff the Mommy told the stupid little boy as they sat in traffic. This is how far back she was going nuts.

This one day, the kid had been sitting in class when a lady from the school office had come to tell him his dentist appointment was canceled. A minute later, he'd raised his hand and asked to go to the bathroom. There never was any appointment. Sure, somebody had called, saying they were from the dentist, but this was a new secret signal. He went out a side door by the cafeteria, and there she was waiting in a gold car.

This was the second time the Mommy came back to claim him.

She rolled down the window and said, "Do you know why Mommy was in jail this time?"

"For changing the hair colors?" he said.

See also: The malicious mischief.

See also: The second-degree assault.

She leaned over to open the door and never stopped talking. Not for days and days.

If you're ever in the Hard Rock Café, she told him, and they announce "Elvis has left the building," that means all the servers need to go to the kitchen and find out what dinner special has just sold out.

These are the things people tell you when they won't tell you the truth.

In a Broadway theater, announcing "Elvis has left the building" means a fire.

In a grocery store, paging Mr. Cash is a call for an armed security guard. Paging "Freight check to Women's Clothing" means somebody is shoplifting in that department. Other stores page a fake woman named Sheila. "Sheila to the front" means somebody is shoplifting in the front of the store. Mr. Cash and Sheila and Nurse Flamingo are always bad news.

The Mommy shut off the engine and sat with one hand gripping the steering wheel at twelve o'clock, and with her other hand she snapped her fingers for the boy to repeat stuff back to her. The insides of her nose were dark with dried blood. Twisted old tissues smeared with more old blood were on the car floor. Some blood was on the dashboard from when she sneezed. On the inside of the windshield was some more.

"Nothing you learn in school is this important," she said. "This stuff you're learning here will save your life."

She snapped her fingers. "Mr. Amond Silvestiri?" she said. "If he's paged, what should you do?"

At some airports, paging him means a terrorist with a bomb. "Mr. Amond Silvestiri, please meet your party at gate ten on the D concourse" means that's where the SWAT teams will find their man.

Mrs. Pamela Rank-Mensa means a terrorist in the airport with just a gun.

"Mr. Bernard Wellis, please meet your party at gate sixteen on the F concourse" means somebody holding a knife to the throat of a hostage there.

The Mommy set the parking brake and snapped her fingers again. "Quick like a bunny. What's Miss Terrilynn Mayfield mean?"

"Nerve gas?" the boy said.

The Mommy shook her head.

"Don't tell me," the boy said. "A rabid dog?"

The Mommy shook her head.

Outside the car, the tight mosaic of cars was packed around them. Helicopters beat the air above the freeway.

The boy tapped his forehead and said, "Flamethrower?"

The Mommy said, "You're not even trying. Do you want a clue?"

"Drug suspect?" he said, then, "Yeah, maybe a clue."

And the Mommy said, "Miss Terrilynn Mayfield . . . now be thinking about cows and horses."

And the boy screamed, "Anthrax!" He pounded his forehead with his fists and said, "Anthrax. Anthrax. Anthrax." He pounded his head and said, "How come I forget so fast?"

With her free hand the Mommy messed his hair and said, "You're doing good. You even remember half of these and you'll outlive most people."

Everywhere they went, the Mommy found traffic. She listened for radio bulletins about where not to go, and found those tie-ups. She found gridlock. She found jams. She searched for car fires or open drawbridges. She didn't like driving fast, but wanted to look busy. In traffic, she couldn't do anything and it wasn't her fault. They'd be trapped. Hidden and secure.

The Mommy said, "I'll give you an easy one." She closed her eyes and smiled, then opened them and said, "At any store, what's it mean when they ask for quarters on checkstand five?"

They were both wearing the same clothes from the day she had picked him up after school. In whatever motel they got, when he crawled into bed the Mommy snapped her fingers and asked for his pants, his shirt, his socks, his underpants, until he'd passed them all out from under the covers. In the morning when she gave them back, sometimes they were washed.

When a cashier asks for quarters, the boy said, they mean a pretty woman is standing there and everybody should come look at her.

"Well, there's more to it than that," the Mommy said. "But yes."

Sometimes the Mommy went to sleep against the car door

and all the other cars drove away from around them. If the motor was on, sometimes red dashboard lights the boy didn't even know were there would light up to show all kind of emergencies. These times, smoke came out through the crack around the hood, and the motor stopped by itself. Cars stuck behind them would honk. The radio talked about a new tie-up, a stalled car in the center lane of the freeway, blocking traffic.

With people honking and looking in the windows at them, being on the radio, the stupid little boy figured this was being famous. Until the car horns woke her up, the little boy just waved. He thought about the fat Tarzan with the monkey and the chestnuts. The way the man could still smile. The way humiliation is humiliation only when you choose to suffer.

The little boy smiled back at all the angry faces glaring in at him.

And the little boy blew kisses.

When a truck honked its horn, then the Mommy jumped awake. Then slow again, she pushed most of the hair off her face for a minute. She pushed a white plastic tube up one nostril and breathed in. Another minute of nothing went by before she took the tube out and squinted at the little boy sitting next to her in the front seat. She squinted at the new red dash lights.

The tube was smaller than her lipstick, with a hole to smell through at one end and something that stunk inside. After she smelled it, there was always blood on the tube.

"You're in, what?" she said. "First? Second grade?"

Fifth, the boy said.

"And at this phase your brain weighs, three? Four pounds?"

In school, he got straight A's.

"So that makes you, what?" she said. "Seven years old?"

Nine.

"Well, Einstein, everything those foster parents of yours have told you," the Mommy said, "you can forget it."

She said, "Those foster families, they don't know what's important."

Right over them was a helicopter flying in one place, and the boy leaned so he could look straight up at it through the blue part at the top of the windshield.

The radio talked about a gold Plymouth Duster blocking the center lane of traffic on the beltway. The car appeared to be overheating.

"Screw history. All these fake people, they're the most important people for you to know," the Mommy said.

Miss Pepper Haviland is the Ebola virus. Mr. Turner Anderson means somebody just threw up.

The radio said emergency crews were being dispatched to help clear the stalled car.

"All that stuff they're teaching you about algebra and macroeconomics, forget it," she said. "You tell me, what does it get you if you can square root a triangle and then some terrorist shoots you in the head? It gets you nothing! This is the real education you need."

Other cars edged around them and took off squealing fast and disappeared to other places.

"I want you to know more than just what people think is safe to tell you," she said.

The boy said, "Like what more?"

"Like, when you're thinking about the rest of your life," she said, and she put her hand over her eyes, "you're never really thinking more than a couple years down the road."

And what else she said is, "By the time you're thirty, your worst enemy is yourself."

Another thing she said was, "The Enlightenment is over. What we're living in now is the *Dis-Enlightenment*."

The radio said the police had been notified about the stalled car.

The Mommy turned up the radio, loud. "Damn," she said. "Please tell me that's not us."

"It said a gold Duster," the boy said. "That's our car."

And the Mommy said, "That shows how little you know."

She opened her door and said to slide over and get out on her side. She watched the fast cars just missing, driving past them. "This isn't our car," she said.

The radio yelled how it appeared the occupants were abandoning the vehicle.

The Mommy shook her hand for him to take. "I'm not your mother," she said. "It's nothing like that." Under her fingernails was more dried nose blood.

The radio yelled after them. The driver of the gold Duster and a small child were now a hazard themselves as they were attempting to dodge across four lanes of freeway traffic.

She said, "I figure we have about thirty days to pile up a lifetime of happy adventures. That's until my credit cards run out."

She said, "That's thirty days unless we get caught, first."

Cars honked and swerved. The radio yelled after them. Helicopters roared closer down.

And the Mommy said, "Now just like with 'The Blue Danube Waltz,' hold on to my hand, tight." She said, "And don't think." She said, "Just run."

Chapter 16

The next patient is a female, about twenty-nine years old, with a mole high on the inside of her thigh that doesn't look right. It's hard to tell in this light, but it looks too big, asymmetrical, with shades of blue and brown. The edges are irregular. The skin around it abraded.

I ask her if she's been scratching it.

And is there any history of skin cancer in her family?

Sitting next to me with his yellow legal pad on the table in front of him, Denny's holding one end of a cork over his cigarette lighter, turning the cork until the end is burned black, and Denny says, "Dude, for serious." He says, "You've got some weird hostility tonight. Did you act out?"

He says, "You always hate the whole world after you get laid."

The patient falls to her knees, her knees spread wide apart. She leans back and starts to pump herself at us in slow motion. Just by contracting her butt muscles, she tosses her shoulders, her breasts, her mons pubis. Her entire body lunges at us in waves.

The way to remember the symptoms of melanoma is the letters ABCD.

Asymmetrical shape.

Border irregularity.

Color variation.

Diameter larger than about six millimeters.

She's shaved. Tanned and oiled so smooth and perfect, she looks less like a woman than just another place to swipe your credit card. Pumping herself in our faces, the murky blend of red and black light makes her look better than she really is. The red lights erase scars and bruises, zits, some kinds of tattoos, plus stretch and track marks. The black lights make her eyes and teeth glow bright white.

It's funny how the beauty of art has so much more to do with the frame than with the artwork itself.

The light trick makes even Denny look healthy, his chickeny wing arms coming out of a white T-shirt. His legal pad glows yellow. He curls his bottom lip inside, biting it as he looks from the patient to his work, and back to the patient.

Pumping herself in our faces, yelling against the music, she says, "What?"

She looks like a natural blonde, a high risk factor, so I ask, has she had any recent unexplained weight loss?

Not looking at me, Denny says, "Dude, do you know how much a real model would cost me?"

Back at him, I say, "Dude, don't forget to sketch her ingrown hairs."

To the patient, I ask, has she noticed any changes in her cycle or in her bowel movements?

Kneeling in front of us, spreading her black-polished fingernails open on either side of herself and leaning back, looking down the arched length of her torso at us, she says, "What?"

Skin cancer, I yell, is the most common cancer in women between the ages of twenty-nine and thirty-four.

I yell, "I'll need to feel your lymph nodes."

And Denny says, "Dude, you want to know what your mom told me or not?"

I yell, "Just let me palpate your spleen."

And sketching fast with the burned cork, he says, "Do I sense a shame cycle?"

The blonde hooks her elbows behind her knees and rolls back onto her spine, twisting a nipple between the thumb and forefinger of each hand. Stretching her mouth wide open, she curls her tongue at us, then says, "Daiquiri." She says. "My name's Cherry Daiquiri. You can't touch me," she says, "but where's this mole you're talking about?"

The way to remember every step to a physical examination is CHAMP FASTS. It's what they call a *mnemonic* in medical school. The letters stand for:

Chief Complaint.

History of Illness.

Allergies.

Medications.

Past Medical History.

Family History.

Alcohol.

Street Drugs.

Tobacco.

Social History.

The only way to get through medical school is mnemonics.

The girl before this one, another blonde but with the kind of hard old-fashioned boob job you could chin yourself on, this last patient smoked a cigarette as part of her act, so I asked if she had any persistent back or abdominal pain. Had she experienced any loss of appetite, any general malaise? If this was how she made her living, I said, she'd better make sure and get regular smears.

"If you smoke more than a pack a day," I said. "This way, I mean."

A conization wouldn't be a bad idea, I told her, or at the very least a D and C.

She gets down on her hands and knees, rotating her open butt, her puckered pink trapdoor in slow motion, and looks back over her shoulder at us and says, "What's this 'conization' scene?"

She says, "Is that something new you're into?" and exhales smoke in my face.

Sort of exhales.

It's when you razor out a cone-shaped sample of the cervix, I tell her.

And she goes pale, pale even under her makeup, even under the wash of red and black light, and pulls her legs back together. She puts out her cigarette in my beer and says, "You have one sick issue with women," and goes off to the next guy down along the stage.

After her I yell, "Every woman is just a different kind of problem."

Still holding his cork, Denny picks up my beer and says,

"Dude, waste not . . ." then pours everything except the drowned butt into his own glass. He says, "Your mom talks a lot about some Dr. Marshall. She says he's promised to make her young again," Denny says, "but only if you cooperate."

And I say, "She. It's Dr. Paige Marshall. She's a woman."

Another patient presents herself, a curly-haired brunette, about twenty-five years old, exhibiting a possible folic acid deficiency, her tongue red and glazed-looking, her abdomen slightly distended, her eyes glassy. I ask, can I listen to her heart. For palpitations. For rapid heartbeat. Has she had any nausea or diarrhea?

"Dude?" Denny says.

The questions to ask about pain are COLDERRA: Characteristics, Onset, Location, Duration, Exacerbation, Relief, Radiation, and Associated Symptoms.

Denny says, "Dude?"

The bacteria called *Staphylococcus aureus* will give you STAPHEO: Skin Infections, Toxic Shock Syndrome, Abscesses, Pneumonia, Hemolysis, Endocarditis, and Osteomyelitis.

"Dude?" Denny says.

The diseases a mother can pass to her baby are TORCH: Toxoplasmosis, Other (meaning syphilis and HIV), Rubella, Cytomegalovirus, and Herpes. It helps if you can picture a mother *passing the torch* to her baby.

Like mother, like son.

Denny snaps his fingers in my face. "What's up with you? How come you're being like this?"

Because it's the truth. This is the world we live in. I've been there, taken the MCAT. The Medical College Admission Test. I went to the USC School of Medicine long enough to know that a mole is never just a mole. That a simple headache means brain tumors, means double vision, numbness, vomiting followed by seizures, drowsiness, death.

A little muscle twitch means rabies, means muscle cramps, thirst, confusion, and drooling, followed by seizures, coma, death. Acne means ovarian cysts. Feeling a little tired means tuberculosis. Bloodshot eyes mean meningitis. Drowsiness is the first sign of typhoid. Those floaters you see cross your eyes on sunny days, they mean your retina is detaching. You're going blind.

"See how her fingernails look," I tell Denny, "that's a sure sign of lung cancer."

If you're confused, that means renal shutdown, severe kidney failure.

You learn all this during Physical Examination, your second year in medical school. You learn all this, and there's no going back.

Ignorance *was* bliss.

A bruise means cirrhosis of the liver. A belch means colorectal cancer or esophageal cancer or at the very least a peptic ulcer.

Every little breeze seems to whisper squamous carcinoma.

Birds in the trees seem to twitter histoplasmosis.

Everybody you see naked, you see as a patient. A dancer could have clear lovely eyes and hard brown nipples, but if her breath is bad she has leukemia. A dancer might have thick, long, clean-looking hair, but if she scratches her scalp, she has Hodgkin's lymphoma.

Page by page, Denny fills up his pad with figure studies, beautiful women smiling, thin women blowing him kisses, women with their faces tilted down, but their eyes looking up at him through falls of hair.

"Losing your sense of taste," I tell Denny, "means oral cancers."

And without looking at me, looking back and forth between

his sketch and the new dancer, Denny says, "Then, dude, you got that cancer a long time ago."

Even if my mom died, I'm not sure if I'd want to go back and get readmitted before my credits start to expire. As it is, I already know way more than I'm comfortable with.

After you find out all the things that can go wrong, your life becomes less about living and more about waiting. For cancer. For dementia. Every look in a mirror, you scan for the red rash that means shingles. See also: Ringworm.

See also: Scabies

See also: Lyme disease, meningitis, rheumatic fever, syphilis.

The next patient who presents herself is another blonde, thin, maybe a little too thin. A spinal tumor probably. If she has a headache, a low fever, a sore throat, she has polio.

"Go like this," Denny yells up to her, and he covers his eyeglasses with his open hands.

The patient does this.

"Beautiful," Denny says, sketching a study fast. "How about if you open your mouth a little."

And she does.

"Dude," he says. "Workshop models are *never* this hot."

All I can see is she's not a very good dancer and, for sure, this lack of coordination means amyotrophic lateral sclerosis.

See also: Lou Gehrig's disease.

See also: Total paralysis. See also: Difficulty breathing. See also: Cramps, tiredness, crying.

See also: Death.

With the edge of his hand, Denny smears the cork lines to add shadow and depth. It's the woman onstage with her hands over her eyes, her mouth slightly open, and Denny picks at it fast, his eyes going back to the woman for details, her belly button, the curve of her hipbones. My only gripe is the way Denny draws women is not the way they look for real. In Denny's version, the cheesy thighs on some woman will look rock-solid. The bagged-out eyes on some other woman will become clear and toned underneath.

"You got any cash left over, dude?" Denny says. "I don't want her to move on just yet."

But I'm broke, and the girl moves on to the next guy down along the stage.

"Let's see, Picasso," I tell him.

And Denny scratches under his eye and leaves a big smudge of soot. Then he tips the legal pad enough for me to see a naked woman with her hands over her eyes, sleek and tensing every muscle tight, none of her looks trashed by gravity or ultraviolet light or poor nutrition. She's smooth but soft. Flexed but relaxed. She's a total physical impossibility.

"Dude," I say, "you made her look too young."

The next patient is Cherry Daiquiri again, coming back around, not smiling this time, sucking hard on the inside of one cheek and asking me, "This mole I have? You sure it's cancer? I mean, I don't know, but how scared should I be . . . ?"

Without looking at her, I hold up one finger. This is international sign language for *Please wait. The doctor will see you shortly*.

"No way are her ankles that thin," I tell Denny. "And her ass is way bigger than you have there."

I lean over to see what Denny's doing, then look down the stage to the last patient. "You need to make her knees lumpier," I say.

The downstage dancer gives me a filthy look.

Denny just keeps sketching. He makes her eyes huge. He fixes her split ends. He gets everything all wrong.

"Dude," I say. "You know, you're not a very good artist."

106

I say, "For serious, dude, I don't see that at all."

Denny says, "Before you go trash the whole world, you need to be calling your sponsor, bad." He says, "And in case you still give a shit, your mom said you need to read what's in her dictionary."

To Cherry crouching there in front of us, I say, "If you're really serious about saving your life, I'm going to have to talk to you someplace private."

"No, not *dictionary*," Denny says, "it's *diary*. In case you ever wonder where you really come from, it's all in her diary."

And Cherry dangles one leg over the edge and starts climbing down off the stage.

I ask him, what's in my mom's diary?

And drawing his little pictures, seeing the impossible, Denny says, "Yeah, diary. Not dictionary, dude. The stuff about your real dad is in her diary."

Chapter 17

At St. Anthony's, the front desk girl yawns behind her hand, and when I ask if maybe she wants to go get a cup of coffee, then she looks at me sideways and says, "Not with you."

And really, I'm not hitting on her. I'll watch her desk long enough for her to go get some coffee. This isn't a come-on.

Really.

I say, "Your eyes look tired."

All she does all day is sign a few people in and out. She watches the video monitor that shows the insides of St. An-

thony's, each corridor, the dayroom, the dining room, the garden, the screen switching from one to the next every ten seconds.
The screen grainy, black-and-white. On the monitor, the dining
room shows for ten seconds, empty with all the chairs upside
down on each table, their chrome legs in the air. A long corridor
appears for the next ten seconds with somebody heaped on a
bench against one wall.

Then for the next ten furry black-and-white seconds, there's
Paige Marshall pushing my mom in a wheelchair down some
other long corridor.

The front desk girl says, "I'll only be gone a minute."

Next to the video monitor is an old speaker. Covered in
nubby sofa mohair is this old radio kind of speaker with a dial
switch surrounded by numbers. Each number is some room in
St. Anthony's. On the desk is a microphone you can use to make
announcements. By turning the dial switch to a number, you can
listen in on any room in the building.

And for just a moment, my mom's voice comes from the
speaker, saying, "I've defined myself, all my life, by what I was
against . . ."

The girl switches the intercom dial to nine, and now you can
hear Spanish radio and the clatter of metal pans back in the
kitchen, back where the coffee is.

I tell the girl, "Take your time." And, "I'm not the monster
you maybe heard from some of the bitter, angry types around
here."

Even with me being so nice, she puts her purse in her desk
and locks it. She says, "This won't take me more than a couple
minutes. Okay?"

Okay.

Then she's gone through the security doors, and I'm sitting
behind her desk. Watching the monitor: the dayroom, the gar-

den, some corridor, each for ten seconds. Watching for Paige Marshall. With one hand, I'm dial-switching from number to number, listening in each room for Dr. Marshall. For my mom. In black-and-white, almost live.

Paige Marshall with all her skin.

Another question from the sex addict checklist:

Do you cut the inside out of your pants pockets so you can masturbate in public?

In the dayroom is some grayhead, facedown in a puzzle.

In the speaker there's just static. White noise.

Ten seconds later, in the crafts room is a table of old women. Women I confessed to, for wrecking their cars, for wrecking their lives. Taking the blame.

I turn up the volume and put my ear against the cloth of the speaker. Not knowing which number means which room, I dial-switch through the numbers and listen.

My other hand I slip into what used to be my britches pocket.

Going number to number, somebody's sobbing on number three. Wherever that is. Somebody's swearing on five. Praying on eight. Wherever that is. The kitchen again on nine, the Spanish music.

The monitor shows the library, another corridor, then it shows me, a grainy black-and-white me, crouched behind the front desk, peering into the monitor. Me with one hand crabbed around the intercom control dial. My other blurry hand is jammed to the elbow inside my britches. Watching. A camera on the lobby ceiling watching me.

Me watching for Paige Marshall.

Listening. For where to find her.

"Stalking" isn't the right word, but it's the first word that comes to mind.

The monitor shows me one old woman after another. Then for ten seconds, there's Paige pushing my mom in a wheelchair down another corridor. Dr. Paige Marshall. And I dial around until I hear my mom's voice.

"Yes," she says, "I fought *against* everything, but more and more I worry that I was never *for* anything."

The monitor shows the garden, old women hunched over walkers. Mired in gravel.

"Oh, I can criticize and complain and judge everything, but what does that get me?" my mom keeps saying in voice-over as the monitor cycles to show other rooms.

The monitor shows the dining room, empty.

The monitor shows the garden. More old people.

This could be some very depressing website. Death Cam.

Some kind of black-and-white documentary.

"Griping isn't the same as creating something," my mom's voice-over says. "Rebelling isn't rebuilding. Ridiculing isn't replacing . . ." And the voice in the speaker fades out.

The monitor shows the dayroom, the woman facedown in her puzzle.

And I dial-switch from number to number, searching.

On number five, her voice is back. "We've taken the world apart," she says, "but we have no idea what to do with the pieces . . ." And her voice is gone, again.

The monitor shows one empty corridor after another stretching into darkness.

On number seven, the voice comes back: "My generation, all of our making fun of things isn't making the world any better," she says. "We've spent so much time judging what other people created that we've created very, very little of our own."

Out of the speaker, her voice says, "I used rebellion as a way to hide out. We use criticism as a fake participation."

The voice-over says, "It only looks as if we've accomplished something."

The voice-over says, "I've never contributed anything worthwhile to the world."

And for ten seconds, the monitor shows my mom and Paige in the corridor just outside the crafts room.

Out of the speaker, scratchy and far away, Paige's voice says, "What about your son?"

My nose pressed to the monitor, I'm so close.

And now the monitor shows me with my ear pressed to the speaker, one hand shaking something, fast, inside my pant leg.

In voice-over, Paige says, "What about Victor?"

And for serious, I am so ready to trigger.

And my mom's voice says, "Victor? No doubt Victor has his own way of escaping."

Then her voice-over laughs and says, "Parenthood is the opiate of the masses!"

And now on the monitor, the front desk girl is standing right behind me with a cup of coffee.

Chapter 18

My next visit, my mom's thinner, if that's possible. Her neck looks as small around as my wrist, the yellow skin sunk into deep hollows between her cords and throat. Her face doesn't hide the skull inside. She rolls her head to one side so she can see me in the doorway, and some kind of gray jelly is caked in the corners of each eye.

The blankets are slack and tented empty between the two peaks of her hipbones. The only other landmarks you can recognize are her knees.

She twines one terrible arm through the chrome bed rail, terrible and thin as a chicken foot reaching toward me, and she swallows. Her jaws work with effort, her lips webbed with spit, and then she says it, reaching out, she says it.

"Morty," she says, "I am not a pimp." Her hands knotted in fists, she shakes them in the air and says, "I'm making a feminist statement. How can it be prostitution if all the women were dead?"

I'm here with a nice bunch of flowers and a get-well card. This is right after work, so I'm in my britches and waistcoat. My buckle shoes and the clocked stockings that show off my skinny calves are spattered with mud.

And my mom says, "Morty, you have to get the whole case thrown out of court." And she sighs back into her stack of pillows. Drool from her mouth has turned the white pillowcase light blue where it meets the side of her face.

A get-well card is not going to fix this.

Her hand claws the air, and she says, "Oh, and Morty, you need to call Victor."

Her room has that smell, the same smell as Denny's tennis shoes in September after he's worn them all summer without socks.

A nice bunch of flowers won't even make a dent.

In my waistcoat pocket is her diary. Stuck in the diary is a past-due bill from the care center. I stick the flowers in her bedpan while I go hunt for a vase and maybe something to feed her. As much of that chocolate pudding stuff as I can carry. Something I can spoon into her mouth and make her swallow.

The way she looks I can't bear to be here and I can't bear to not be here. As I leave she says, "You've got to get busy and find Victor. You have to make him help Dr. Marshall. Please. He has to help Dr. Marshall save me."

114

As if anything ever happens by accident.

Outside in the hallway is Paige Marshall, wearing her glasses, reading something off a clipboard. "I just thought you'd like to know," she says. She leans back against the handrail that lines the hallway and says, "Your mother is down to eighty-five pounds this week."

She moves the clipboard behind her back, gripping it and the handrail with both hands. The way she stands puts her breasts forward. Tilts her pelvis at me. Paige Marshall runs her tongue along the inside of her bottom lip and says, "Have you thought any more about taking some action?"

Life support, tube feeding, artificial respirators—in medicine they call this stuff "heroic measures."

I don't know, I say.

We stand there, waiting for each other to give an inch.

Two smiling old ladies wander past us, and one points and says to the other, "There's that nice young man I told you about. He's the one who strangled my pet cat."

The other lady, her sweater is buttoned wrong, and she says, "You don't say." She says, "He beat my sister almost to death one time."

They wander away.

"It's sweet," Dr. Marshall says, "what you're doing, I mean. You're giving these people completion on the biggest issues in their lives."

The way she looks right now, you have to think about multiple car pile-ups. Imagine two bloodmobiles colliding head on. The way she looks, you'd have to think of mass graves to even log thirty seconds in the saddle.

Think of spoiled cat food and ulcerated cankers and expired donor organs.

That's how beautiful she looks.

If she'll excuse me, I still need to find some pudding.

She says, "Is it that you have a girlfriend? Is that your reason?"

The reason why we didn't have sex in the chapel a few days ago. The reason why even with her naked and ready, I couldn't. The reason why I ran.

For a complete listing of other girlfriends, please refer to my fourth step.

See also: Nico.

See also: Leeza.

See also: Tanya.

Dr. Marshall tilts her pelvis at me and says, "Do you know how most patients like your mother die?"

They starve. They forget how to swallow and breathe food and drink into their lungs by accident. Their lungs fill with rotting matter and liquid, they develop pneumonia, and they die.

I say, I know.

I say maybe there's worse things you can do than just letting somebody old die.

"This isn't just some old person," Paige Marshall says. "This is your mother."

And she's almost seventy years old.

"She's sixty-two," Paige says. "If there's anything you can do to save her and you don't, you're killing her with neglect."

"In other words," I say, "I should *do* you?"

"I've heard about your track record from some of the nurses," Paige Marshall says. "I know you have no issues around recreational sex. Or is it just me? Am I just not your type? Is that it?"

The two of us get quiet. A certified nurse's aide walks past, pushing a cart of bundled sheets and damp towels. Her shoes have rubber soles and the cart has rubber wheels. The floor is ancient cork tile polished dark with traffic, so she goes by without a sound, just the stale trailing urine smell.

"Don't get me wrong," I say. "I want to fuck you. I really want to fuck you."

Down the hall, the nurse's aide stops and looks back at us. She says, "Hey Romeo, why don't you give poor Dr. Marshall a break?"

Paige says, "It's fine, Miss Parks. This is between Mr. Mancini and myself."

We both stare back until she smirks and pushes her cart off around the next corner. Her name's Irene, Irene Parks, and yeah, okay, we did it in her car in the parking lot about this time last year.

See also: Caren, RN.

See also: Jenine, CNA.

At the time, I thought each of them was going to be somebody special, but without their clothes, they could've been anybody. Now her ass is about as inviting as a pencil sharpener.

To Dr. Paige Marshall I say, "There you are so wrong." I say, "I want to fuck you so bad I can taste it." I say, "And no, I don't want anybody to die, but I don't want my mom back the way she's always been."

Paige Marshall exhales. She sucks her mouth into a tight little knot and just glares at me. She holds her clipboard to her chest with her arms crossed over it.

"So," she says. "This hasn't anything to do with sex. You just don't want your mother to recover. You just can't deal with strong women, and you think that if she dies, then your issue about her will also."

From her room, my mom calls, "Morty, what am I paying you for?"

Paige Marshall says, "You can lie to my patients and complete their life conflicts, but don't lie to yourself." Then she says, "And don't lie to me."

Paige Marshall says, "You'd rather see her dead than see her recover."

And I say, "Yes. I mean, no. I mean, I don't know."

All my life, I've been less my mother's child than her hostage. The subject of her social and political experiments. Her own private lab rat. Now she's mine, and she's not going to escape by dying or getting better. I just want one person I can rescue. I want one person who needs me. Who can't live without me. I want to be a hero, but not just one time. Even if it means keeping her crippled, I want to be someone's constant savior.

"I know, I know, I know this sounds terrible," I say, "but I don't know. . . . This is what I think."

Here's where I should tell Paige Marshall what I really think.

I mean, I'm just tired of being wrong all the time just because I'm a guy.

I mean, how many times can everybody tell you that you're the oppressive, prejudiced enemy before you give up and become the enemy. I mean, a male chauvinist pig isn't born, he's made, and more and more of them are being made by women.

After long enough, you just roll over and accept the fact that you're a sexist, bigoted, insensitive, crude, cretinist cretin. Women are right. You're wrong. You get used to the idea. You live down to expectations.

Even if the shoe doesn't fit, you'll shrink into it.

I mean, in a world without God, aren't mothers the new god? The last sacred unassailable position. Isn't motherhood the last perfect magical miracle? But a miracle that's impossible for men.

And maybe men say they're glad not to give birth, all the pain and blood, but really that's just so much sour grapes. For sure, men can't do anything near as incredible. Upper body strength, abstract thought, phalluses—any advantages men appear to have are pretty token.

You can't even hammer a nail with a phallus.

Women are already born so far ahead ability-wise. The day men can give birth, that's when we can start talking about equal rights.

I don't tell Paige all that.

Instead, I say how I just want to be one person's guardian angel.

"Revenge" isn't the right word, but it's the first word that comes to mind.

"Then save her by fucking me," says Dr. Marshall.

"But I don't want her saved all the way," I say. I'm terrified of losing her, but if I don't, I may lose myself.

There's still my mom's red diary in my coat pocket. There's still the chocolate pudding to get.

"You don't want her to die," Paige says, "and you don't want her to recover. Just what do you want?"

"I want somebody who can read Italian," I say.

Paige says, "Like what?"

"Here," I say and show her the diary. "It's my mom's. It's in Italian."

Paige takes the book and leafs through it. Her ears look red and excited around the edge. "I took four years of Italian as an undergrad," she says. "I can tell you what it says."

"I just want to keep control," I say. "For a change, I want to be the adult."

Still leafing through the book, Dr. Paige Marshall says, "You want to keep her weak so you're always the one in charge." She looks up at me and says, "It sounds as if you'd like to be God."

Chapter 19

Black-and-white chickens stagger around Colonial Dunsboro, chickens with their heads flattened. Here are chickens with no wings or only one leg. There are chickens with no legs, swimming with just their ragged wings through the barnyard mud. Blind chickens without eyes. Without beaks. Born that way. Defective. Born with their little chicken brains already scrambled.

There's an invisible line between science and sadism, but here it's made visible.

It's not that my brains are going to fare much better. Just look at my mom.

Dr. Paige Marshall should see them all struggle along. Not that she'd understand.

Denny here with me, Denny reaches into the back of his pants and pulls out a page of the classified ads from the newspaper all folded up in a little square. For sure this is contraband. His Royal High Governorship sees this and Denny's going to be banished to unemployment. For real, right out in the barnyard in front of the cow shed, Denny hands me this newspaper page.

Except for the newspaper, we're being so authentic it's like nothing we're wearing's even been washed in this century.

People are snapping pictures, trying to take some part of you home as a souvenir. People point video cameras, trying to trap you into their vacation. They're all shooting you, shooting the crippled chickens. Everybody's trying to make every minute of the present last forever. Preserve every second.

Inside the cow shed, there's the gurgle of somebody sucking air through a bong. You can't see them, but there's that silent tension of a bunch of people leaned together in a circle, trying to hold their breath. A girl coughs. Ursula, the milkmaid. There's so much reefer in there a cow coughs.

This is when we're supposed to be harvesting dried cow things, you know, cow piles, and Denny goes, "Read it, dude. The circled ad." He opens the page for me to see. "That ad, there," he says. There's one little classified circled in red ink.

With the milkmaid around. The tourists. There's nothing less than a trillion ways we're about to get caught. For real, Denny could not be more obvious.

Against my hand, the paper's still warm from Denny's butt,

and when I go, "Not here, dude," and try to give the paper back . . .

When I do that, Denny says, "Sorry, I didn't mean to, you know, incriminate you. If you want, I can just read it for you."

The grade-schoolers who come here, it's a big deal for them to visit the henhouse and watch the eggs hatch. Still, a regular chick isn't as interesting as, say, a chicken with only one eye or a chicken with no neck or with a stunted paralyzed leg, so the kids shake the eggs. Shake them hard and put them back to hatch.

So if what's born is deformed or insane? It's all for the sake of education.

The lucky ones are just born dead.

Curiosity or cruelty, for sure, me and Dr. Marshall would go around and around on this point.

I shovel up some cow piles, careful so they don't break in half. So the wet insides don't stink. With all the cow crap on my hands, I have to not bite my nails.

Next to me, Denny reads:

"Free to good home, twenty-three-year-old male, recovering self-abuser, limited income and social skills, house-trained." Then he reads a phone number. It's his phone number.

"It's my folks, dude, that's their phone number," Denny says. "It's like they're hinting."

He found this left on his bed last night.

Denny says, "They mean me."

I say I understand that part. With a wood shovel, I'm still getting the poops, piling them in a big woven thing. You know. A basket thing.

Denny says, can he come live with me?

"We're talking plan Z here," Denny says. "I'm only asking you as a last resort."

Because he doesn't want to bug me or because he's not nuts about living with me, I don't ask.

You can smell corn chips on Denny's breath. Another violation of historic character. He's such a shit magnet. The milkmaid, Ursula, comes out of the cow shed and looks at us with her stoner eyes just about filled with blood.

"If there was a girl you liked," I say to him, "if she wanted to have sex just so she could get pregnant, would you?"

Ursula grabs her skirts up and comes stomping through the cow poop in her wooden clogs. She kicks a blind chicken that's in her way. Somebody snaps her picture, kicking. A married couple start to ask Ursula to hold their baby for a picture, but then maybe they see her eyes.

"I don't know," Denny says. "A baby's not like having a dog. I mean, a baby lives a *long* time, dude."

"But what if she wasn't planning to have the baby?" I say.

Denny's eyes go up and then down, looking at nothing, then he looks at me. "I don't understand," he says. "You mean like sell it?"

"I mean like sacrifice it," I say.

And Denny says, "Dude."

"Just supposing," I say, "she's going to scramble its little unborn fetus brain and suck the mess out with a big needle and then inject that stuff into the head of somebody you know who has brain damage, to cure them," I say.

Denny's lips hang open a crack. "Dude, you don't mean *me,* do you?"

I mean my mom.

It's called a neural transplant. Some people call it a neural graft, and it's the only effective way to rebuild my mom's brain at this late stage. It would be better known except for problems getting, you know, the key ingredient.

"A ground-up baby," Denny says.

I say, "A fetus."

Fetal tissue, Paige Marshall said. Dr. Marshall with her skin and her mouth.

Ursula stops next to us, and she points at the newspaper in Denny's hand. She says, "Unless the date on that's 1734, you're fucked. That's a violation of character."

The hair on Denny's head is trying to grow back, except some is ingrown and trapped under red or white pimples.

Ursula steps away, then turns back. "Victor," she says, "if you need me, I'll be churning."

I say, later. And she slogs off.

Denny says, "Dude, so it's like a choice between your mom and your firstborn?"

It's not a big deal, the way Dr. Marshall sees it. We do it every day. Kill the unborn to save the elderly. In the gold wash of the chapel, breathing her reasons into my ear, she asked, every time we burn a gallon of gas or an acre of rain forest, aren't we killing the future to preserve the present?

The whole pyramid scheme of Social Security.

She said, with her breasts wedged between us, she said, I'm doing this because I care about your mother. The least you could do is your small part.

I didn't ask what she meant by *small part*.

And Denny says, "So tell me the truth about yourself."

I don't know. I couldn't go through with it. With the fucking part.

"No," Denny says. "I mean, did you read your mom's diary yet?"

No, I can't. I'm a little stuck around this dicey baby-killing issue.

Denny looks me hard in the eye and says, "Are you really, like, a cyborg? Is that your mom's big secret?"

"A what?" I say.

"You know," he says, "an artificial humanoid created with a limited life span, but implanted with false childhood memories so you think you're really a real person, except you're really going to die soon?"

And I look at Denny hard and say, "So, dude, my mom told you I'm some kind of a *robot*?"

"Is that what her diary says?" Denny says.

Two women come up, holding out a camera, and one says, "Do you mind?"

"Say cheese," I tell them and snap their picture smiling in front of the cow shed, then they walk away with another fleeting memory that almost got away. Another petrified moment to treasure.

"No, I haven't read the diary," I say. "I haven't fucked Paige Marshall. I can't do jack shit until I decide about this."

"Okay, okay," Denny says, to me he says, "then are you really just a brain in a pan somewhere being stimulated with chemicals and electricity into thinking you have a real life?"

"No," I go. "I'm definitely not a brain. That's not it."

"Okay," he says. "Maybe you're an artificially intelligent computer program that interacts with other programs in a simulated reality."

And I go, "What does that make you?"

"I'd be just another computer," Denny says. Then he says, "I get your point, dude. I can't even figure out change for the bus."

Denny narrows his eyes and tilts his head back, looking at me with one eyebrow cocked. "Here's my last guess," he says.

He says, "Okay, the way I figure it, you're just the subject of

125

an experiment and the whole world you know is just an artificial construct populated by actors who play the roles of everybody in your life, and the weather is just special effects and the sky is painted blue and the landscape everywhere is just a set. Is that it?"

And I go, "Huh?"

"And I'm really a brilliantly talented and gifted actor," Denny says, "and I'm just pretending to be your stupid masturbation-addicted loser best friend."

Somebody snaps a picture of me gritting my teeth.

And I look at Denny, and say, "Dude, you're not pretending anything."

At my elbow is some tourist guy grinning at me. "Victor, hey," he says. "So this is where you work."

Where he knows me from, I haven't the foggiest.

Medical school. College. A different job. Or it could be he's just another sex maniac from my group. It's funny. He doesn't look like a sexaholic, but nobody ever does.

"Hey, Maude," he says and elbows the woman he's with. "This is the guy I'm always telling you about. I saved this guy's life."

And the woman says, "Oh my gosh. So it's true?" She pulls her head into her shoulders and rolls her eyes. "Reggie here is always bragging about you. I guess I always thought he was exaggerating."

"Oh, yeah," I say. "Old Reg here, yeah, he saved my life."

And Denny says, "Anymore, who hasn't?"

Reggie says, "Are you making out okay these days? I tried to send as much cash as I could. Was it enough to take care of that wisdom tooth you needed yanked?"

And Denny says, "Oh, for crying out loud."

A blind chicken with half a head and no wings, shit smeared all over it, stumbles up against my boot, and when I reach down to pet it, the thing's shivering inside its feathers. It makes a soft clucking, cooing sound that's almost a purr.

It's nice to see something more pathetic than I feel right now.

Then I catch myself with a fingernail in my mouth, cow crap. Chicken shit.

See also: Histoplasmosis. See also: Tapeworms.

And I go, "Yeah, the money." I say, "Thanks, dude." And I spit. Then I spit again. There's the click of Reggie taking my picture. Just another stupid moment people have to make last forever.

And Denny looks at the newspaper in his hand and says, "So, dude, can I come live at your mom's house? Yes or no?"

Chapter 20

The Mommy's three-o'clock appointment would show up clutching a yellow bath towel, and around his finger would be the blank groove where there should be a wedding ring. The second the door was locked, he'd try and give her the cash. He'd start to take off his pants. His name was Jones, he'd tell her. His first name Mister.

Guys here to see her for the first time were all the same. She'd tell him, pay me after. Don't be in such a rush. Keep all your clothes on. There's no hurry.

She'd tell him the appointment book was full of Mr. Joneses, Mr. Smiths, John Does, and Bob Whites, so he'd better come up with a better alias. She'd tell him to lie down on the couch. Close the blinds. Dim the lights.

This is how she could make a pile of money. It didn't violate the terms of her parole, but only because the parole board lacked imagination.

To the man on the couch, she'd say, "Shall we get started?"

Even if a guy said he wasn't after sex, the Mommy would still tell him to bring a towel. You brought a towel. You paid in cash. Don't ask her to bill you later or bill some insurance company, because she just couldn't be bothered. You pay cash, then you file the claim.

You only get fifty minutes. Guys had to know what they wanted.

This means the woman, the positions, the setting, the toys. Don't spring anything fancy on her at the last minute.

She'd tell Mr. Jones to lie back. Close his eyes.

Allow all the tension in your face to melt away. Your forehead first; let it go slack. Relax the spot between your eyes. Imagine your forehead smooth and relaxed. Then the muscles around your eyes, smooth and relaxed. Then the muscles around your mouth. Smooth and relaxed.

Even if guys said they were just looking to lose some weight, they wanted sex. If they wanted to quit smoking. Manage stress. Quit biting their nails. Cure hiccups. Stop drinking. Clear up their skin. Whatever the issue, it was because they weren't getting laid. Whatever they said they wanted, they'd get sex here and the problem was solved.

If the Mommy was a compassionate genius or a slut, you don't know.

Sex pretty much cures everything.

She was the best therapist in the business, or she was a whore that fucked with your mind. She didn't like being so slam bam with her clients, but she'd never planned to earn a living this way.

This kind of session, the sex kind, had first happened by accident. A client who wanted to quit smoking wanted to be regressed to the day he was eleven and took his first puff. So he could remember how bad it tasted. So he could quit by going back and never starting. That was the basic idea.

On his second session, this client wanted to meet with his father, who was dead of lung cancer, just to talk. This is still pretty much normal. People want to meet with famous dead people all the time, for guidance, for advice. It was so real that on his third session, the client wanted to meet Cleopatra.

To each client, the Mommy said, let all the tension drain from your face to your neck, then from your neck to your chest. Relax your shoulders. Allow them to roll back and press into the couch. Imagine a heavy weight pressing your body, settling your head and arms deeper and deeper into the cushions of the couch.

Relax your arms, your elbows, your hands. Feel the tension trickle down into each finger, then relax and imagine the tension draining out through each fingertip.

What she did was put him in a trance, hypnotic induction, and guide the experience. He wasn't going back in time. None of it was real. What was most important is he wanted this to happen.

The Mommy, she just gave the play-by-play story. The blow-by-blow description. The color commentary. Imagine listening to a baseball game over the radio. Imagine how real it can seem. Now imagine it from inside a heavy theta-level trance, a deep trance where you hear and smell. You taste and feel. Imagine Cleopatra rolling out of her carpet, naked and perfect and everything you've always wanted.

130

Imagine Salome. Imagine Marilyn Monroe. If you could go back to any period in history and get with any woman, women who would do everything you could imagine. Incredible women. Famous women.

The theater of the mind. The bordello of the subconscious.

That's how it started.

Sure, what she did was hypnosis, but it wasn't real past-life regression. It was more a kind of guided meditation. She'd tell Mr. Jones to focus on the tension in his chest and let it recede. Let it flow down to his waist, his hips, his legs. Imagine water spiraling down a drain. Relax each part of your body, and let the tension flow down to your knees, your shins, your feet.

Imagine smoke drifting away. Let it diffuse. Watch it vanish. Disappear. Dissolve.

In her appointment book, next to his name it said Marilyn Monroe, the same as most guys here for their first time. She could live on just doing Marilyn. She could live on just doing Princess Diana.

To Mr. Jones, she said, imagine you're looking up at a blue sky, and imagine a tiny airplane skywriting the letter Z. Then let the wind erase the letter. Then imagine the plane writing the letter Y. Let the wind erase it. Then the letter X. Erase it. Then the letter W.

Let the wind erase it.

All she really did was set the stage. She just introduced men to their ideal. She set them up on a date with their subconscious because nothing is as good as you can imagine it. No one is as beautiful as she is in your head. Nothing is as exciting as your fantasy.

Here you'd have the sex you'd only dreamt about. She'd set the stage and make the introductions. The rest of the session, she'd watch the clock and maybe read a book or do a crossword puzzle.

Here you'd never be disappointed.

Buried deep in his trance, a guy would lie there and twitch and hump, a dog chasing rabbits in a dream. Every few guys, she'd get a screamer or a moaner or a groaner. You have to wonder what the people in the room next door would think. Guys in the waiting room heard the fuss, and it would drive them wild.

After the session, a guy would be soaked with sweat, his shirt wet and sticking to him, his pants stained. Some could pour the sweat out of their shoes. They could shake it out of their hair. The couch in her office was Scotchgarded, but it never really got a chance to really dry out. Now it's sealed inside a clear plastic slipcover, more to keep the years of mess inside it than to protect it from the outside world.

So guys each had to bring a towel, in their briefcases, in paper bags, in their gym bags with a clean change of clothes. In between clients, she'd spray around air fresheners. She'd open the windows.

To Mr. Jones, she'd say, make all the tension in your body collect in your toes, then drain out. All the tension. Imagine your whole body slack. Relaxed. Collapsed. Relaxed. Heavy. Relaxed. Empty. Relaxed.

Breathe with your stomach instead of your chest. In, and then out.

In, and then out.

Breathing in.

And then out. Smooth and even.

Your legs are tired and heavy. Your arms are tired and heavy.

At first, what the stupid little boy remembers is the Mommy did house cleansings, not any kind of vacuuming and dusting, but spiritual cleaning, exorcisms. The hardest part was getting the people at the Yellow Pages to run her ad under the heading "Exorcist." You go and burn sage. Say the Lord's Prayer and walk around. Maybe beat a clay drum. Declare the house clean. Clients will pay for just doing that.

Cold spots, bad smells, eerie feelings—most people don't need an exorcist. They need a new furnace or a plumber or an interior decorator. The point is, it's not important what you think. What's important is that they're sure they have a problem. Most of those jobs come through realtors. In this city, we have a real estate disclosure law, and people will admit to the dumbest faults, not just asbestos and buried oil tanks, but ghosts and poltergeists. Everybody wants more excitement from their life than they'll ever get. Buyers on the verge of closing, they'll need a little reassurance about the house. The realtor calls, and you put on a little show, burn some sage, and everybody wins.

They get what they want, plus a good story to tell. An experience.

Then came Feng Shui, the kid remembers, and the clients wanted an exorcism *and* they wanted her to tell them where to put the sofa. Clients would ask where did the bed need to go to avoid being in the path of cutting chi from the corner of the dresser. Where should they hang mirrors to bounce the flow of chi back upstairs or away from open doors. It turned into that kind of job. This is what you do with a graduate degree in English.

Just her résumé was proof of reincarnation.

With Mr. Jones, she'd run through the alphabet backwards. She'd tell him, you are standing in a grassy meadow, but now the clouds will descend, coming lower and lower, settling over you until they're all around you in a dense fog. A dense, bright fog.

Imagine standing in a bright, cool fog. The future is to your right side. The past to your left. The fog is cool and wet on your face.

Turn to your left and start walking.

133

Imagine, she'd tell Mr. Jones, a shape just ahead of you in the fog. Keep walking. Feel the fog start to lift. Feel the sun bright and warm on your shoulders.

The shape is closer. With every step, the shape is more and more clear.

Here, in your mind, you have complete privacy. Here there's no difference between what is and what could be. You're not going to catch any disease. Or crab lice. Or break any law. Or settle for any less than the best of everything you can imagine.

You can do anything you can imagine.

She'd tell each client, breathe in. Then out.

You can have anyone. Anywhere.

In. Then out.

From Feng Shui, she went to channeling. Ancient gods, enlightened warriors, dead pets, she'd faked them. Channeling led to hypnosis and past-life regression. Regressing people led her here, to nine clients every day at two hundred bucks per. To guys in the waiting room all day. To wives calling and yelling at the little boy:

"I know he's there. I don't know what he claims, but he's married."

To wives sitting in cars outside, calling on car phones to say:

"Don't think I don't know what's going on up there. I've followed him."

It's not as if the Mommy started with the idea of summoning up the most powerful women in history to give hand jobs, blow jobs, half-and-half, and round-the-world.

It just snowballed. The first guy talked. A friend of his called. A friend of the second guy called. At first, they all asked for help to cure something legit. Smoking or chewing tobacco. Spitting in public. Shoplifting. Then they just wanted sex. They wanted

Clara Bow and Betsy Ross and Elizabeth Tudor and the Queen of Sheba.

And every day she was running down to the library to research the next day's women, Eleanor Roosevelt, Amelia Earhart, Harriet Beecher Stowe.

In, and then out.

Guys called wanting to pork Helen Hayes, Margaret Sanger, and Aimee Semple McPherson. They wanted to bone Edith Piaf, Sojourner Truth, and the Empress Theodora. And at first it bothered the Mommy, how all these guys were obsessed with only dead women. And how they never asked for the same woman twice. And no matter how much detail she put into a session, they only wanted to pork and bone, slam and bump, shaft, hole, screw, drill, pound, pile-drive, core, and ride.

And sometimes a euphemism just isn't.

Sometimes a euphemism is more true than what it's supposed to hide.

And this really wasn't about sex.

These guys meant just what they asked for.

They didn't want conversation or costumes or historical accuracy. They wanted Emily Dickinson naked in high heels with one foot on the floor and the other up on her desk, bent over and running a quill pen up the crack of her butt.

They'd pay two hundred bucks to go into a trance and find Mary Cassatt wearing a push-up bra.

It wasn't every man who could afford her, so she'd get the same type again and again. They'd park their minivans six blocks away and hurry over to the house, staying near the buildings, each guy dragging his shadow. They'd stumble in wearing dark glasses, then wait behind open newspapers and magazines until their name was called. Or their alias. If the Mommy and the stupid little boy ever met them in public, these men would pretend not to know her. In public, they'd have wives. In the supermarket, they'd have kids. In the park, dogs. They'd have real names.

They'd pay her with damp twenties and fifties from sopping wet wallets full of sweaty photos, library cards, charge cards, club memberships, licenses, change. Obligations. Responsibility. Reality.

Imagine, she'd tell each client, the sun on your skin. Feel the sun get warmer and warmer with each breath you exhale. The sun bright and warm on your face, your chest, your shoulders.

Breathe in. Then out.

In. Then out.

Her repeat customers, now they all wanted girl-on-girl shows, they'd want a two-girl party, Indira Gandhi and Carol Lombard. Margaret Mead and Audrey Hepburn and Dorothea Dix. Repeat clients didn't even want to be real themselves. The bald ones would ask for full, thick hair. The fat ones asked for muscle. The pale, tans. After enough sessions, every man would ask for a strutting, foot-long erection.

So it wasn't real past-life regression. And wasn't love. It wasn't history, and wasn't reality. It wasn't television, but it happened in your mind. It was a broadcast, and she was the sender.

It wasn't sex. She was just the tour guide for a wet dream. A hypno lap dancer.

Each guy kept his pants on for damage control. Containment. The mess went way beyond just peter tracks. And it paid a fortune.

Mr. Jones would get the standard Marilyn experience. He'd be rigid on the couch, sweating and mouth-breathing. His eyes rolled back. His shirt would go dark under the arms. His crotch would tent up.

Here she is, the Mommy would tell Mr. Jones.

The fog is gone and it's a shining, hot day. Feel the air on your bare skin, your bare arms and legs. Feel yourself getting warmer with every breath you breathe out. Feel yourself growing longer and thicker. Already you're harder and heavier, more purple and throbbing than you've ever felt.

Her watch said they had about forty minutes before the next client.

The fog is gone, Mr. Jones, and the shape just in front of you is Marilyn Monroe in a tight satin dress. Golden and smiling, her eyes half closed, her head tilts back. She stands in a field of tiny flowers and lifts her arms, and as you step closer her dress slips to the ground.

To the stupid little boy, the Mommy used to say this wasn't sex. These weren't real women as much as they were symbols. Projections. Sex symbols.

The power of suggestion.

To Mr. Jones, the Mommy would say, "Have at her."

She'd say, "She's all yours."

Chapter 21

That first night, Denny's outside the front door holding something wrapped in a pink baby blanket. This is all through the peephole in my mom's door: Denny in his giant plaid coat, Denny cradling some baby to his chest, his nose bulging, his eyes bulging, everything bulging because of the peephole lens. Everything distorted. His hands clutching the bundle are white with the effort.

And Denny yells, "Open up, dude!"

And I open the door as far as the burglar chain will go. I go, "What you got there?"

And Denny tucks the blanket around his little bundle and says, "What's it look like?"

"It looks like a baby, dude," I say.

And Denny says, "Good." He hefts the pink bundle and says, "Let me in, dude, this is getting heavy."

Then I slip the chain. I step aside, and Denny charges in and over to one living-room corner, where he heaves the baby onto the plastic-covered sofa.

The pink blanket rolls and out rolls a rock, gray and granite-colored, scrubbed and smooth-looking. No baby, for real, just this boulder.

"Thanks for the baby idea," Denny says. "People see a young guy with a baby, and they're sweet to you," he says. "They see a guy carrying a big rock, and they get all tensed up. Especially if you want to bring it on the bus."

He tucks one edge of the pink blanket under his chin and starts folding it against his front and says, "Plus, with a baby you always get a seat. And if you forget your money they don't kick you off." Denny flops the folded blanket over his shoulder and says, "This your mom's house?"

The dining-room table is covered with today's birthday cards and checks, my thank-you letters, the big book of who and where. Beside that's my mom's old ten-key adding machine, the kind with a long slot-machine handle you pull along one side. Sitting back down, I start doing today's deposit slip and say, "Yeah, it's her house until the property tax people kick me out in a few months."

Denny says, "It's good you got a whole house, since my folks want all my rocks to move out with me."

"Dude," I say. "How many do you got?"

He's got a rock for every day he has sobriety, Denny says. It's what he does at night to stay occupied. Find rocks. Wash them.

Haul them home. It's how his recovery is going to be about doing something big and good instead of just not doing little bad shit.

"It's so I don't act out, dude," he says. "You have no idea how tough it is to find good rocks in a city. I mean, not like chunks of concrete or those plastic rocks people hide their extra keys inside."

The total for today's checks is seventy-five bucks. All from strangers who Heimlich Maneuvered me in some restaurant somewhere. This is nowhere near what I figure a stomach tube has got to cost.

To Denny, I say, "So how many days you got so far?"

"One hundred and twenty-seven rocks' worth," Denny says. He comes around the table next to me, looking at the birthday cards, looking at the checks, and says, "So where's your mom's famous diary?"

He picks up a birthday card.

"You can't read it," I say.

Denny says, "Sorry, dude," and starts to put the card down.

No, I tell him. The diary. It's written in some foreign language. That's why he can't read it. I can't read it. How my mom thinks is she probably wrote it that way so I'd never sneak through it when I was a kid. "Dude," I say, "I think it's Italian."

And Denny goes, "Italian?"

"Yeah," I go, "you know, like spaghetti?"

Still with his big plaid coat on, Denny says, "You eat yet?"

Not yet. I seal the deposit envelope.

Denny says, "You think they're going to banish me tomorrow?"

Yes, no, probably. Ursula saw him with the newspaper.

The deposit slip is ready for the bank tomorrow. All the thank-you letters, the underdog letters, are signed and stamped and ready to mail. I get my coat from the sofa. Next to it, Denny's rock is squashing the springs down.

"So what's with these rocks," I say.

Denny's opened the front door, and he's standing there while I turn off some lights. In the doorway, he says, "I don't know. But rocks are like, you know, *land*. It's like these rocks are a kit. It's land, but with some assembly required. You know, landowner-ship, but for right now it's indoors."

I say, "For sure."

We go out and I lock the door behind us. The night sky is all fuzzy with stars. All out of focus. There's no moon.

Outside on the sidewalk, Denny looks up at the mess and says, "What I think happened is when God wanted to make the earth out of chaos, the first thing he did was just get a lot of rocks together."

While we walk, his new obsessive compulsion has my eyes already scanning vacant lots and places for rocks we can pick up.

Walking down to the bus stop with me, still with the pink baby blanket folded over his shoulder, Denny says, "I only take the rocks nobody wants." He says, "I'll just get one rock every night. Then I figure I'll figure out the next part, you know—next."

It's such a creepy idea. Us taking home rocks. We're collecting land.

"You know that girl, Daiquiri?" Denny says. "The dancer with the cancery mole." He says, "You didn't sleep with her, did you?"

We're shoplifting real property. Burgling terra firma.

And I say, "Why not?"

We're just an outlaw couple of land rustlers.

And Denny says, "Her real name is Beth."

The way Denny thinks, he's probably got plans to start his own planet.

Chapter 22

Dr. Paige Marshall stretches a string of something white tight between her two gloved hands. She stands over a deflated old woman in a recliner chair, and Dr. Marshall says, "Mrs. Wintower? I need you to open your mouth as wide as you can."

Latex gloves, the yellow way they make your hands look, this is just how cadaver skin looks. The medical cadavers from first-year anatomy with their shaved heads and pubic hair. The little stubble of the hairs. The skin could be chicken skin, cheap stewing chicken, turning yellow and dimpled with follicles. Feathers or hair, it's all just keratin. The muscles of the human thigh look the same as dark-meat turkey. During first-year anatomy, you can't look at chicken or turkey and not be eating a cadaver.

The old woman tilts her head back to show her teeth wedged in their brown curve. Her tongue coated white. Her eyes are closed. This is how all these old women look at Communion, at Catholic Mass, when you're an altar boy and have to follow along with the priest as he puts the wafer on tongue after old tongue. The church says you can receive the Host into your hand, then feed yourself, but not these old ladies. In church, you'll still look down the Communion rail and see two hundred open mouths, two hundred old ladies stretching their tongues toward salvation.

Paige Marshall leans in and forces the white string between the old woman's teeth. She pulls, and when the string twangs out from the mouth, some soft gray bits flick out. She runs the string between two more teeth, and the string comes out red.

For bleeding gums, see also: Oral cancers.

See also: Necrotizing ulcerative gingivitis.

The only good part about being an altar boy is you get to hold the paten under the chin of each person receiving Communion. This is a gold platter on a stick you use to catch the Host if it falls. Even if a Host hits the floor, you still have to eat it. At this point it's consecrated. It's become the body of Christ. The flesh incarnate.

I watch from behind while Paige Marshall puts the bloody string back into the old woman's mouth again and again. Gray and white bits of smear collect on the front of Paige's lab coat. Little specks of pink.

A nurse leans in the doorway and says, "Everybody okay in here?" To the old woman in the chair, she says, "Paige isn't hurting you, is she?"

The woman gargles an answer.

The nurse says, "What was that?"

The old woman swallows and says, "Dr. Marshall is very gentle. She's more gentle than when you do my teeth."

"Almost done," Dr. Marshall says. "You are being so good, Mrs. Wintower."

And the nurse shrugs and leaves.

The good part of being an altar boy is when you hit somebody in the throat with the paten. People on their knees with their hands clasped in prayer, the little gaggy face they make right at the moment they are being so divine. I loved that.

As the priest puts the host on their tongue, he'll say, "Body of Christ."

And the person kneeling for Communion will say, "Amen."

What's best is to hit their throat so the "Amen" comes out as a ga-ga baby sound. Or they make a duck quack. Or chicken cluck. Still, you had to do this by accident. And you had to not laugh.

"All done," Dr. Marshall says. She straightens up, and when she goes to toss the bloody string in the trash she sees me.

"I didn't want to interrupt," I say.

She's helping the old woman out of the recliner and says, "Mrs. Wintower? Can you send Mrs. Tsunimitsu in to see me?"

Mrs. Wintower nods. Through her cheeks, you can see her tongue stretching around inside her mouth, feeling her teeth, sucking her lips into a tight pucker. Before she steps out into the hallway, she looks at me and says, "Howard, I've forgiven you for cheating on me. You don't have to keep coming around."

"Remember to send in Mrs. Tsunimitsu," says Dr. Marshall.

And I say, "So?"

And Paige Marshall says, "So I have to do dental hygiene all day. What do you need?"

I need to know what it says in my Mom's diary.

"Oh, that," she says. She's snapping off her latex gloves and stuffing them into a hazardous-waste canister. "The only thing that diary proves is your mother was delusional since before you were born."

Delusional how?

Paige Marshall looks at a clock on the wall. She waves at the chair, the vinyl leather-look recliner Mrs. Wintower just left, and says, "Take a seat." She's stretching on a new pair of latex gloves.

She wants to floss my teeth?

"It will help with your breath," she says. She spools out a length of dental floss, and says, "Sit, and I'll tell you what's in the diary."

So I sit, and my weight pushes a cloud of bad stink out of the recliner.

"That wasn't me," I say. "That smell, I mean. I didn't do that."

And Paige Marshall says, "Before you were born, your mother spent some time in Italy, right?"

"So that's the big secret?" I say.

And Paige says, "What?"

That I'm *Italian?*

"No," Paige says. She leans into my mouth. "But your mother is Catholic, isn't she?"

The string hurts as she snaps it between a couple teeth.

"Please be joking," I say. Around her fingers, I say, "I'm not Italian *and* Catholic! This is too much to bear."

I tell her I already know all this.

And Paige says, "Shut up." She leans back.

"So who's my father?" I say.

She leans into my mouth, and the string snaps between two back teeth. The taste of blood pools around the base of my tongue. She's squinting her attention deep into me, and says, "Well, if you believe in the Holy Trinity, you're your own father."

145

I'm my own father?

Paige says, "My point is that your mother's dementia appears to go back to before you were born. According to what's written in her diary, she's been deluded since at least her late thirties."

She twangs the string out and bits of mouth food flick onto her coat.

And I ask, what does she mean *the Holy Trinity?*

"You know," Paige says. "The Father, the Son, the Holy Ghost. Three in one. Saint Patrick and the shamrock." She says, "Could you open a little wider?"

So just frigging tell me, flat out, I ask her, what does my mom's diary say about me?

She looks at the bloody string just yanked out of my mouth, and she looks down at my bits of blood and food flicked onto her lab coat and says, "It's a fairly common delusion among mothers." She leans in with the string and loops it around another tooth.

Bits of stuff, half-digested stuff I didn't know was there, it's all breaking loose and coming out. With her pulling my head around by the floss, I could be a horse in harness at Colonial Dunsboro.

"Your poor mother," Paige Marshall says, looking through the blood flecked on her eyeglass lenses, "she's so delusional she truly believes you're the second coming of Christ."

Chapter 23

Anytime somebody in a new car offered them a ride, the Mommy told the driver, "No."

They'd stand at the side of the road and watch the new Cadillac or the Buick or Toyota disappear, and the Mommy would say, "The smell of a new car is the smell of death."

This was the third or fourth time she came back to claim him.

The glue and resin smell in new cars is formaldehyde, she'd tell him, the same thing they use to preserve dead bodies. It's in new houses and new furniture. It's called off-gassing. You can inhale formaldehyde from new clothes. After you inhale enough, expect stomach cramps, vomiting, and diarrhea.

See also: Liver failure.

See also: Shock.

See also: Death.

If you're looking for enlightenment, the Mommy said, a new car isn't the answer.

Along the side of the road would be foxgloves blooming, tall stalks of purple-and-white flowers. "Digitalis," the Mommy said, "doesn't work, either."

From eating foxglove flowers, you get nausea, delirium, and blurred vision.

Above them, a mountain held itself against the sky, catching clouds and coated with pine trees and then some snow higher up. It was so big that no matter how long they walked, it was still in the same place.

The Mommy took the white tube out of her purse. She pinched onto one shoulder of the stupid little boy for balance and sniffed hard with the tube stuck up one side of her nose. Then she dropped the tube onto the gravel edge of the road and just stood looking at the mountain.

This was a mountain so big they would always be walking past it.

When the Mommy let go, the stupid boy picked up the tube. He wiped the blood off with his shirttail and handed it back to her.

"Trichloroethane," the Mommy said and held the tube for him to see. "All my extensive testing has shown this to be the best treatment for a dangerous excess of human knowledge."

She buried the tube back in her purse.

"That mountain, for example," she said. She took the boy's

stupid chin between her thumb and forefinger and made him look with her. "That big glorious mountain. For one transitory moment, I think I may have actually seen it."

Another car slowed down, something brown and four-door, something too late-model, so the Mommy waved it away.

For one flash, the Mommy had seen the mountain without thinking of logging and ski resorts and avalanches, managed wildlife, plate tectonic geology, microclimates, rain shadow, or yin-yang locations. She'd seen the mountain without the framework of language. Without the cage of associations. She'd seen it without looking through the lens of everything she knew was true about mountains.

What she'd seen in that flash wasn't even a "mountain." It wasn't a natural resource. It had no name.

"That's the big goal," she said. "To find a cure for knowledge."

For education. For living in our heads.

Cars went by on the highway, and the Mommy and little boy kept walking with the mountain still sitting there.

Ever since the story of Adam and Eve in the Bible, humanity had been a little too smart for its own good, the Mommy said. Ever since eating that apple. Her goal was to find, if not a cure, then at least a treatment that would give people back their innocence.

Formaldehyde didn't work. Digitalis didn't work.

None of the natch highs seemed to do the job, not smoking mace or nutmeg or peanut skins. Not dill or hydrangea leaves or lettuce juice.

At night, the Mommy used to sneak the little boy through the backyards of other people. She'd drink the beer people left out for slugs and snails, and she'd nibble their jimson weed and nightshade and catnip. She'd squeeze up next to parked cars and smell inside their gas tank. She'd unscrew the cap in their lawn and smell their heating oil.

"I figure if Eve could get us into this mess, then I can get us out," the Mommy said. "God really likes to see a go-getter."

Other cars slowed down, cars with families, full of luggage and family dogs, but the Mommy just waved them all past.

"The cerebral cortex, the cerebellum," she said, "that's where your problem is."

If she could just get down to using only her brain stem, she'd be cured.

This would be somewhere beyond happiness and sadness.

You don't see fish agonized by wild mood swings.

Sponges never have a bad day.

The gravel crushed and shifted under their feet. The cars going by made their own hot wind.

"My goal," the Mommy said, "is not to uncomplicate my life."

She said, "My goal is to uncomplicate *myself*."

She told the stupid little boy, morning glory seeds didn't work. She'd tried them. The effects didn't last. Sweet potato leaves didn't work. Neither did pyrethrum extracted from chrysanthemums. Neither would sniffing propane. Neither did the leaves of rhubarb or azaleas.

After a night in someone's yard, the Mommy left a bite out of almost every plant for people to find.

Those cosmetic drugs, she said, those mood equalizers and antidepressants, they only treat the symptoms of the bigger problem.

Every addiction, she said, was just a way to treat this same problem. Drugs or overeating or alcohol or sex, it was all just another way to find peace. To escape what we know. Our education. Our bite of the apple.

Language, she said, was just our way to explain away the wonder and the glory of the world. To deconstruct. To dismiss. She said people can't deal with how beautiful the world really is. How it can't be explained and understood.

Ahead of them on the highway was a restaurant parked all around with trucks bigger than the restaurant itself. Some of the new cars the Mommy didn't want were parked there. You could smell a lot of different food being fried in the same hot oil. You could smell the truck engines idle.

"We don't live in the real world anymore," she said. "We live in a world of symbols."

The Mommy stopped and put her hand in her purse. She held the boy's shoulder and stood looking up at the mountain. "Just one last little peek at reality," she said. "Then we'll have lunch."

Then she put the white tube in her nose and breathed in.

Chapter 24

According to Paige Marshall, my mom came from Italy already pregnant with me. This was the year after somebody had broken into a church in northern Italy. This is all in my mom's diary.

According to Paige Marshall.

My mom had gambled on some new kind of fertility treatment. She was almost forty. She wasn't married, she didn't want a husband, but somebody had promised her a miracle.

This same somebody, they knew somebody who'd stolen a

shoe box from under the bed of a priest. In that shoe box was the last earthly remains of a man. Somebody famous.

It was his foreskin.

This was a religious relic, the kind of bait used to draw crowds into churches during the Middle Ages. This is only one of several famous penises still around. In 1977, an American urologist bought the inch-long dried penis of Napoleon Bonaparte for about four thousand dollars. Rasputin's foot-long penis is supposed to lie on velvet in a polished wooden box in Paris. John Dillinger's twenty-inch monster is supposed to be bottled in formaldehyde at the Walter Reed Army Medical Center.

According to Paige Marshall, it's in my mom's diary that six women were offered embryos created from this genetic material. Five of those never came to term.

The sixth is me. It was the foreskin of Jesus Christ.

This is how crazy my mom was. Even twenty-five years ago, she was this cracked.

Paige laughed and leaned in to floss the teeth of another old woman.

"You have to give your mother credit for originality," she said.

According to the Catholic Church, Jesus was reunited with the foreskin at his resurrection and ascension. According to the story of Saint Teresa of Avila, when Jesus appeared to her and took her as his bride, he used the foreskin as her wedding ring.

Paige snapped the string out from between the woman's teeth and flicked blood and food onto the lenses of her own black glasses. The black brain of her hair tilted from side to side as she tried to see the old woman's top row of teeth.

She said, "Even if your mother's story is true, there's no proof the genetic material came from the actual historical figure. It's more likely your father was just some poor Jewish nobody."

The old woman in the recliner, stretching her mouth around Dr. Marshall's hands, rolled her eyes to stare at me.

And Paige Marshall said, "This should make it okay for you to cooperate."

Cooperate?

"With my course of treatment for your mother," she said.

To kill an unborn baby. I said, even if I wasn't him, I still didn't think Jesus would approve.

"Of course he would," Paige said. She snapped the string to flick a lump of tooth jam at me. "Didn't God sacrifice his own son to save people? Isn't that the story?"

Here it is again, the fine line between science and sadism. Between a crime and a sacrifice. Between murdering your own child and what Abraham almost did to Isaac in the Bible.

The old woman pulled her face away from Dr. Marshall, tonguing the string and bits of bloody food out of her mouth. She looked at me and said in her creaking voice, "I know you."

As automatic as sneezing, I said, I'm sorry. Sorry I fucked her cat. Sorry I drove over her flower beds. Sorry I shot down her husband's fighter plane. Sorry I flushed her hamster down the toilet. I sighed at her and said, "Did I forget anything?"

Paige said, "Mrs. Tsunimitsu, I need you to open wide for me."

And Mrs. Tsunimitsu said, "I was with my son's family, dining out, and you almost choked to death." She says, "My son saved your life."

She says, "I was so proud of him. He still tells people that story."

Paige Marshall looks up at me.

"Secretly," Mrs. Tsunimitsu said, "I think my son, Paul, always felt like a coward until that night."

154

Paige sat back and looked from the old woman to me, back and forth.

Mrs. Tsunimitsu clasped her hands together below her chin, closed her eyes, and smiled. She said, "My daughter-in-law had wanted a divorce, but after she saw Paul save you, she fell back in love."

She said, "I knew you were faking. Everybody else saw what they wanted to see."

She said, "You have an enormous capacity for love in you."

The old woman sat there smiling and said, "I can tell you have the most generous of hearts."

And fast as sneezing, I told her:

"You're a fucking wrinkled old lunatic."

And Paige winces.

I tell everybody, I'm tired of being jerked around. Okay? So let's just not pretend. I don't have fuck for a heart. You people are not going to make me feel anything. You are not going to get to me.

I'm a stupid, callous, scheming bastard. End of story.

This old Mrs. Tsunimitsu. Paige Marshall. Ursula. Nico, Tanya, Leeza. My mom. Some days, life just looks like me versus every stupid chick in the whole damn world.

With one hand, I grab Paige Marshall around the arm and yank her toward the door.

Nobody's going to trick me into feeling Christlike.

"Listen to me," I say. I shout, "If I wanted to feel anything, I'd go to a frigging movie!"

And old Mrs. Tsunimitsu smiles and says, "You can't deny the goodness of your true nature. It's shining for everyone to see."

To her I say, shut up. To Paige Marshall I say, "Come on."

I'll prove to her I'm no Jesus Christ. Anybody's true nature is bullshit. There is no human soul. Emotion is bullshit. Love is bullshit. And I'm dragging Paige down the hallway.

We live and we die and anything else is just delusion. It's just passive chick bullshit about feelings and sensitivity. Just made-up subjective emotional crap. There is no soul. There is no God. There's just decisions and disease and death.

What I am is a dirty, filthy, helpless sexaholic, and I can't change, and I can't stop, and that's all I'll ever be.

And I'll prove it.

"Where are you taking me?" Paige says, stumbling, her glasses and lab coat still flecked with food and blood.

Already, I'm imagining junk so as not to trigger too fast, stuff like pets soaked in gasoline and set on fire. I'm picturing the dumpy Tarzan and his trained chimp. I'm thinking, here's just another stupid chapter in my fourth step.

To make time stand still. To fossilize this moment. To make the fucking last forever.

I'm taking her in the chapel, I tell Paige. I'm the child of a lunatic. Not a child of God.

Let God prove me wrong. He can nail me with a lightning bolt.

I'm going to take her on the frigging altar.

Chapter 25

It was malicious endangerment this time or reckless abandonment or criminal neglect. There were so many laws the little boy couldn't keep them straight.

It was third-degree harassment or second-degree disregard, first-degree disdain or second-degree nuisance, and it got so the stupid kid was terrified to do anything except what everybody else did. Anything new or different or original was probably against the law.

Anything risky or exciting would land you in jail.

That's why everybody was so eager to talk to the Mommy.

She'd been out of jail for only a couple weeks this time, and already stuff had started to happen.

There were so many laws and, for sure, about countless ways you could screw up.

First the police asked about the coupons.

Somebody had gone to a downtown copy shop and used a computer to design and print hundreds of coupons that promised a free meal for two, a seventy-five-dollar value with no expiration date. Each coupon was folded inside a cover letter that thanked you for being such a valued customer and said the enclosed coupon was a special promotion.

All you had to do was eat dinner at the Clover Inn Restaurant.

When the server presented the bill, you could just pay with the coupon. Tip included.

Somebody did all that. Mailed out hundreds of these coupons.

It had all the earmarks of an Ida Mancini stunt.

The Mommy had been a server at the Clover Inn for her first week out of the halfway house, but she got fired for telling people stuff they didn't want to know about their food.

Then she just disappeared. A few days later, an unidentified woman had run screaming down the center aisle of a theater during the quiet, boring part of some big fancy ballet dance.

This is why the police got the stupid little boy out of school one day and brought him downtown. To see if maybe he'd heard from her. From the Mommy. If maybe he knew where she was hiding.

About this same time, several hundred very angry customers flooded into a fur salon with fifty-percent-discount coupons they got in the mail.

About this time, a thousand very scared people arrived at the county sexually transmitted disease clinic, demanding to be tested after they received letters on the county letterhead warning them that some former sex partner had been diagnosed with an infectious disease.

The police detectives took the little stooge downtown in a plain car and then upstairs in a plain building and sat with him and his foster mother, asking, has Ida Mancini attempted to contact you?

Have you any idea from where she's receiving funds?

Why do you think she's doing these awful things?

And the little boy just waited.

Help would come soon enough.

The Mommy, she used to tell him she was sorry. People had been working for so many years to make the world a safe, organized place. Nobody realized how boring it would become. With the whole world property-lined and speed-limited and zoned and taxed and regulated, with everyone tested and registered and addressed and recorded. Nobody had left much room for adventure, except maybe the kind you could buy. On a roller coaster. At a movie. Still, it would always be that kind of faux excitement. You know the dinosaurs aren't going to eat the kids. The test audiences have outvoted any chance of even a major faux disaster. And because there's no possibility of real disaster, real risk, we're left with no chance for real salvation. Real elation. Real excitement. Joy. Discovery. Invention.

The laws that keep us safe, these same laws condemn us to boredom.

Without access to true chaos, we'll never have true peace.

Unless everything can get worse, it won't get any better.

This is all stuff the Mommy used to tell him.

She used to say, "The only frontier you have left is the world of intangibles. Everything else is sewn up too tight."

Caged inside too many laws.

By intangibles, she meant the Internet, movies, music, stories, art, rumors, computer programs, anything that isn't real. Virtual realities. Make-believe stuff. The culture.

The unreal is more powerful than the real.

Because nothing is as perfect as you can imagine it.

Because it's only intangible ideas, concepts, beliefs, fantasies that last. Stone crumbles. Wood rots. People, well, they die.

But things as fragile as a thought, a dream, a legend, they can go on and on.

If you can change the way people think, she said. The way they see themselves. The way they see the world. If you do that, you can change the way people live their lives. And that's the only lasting thing you can create.

Besides, at some point, the Mommy used to say, your memories, your stories and adventures, will be the only things you'll have left.

At her last trial, before this last time she went to jail, the Mommy had sat up next to the judge and said, "My goal is to be an engine of excitement in people's lives."

She'd stared straight into the stupid little boy's eyes and said, "My purpose is to give people glorious stories to tell."

Before the guards took her into the back wearing handcuffs, she'd shouted, "Convicting me would be redundant. Our bureaucracy and our laws have turned the world into a clean, safe work camp."

She shouted, "We are raising a generation of slaves."

And it was back to prison for Ida Mancini.

"Incorrigible" isn't the right word, but it's the first word that comes to mind.

The unidentified woman, the one who ran down the aisle

during the ballet, she was screaming, "We are teaching our children to be helpless."

Running down the aisle and out a fire exit, she'd yelled, "We're so structured and micromanaged, this isn't a world anymore, it's a damn cruise ship."

Sitting, waiting with the police detectives, the stupid little shitface troublemaker asked if maybe the defense lawyer Fred Hastings could be there, too.

And one detective said a filthy word under his breath.

And right then, the fire alarm bell went off.

And even with the bell ringing, the detectives still asked:

"DO YOU HAVE ANY IDEA HOW TO GET IN TOUCH WITH YOUR MOTHER?"

Screaming against the bell, they asked:

"CAN YOU AT LEAST TELL US WHO SHE MIGHT TARGET NEXT?"

Shouting against the alarm, the foster mother asked:

"DON'T YOU WANT TO HELP US HELP HER?"

And the alarm stopped.

A lady stuck her head in the door and said, "Don't panic, guys. It looks like another false alarm."

A fire alarm is never about a fire, not anymore.

And this dumb-fuck little boy says, "May I use your bathroom?"

Chapter 26

The half-moon looks up at us, reflected in a silver pie tin of beer.
Denny and me kneel in somebody's backyard, and Denny kicks
away the snails and slugs with little kicks of his index finger.
Denny lifts the pie tin, full to the brim, bringing his reflection
and his real face closer and closer until his fake lips meet his own
lips.

Denny drinks about half the beer and says, "This is how they
drink beer in Europe, dude."

Out of slug traps?

"No, dude," Denny says. He hands me the pie tin and says, "Flat and warm."

I kiss my own reflection and drink, the moon watching over my shoulder.

On the sidewalk waiting for us is a baby stroller with its wheels splayed out wider at the bottom than the top. The bottom of the stroller drags against the ground, and wrapped in the pink baby blanket is a boulder of sandstone too big for Denny or me to lift. A pink rubber baby head is balanced inside the top edge of the blanket.

"About having sex in a church," Denny says, "tell me you didn't."

It's not so much that I didn't. I couldn't.

Couldn't bone, shaft, drill, core, screw. All those euphemisms that aren't.

Denny and me, we're just two regular guys taking the baby out for a stroll at midnight. Just a couple of nice young guys in this fine neighborhood of big houses, each set back on its lawn. All these houses with their self-contained, climate-controlled, smug illusion of security.

Denny and me, we're about as innocent as a tumor.

Harmless as a psilocybin toadstool.

This is such a fine neighborhood, even the beer they leave out for the animals is imported from Germany or Mexico. We hop the fence into the next backyard and snoop under the plants for our next round.

Ducking to look under leaves and bushes, I say, "Dude." I say, "You don't think I'm a good-hearted person, do you?"

And Denny says, "Hell no, dude."

After a few blocks, all those backyards of beer, I know Denny's being honest. I say, "You don't think I'm really a secretly sensitive and Christlike manifestation of perfect love?"

"No way, dude," Denny says. "You're an asshole."

And I say, "Thanks. Just checking."

And Denny stands up using just his legs in slow motion, and in a pie tin between his hands is another reflection of the night sky, and Denny says, "Bingo, dude."

About me in the church I tell him, I'm more disappointed in God than in myself. He should've hammered me with a lightning bolt. I mean, God's god. I'm just an asshole. I didn't even take off Paige Marshall's clothes. Still with her stethoscope around her neck, dangling between her breasts, I pushed her back on the altar. I didn't even take off her lab coat.

The stethoscope against her own chest, she said, "Go fast." She said, "I want you to stay in synch with my heart."

It's not fair how a woman never has to think of shit to keep from coming.

And me, I just couldn't. Already, that Jesus idea was just killing my hard-on.

Denny hands me the beer, and I drink. Denny spits out a dead slug and says, "Better drink through your teeth, dude."

Even in a church, even laid up on an altar, without her clothes, Paige Marshall, Dr. Paige Marshall, I didn't want her to become just another piece of ass.

Because nothing is as perfect as you can imagine it.

Because nothing is as exciting as your fantasy.

Breathe in. And then, out.

"Dude," Denny says. "This is got to be my nightcap. Let's get the rock and head home."

And I say, just one more block, okay? Just one more round of backyards. I'm not near drunk enough to forget my day.

This is such a fine neighborhood. I jump the fence to the next backyard and land on my head in somebody's rose bush. Somewhere a dog's barking.

The whole time we were up at the altar, me trying to get my dog hard, the cross, polished and blond wood, was looking down on us. No tortured man. No crown of thorns. No flies circling and sweat. No stink. No blood and suffering, not in this church. No rain of blood. No plague of locusts.

Paige, the whole time with the stethoscope in her ears, just listened to her own heart.

The angels on the ceiling were painted over. The light through the stained-glass window was thick and gold and swimming with dust. The light fell in a thick solid shaft, a warm heavy shaft that spilled on us.

Attention please, would Dr. Freud please pick up the white courtesy telephone.

A world of symbols, not the real world.

Denny looks at me stuck and bleeding from the rose thorns, my clothes ripped, lying in a bush, and says, "Okay, I mean it." He says, "This is, for sure, last call."

The smell of roses, the smell of incontinence at St. Anthony's.

A dog's barking and scratching to get out the back door of the house. A light comes on in the kitchen to show somebody in the window. Then the back-porch light comes on, and it's amazing how fast I tear my ass out of that bush and run to the street.

Coming the other way on the sidewalk are a couple, leaned together and walking with an arm around each other. The woman rubs her cheek on the man's lapel, and the man kisses the crown of her head.

Denny's already pushing the stroller, so fast the front wheels catch in a sidewalk crack, and the baby's rubber head pitches out. Glass eyes staring wide open, the pink head bounces past the happy couple and rolls into the gutter.

To me, Denny says, "Dude, you want to fetch that for me?"

My clothes shredded and gummy with blood, thorns stuck in

my face, I trot past the couple and nab the head out of the leaves and trash.

The man yelps and pulls back.

And the woman says, "Victor? Victor Mancini. Oh, my God."

She must've saved my life, because I don't know who the hell she is.

In the chapel, after I gave up, after we were buttoning our clothes shut, I said to Paige, "Forget fetal tissue. Forget resenting strong women." I say, "You want to know the real reason why I won't fuck you?"

Doing up the buttons of my britches, I told her, "Maybe the truth is I really want to like you instead."

And with both hands above her head, making her black hair brain tight again, Paige said, "Maybe sex and affection aren't mutually exclusive."

And I laughed. My hands tying my cravat, I told her, yes. Yes, they are.

Denny and me, we get to the seven hundred block of, the street sign says Birch Street. To Denny pushing the stroller, I say, "Wrong way, dude." I point behind us and say, "My mom's house is back there."

Denny keeps pushing, the bottom of the stroller making a growling sound against the sidewalk. The happy couple are drop-jawed, still watching us from two blocks back.

I trot along next to him, tossing the pink doll head from hand to hand. "Dude," I say. "Turn back around."

Denny says, "We have to see the eight hundred block first."

What's there?

"It's supposed to be nothing," Denny says. "My Uncle Don used to own it."

The houses end, and the eight hundred block is just land

with more houses on the block after that. The land is just tall grass planted around the edges with old apple trees, their bark all wrinkled and twisting up into the darkness. Inside a bunch of brush, blackberry whips, and scrub, more thorns on every twig, the middle of the land is clear.

On the corner is a billboard sign, plywood painted white with a picture across the top of red-brick houses built against each other and people waving from windows with flower boxes. Under the houses, black words say: Coming Soon Menningtown Country Townhouses. Under the billboard, the ground's snowed with peeling paint chips. Up close, the billboard is curling, the brick townhouses cracked and faded pink.

Denny tips the boulder out of the stroller, and it lands in the tall grass beside the sidewalk. He shakes out the pink blanket and hands me two corners. Between us, we fold it, and Denny says, "If you can have the opposite of a role model, he'd be my Uncle Don."

Then Denny flops the folded blanket into the stroller and starts to push the stroller toward home.

And I call after him, "Dude. You don't want this rock?"

And Denny says, "Those mothers against drunk driving, for sure, they threw a party when they found out old Don Menning was dead."

Wind lifts and crushes the tall grass. Nobody but plants lives here now, and across the dark center of the block you can see the porch lights of houses on the other side. The black zigzags of old apple trees are outlines in between.

"So," I go, "is this a park?"

And Denny says, "Not really." Still walking away, he says, "It's mine."

I pitch the doll head at him and say, "For real?"

"Since my folks called a couple days ago," he says, and he

167

catches the head and drops it into the stroller. Under the street-lights, past everybody's dark house, we walk.

My buckle shoes flashing, my hands stuffed in my pockets, I say, "Dude?" I say, "You don't really think I'm anything like Jesus Christ, do you?"

I say, "Please say no."

We walk.

And pushing his empty stroller, Denny says, "Face it, dude. You nearly did sex on God's table. You're already shame spiraling big-time."

We walk, and the beer's wearing off, and it's a surprise how the night air's so cold.

And I say, "Please, dude. Tell me the truth."

I'm not good and kind and caring or any of that happy horse-shit.

I'm nothing but a thoughtless, brain-dead, loser dude. That I can live with. This is who I am. Just a puss-pounding, seam-reaming, dog-driving, fucking helpless sex addict asshole, and I can't ever, ever let myself forget that.

I say, "Tell me again I'm an insensitive asshole."

Chapter 27

How tonight's supposed to work is I hide in the bedroom closet while the girl's taking a shower. Then when she comes out all shiny with sweat, the air steamy and fogged with hair spray and perfume, she comes out naked except for a lacy bathrobe. Then I jump out with some pantyhose stretched over my face and wearing sunglasses. I throw her on the bed. I put a knife to her throat. Then I rape her.

Simple as that. The shame spiral continues.

Just keep asking yourself: *"What would Jesus NOT do?"*

Only I can't rape her on the bed, she says, the spread is pale pink silk and will spot. And not on the floor because the carpet hurts her skin. We agreed on the floor, but on a towel. Not a good guest towel, she said. She told me she'd leave a ratty towel on the dresser, and I'd need to spread it on the floor ahead of time so as not to break the mood.

She'd leave the bedroom window unlocked before she got in the shower.

So I'm hiding in the closet, naked with all her dry cleaning sticking to me, the pantyhose over my head, wearing sunglasses and holding the dullest knife I could find, waiting. The towel's spread on the floor. The pantyhose are so hot my face is running with sweat. The hair plastered to my head starts to itch.

Not by the window, she'd told me. And not by the fireplace. She said to rape her near the armoire, but not too near. She said to try and spread the towel in a high-traffic area where the carpet wouldn't show as much wear.

This is a girl named Gwen I met in the Recovery section of a bookstore. It's hard to say who picked up whom, but she was pretending to read a twelve-step book about sexual addiction, and I was wearing my lucky camo pants and cruising her over a copy of the same book, and I figured what's one more dangerous liaison.

Birds do it. Bees do it.

I need that rush of endorphins. To tranquilize me. I crave the peptide phenylethylamine. This is who I am. An addict. I mean, who's counting?

In the bookstore coffee shop, Gwen said to get some rope, but not nylon rope because it hurt too much. Hemp gives her an inflamed rash. Black electrical tape would work, too, but not over her mouth, and not duct tape.

"Pulling off duct tape," she said, "is about as erotic as getting my legs waxed."

We compared our schedules, and Thursday was out. Friday I had my regular sexaholics meeting. No chits for me this week. Saturday I spent at St. Anthony's. Most Sunday nights she helped run a bingo event at her church, so we settled on Monday. Monday at nine, not eight, because she worked until late in the evening, and not ten because I had to be at work early the next morning.

So Monday comes. The electrical tape is ready. The towel's spread, and when I leap at her with the knife she says, "Are those my pantyhose you're wearing?"

I twist one of her arms behind her back and put the chilled blade to her throat.

"For crying out loud," she says. "This is way out of bounds. I said you could rape me. I *did not* say you could ruin my pantyhose."

With my knife hand, I grab the front edge of her lacy bathrobe and try to tug it off her shoulder.

"Stop, stop, stop," she says and slaps my hand away, "Here, let me do it. You're just going to ruin it." She twists away from me.

I ask if I can take off my sunglasses.

"No," she says and slips out of her robe. Then she goes to the open closet and hangs the robe on a padded hanger.

But I can't hardly see.

"Don't be so selfish," she says. Naked now, she takes my hand and presses it around one of her wrists. Then she slips her arm behind her back, turning to press her bare back to me. My dog's nosing higher and higher, and her warm slick butt crack's gumming me, and she says, "I need you to be a faceless attacker."

I tell her it's too embarrassing to buy a pair of pantyhose. A guy buying pantyhose is either a criminal or a pervert; either way the cashier will hardly take your money.

"Jeez, quit whining," she says. "Every rapist I've ever been with has brought his own pantyhose."

Plus I tell her, when you're looking at the pantyhose rack, they have all those colors and sizes. Nude, charcoal, beige, tan, black, cobalt, and none of them come in just "head-sized."

She twists her face away and groans. "Can I tell you something? Can I tell you just *one* thing?"

I say, what?

And she says, "Your breath is *really* bad."

Back in the bookstore coffee shop, while we were still scripting, she said, "Make sure and put the knife in a freezer beforehand. I need it to be really really cold."

I asked if maybe we could just use a rubber knife.

And she said, "The knife is very important to my total experience."

She said, "It's best if you put the edge of the knife to my throat before it gets to room temperature."

She said, "But be careful, because if you cut me by accident"—she leaned toward me over the table, jabbing her chin at me—"if you even scratch me, I swear I'll have you in jail before you can get your pants back on."

She sipped her herbal chai and set the cup back in its saucer and said, "My sinuses would appreciate it if you didn't wear any kind of cologne or aftershave or deodorant with a strong scent, because I'm very sensitive."

These horny sexaholic chicks, they have such a high tolerance. They just can't not get banged. They just can't stop, no matter how degrading things get.

God, how I love being codependent.

In the coffee shop, Gwen lifts her purse into her lap and digs around inside it. "Here," she says and unfolds a photocopied list of the details she wants to include. At the top of the list it says:

172

Rape is about power. It is not romantic. Do not fall in love with me. Do not kiss me on the mouth. Do not expect to linger after the act. Do not ask to use my bathroom.

That Monday night in her bedroom, pressed into me naked, she says, "I want you to hit me." She says, "But not too hard and not too soft. Just hit me hard enough so I come."

One of my hands is holding her arm behind her back. She's grinding her butt against me, and she's got a kick-ass tanned little bod except her face is pale and waxy with too much moisturizer. In the mirrored closet door, I can see her front with my face peeking over her shoulder. Her hair and sweat pools in the crack where my chest and her back press together. Her skin has that hot-plastic tanning-bed smell. My other hand is holding the knife, so I ask, does she want me to hit her with the knife?

"No," she says. "That would be stabbing. Hitting someone with a knife is stabbing." She says, "Put the knife down and use your open hand."

So I go to toss the knife.

And Gwen says, "*Not* on the bed."

So I toss the knife on the dresser, and I raise my hand to slap. From behind her, this is really awkward.

And she says, "But not in the face."

So I move my hand a little lower.

And she says, "And do not hit my breasts unless you want to give me lumps."

See also: Cystic mastitis.

She says, "How about if you just slap my ass."

And I say, how about if she just shuts up and lets me rape her my way.

And Gwen says, "If that's how you feel, you can just take your little penis and run along home now."

Since she's just out of the shower, her bush is soft and full, not

173

matted down the way it is when you first take off a woman's underwear. My free hand creeps around to between her legs, and she feels fake, rubbery and plastic. Too smooth. A little greasy.

I say, "What's with your vagina?"

Gwen looks down at herself and says, "What?" She says, "Oh, that. It's a Femidom, a female condom. The edges stick out like that. I don't want you giving me any diseases."

Is it just me, I say, but I thought rape was supposed to be more spontaneous, you know, a crime of passion.

"That shows you don't know shit about how to rape anybody," she says. "A good rapist will plan his crime meticulously. He ritualizes every little detail. This should be almost like a religious ceremony."

What happens here, Gwen says, is sacred.

In the bookstore coffee shop, she'd passed me the photocopied sheet and said, "Can you agree to all these terms?"

The sheet said, *Do not ask where I work.*

Do not ask if you're hurting me.

Do not smoke in my house.

Do not expect to stay the night.

The sheet says, *The safe word is POODLE.*

I ask what she means by a *safe word*.

"If the scene gets too heavy or if it isn't working for one of us," she says, "you just say 'poodle' and the action stops."

I ask if I get to shoot my wad.

"If it's all that important to you," she says.

Then I say, okay, where do I sign?

These pathetic sexaholic chicks. They're so damn dick-hungry.

Without her clothes, she looks a little bony. Her skin feels hot and damp as if you could squeeze out warm soapy water. Her legs are so thin they don't touch until her ass. Her little flat breasts

174

seem to cling to her rib cage. Still holding her arm behind her back, watching ourselves in the mirrored closet door, she has the long neck and sloped shoulders of a wine bottle.

"Stop, please," she says. "You're hurting me. Please, I'll give you money."

I ask, how much?

"Stop, please," she says. "Or I'll scream."

So I drop her arm and step away. "Don't scream," I say. "Just do not scream."

Gwen sighs and then hauls off and punches me in the chest. "You moron!" she says. "I didn't say 'poodle.'"

It's the sexual equivalent of Simon Sez.

She twists back into my grip. Then she walks us over to the towel and says, "Wait." She goes to the dresser and comes back with a pink plastic vibrator.

"Hey," I say, "you're not using that on me."

Gwen shudders and says, "Of course not. This is mine."

And I say, "So what about me?"

And she says, "Sorry, next time bring your own vibrator."

"No," I say, "what about *my penis?*"

And she says, "What *about* your penis?"

And I ask, "How does it fit into all this?"

Settling herself on the towel, Gwen shakes her head and says, "Why do I do this? Why do I always pick the guy who just wants to be nice and conventional? The next thing you'll want to do is marry me." She says, "Just one time, I'd like to have an abusive relationship. Just once!"

She says, "You can masturbate while you rape me. But only on the towel and only if you don't slop any on me."

She spreads the towel out around her ass and pats a little area of terry cloth next to her. "When it's time," she says, "you can put your orgasm right here."

Her hand goes pat, pat, pat.

Uh, okay, I say, now what?

Gwen sighs and sticks the vibrator in my face. "Use me!" she says. "Degrade me, you stupid idiot! Demean me, you jerk-off! Debase me!"

It's not really clear where the switch is, so she has to show me how to turn it on. Then it's buzzing so hard I drop it. Then it's jumping around on the floor, and I have to catch the damn thing.

Gwen brings her knees up and they drop off to each side the way a book drops open, and I kneel on the edge of the towel and work the buzzing tip just inside the soft plastic edges of her. I work my dog with my other hand. Her calves are shaved and taper to curved feet with blue polish on the nails. She's laid back with her eyes closed and her legs spread. Holding her hands together and stretched above her head so her breasts pull up into perfect little handfuls, she says, "No, Dennis, no. I don't want this, Dennis. Don't. No. You can't have me."

And I say, "My name is Victor."

And she says to shut up and let her concentrate.

And I try to give us both a good time, but this is the sex equivalent of rubbing your stomach and patting your head. Either I'm focused on her or I'm focusing on myself. Either way, it's the same as a bad three-way. One of us is always getting left out. Plus the vibrator is slippery and hard to hang on to. It's heating up and smells acrid and smoky as if something's burning inside.

Gwen opens one eye just a sliver, squinting down at my flogging the dog, and says, "*Me* first!"

I'm wrestling my dog. I'm snaking Gwen. I'm snaking Gwen. This feels less like I'm a rapist than I'm a plumber. The edges of the Femidom keep slipping inside, and I have to stop and pick them out with two fingers.

Gwen says, "Dennis, no, Dennis, stop, Dennis," her voice coming up from deep in her throat. She pulls her own hair and gasps. The Femidom slips inside again, and I just let it go. The vibrator tamps it deeper and deeper. She says to play with her nipples with my other hand.

I say, I need my other hand. My dice draw up tight and ready to trigger, and I say, "Oh yeah. Yes. Oh, yeah."

And Gwen says, "Don't you *dare*," and she licks two fingers. She pins her eyes on mine and works her wet fingers between her legs, racing me.

And all I have to do is picture Paige Marshall, my secret weapon, and the race is over.

The second before you trigger, that feeling when your asshole starts to clench, that's when I turn toward the little spot on the towel Gwen said. Feeling stupid and paper-trained, my white soldiers start to toss, and maybe by accident they misjudge the trajectory and toss across her pink bedspread. Her whole big soft puffy pink landscape. Arc after arc sprays out, in hot cramping gobs of all sizes, all over the spread and the pillow shams, and the pink silk bed skirt.

What would Jesus NOT do?

Spunk graffiti.

"Vandalism" isn't the right word, but it's the first word that comes to mind.

Gwen's collapsed on the towel panting with her eyes closed, the vibrator humming inside her. Her eyes rolled back in her head, she's gushing between her fingers and whispering, "I beat you . . ."

She whispers, "You son of a bitch, I beat you . . ."

I'm tucking myself back in my pants and grabbing my coat. White soldier gobs are hanging all over the bed, the drapes, the wallpaper, and Gwen's still lying there, breathing hard, the vibrator angled halfway out of her. A second later, it slips free and flops around on the floor like a fleshy wet fish. It's then Gwen opens her eyes. She starts to push herself up on her elbows before she sees the damage.

I'm halfway out the window when I say, "Oh, by the way . . ."

I say, "Poodle," and behind me I hear her first scream for real.

Chapter 28

In the summer of 1642 in Plymouth, Massachusetts, a teenage boy was accused of buggering a mare, a cow, two goats, five sheep, two calves, and a turkey. This is real history on the books. In accordance with the Biblical laws of Leviticus, after the boy confessed he was forced to watch each animal being slaughtered. Then he was killed and his body heaped with the dead animals and buried in an unmarked pit.

This was before there were sexaholic talk therapy meetings.

This teenager, writing his fourth step must've been a whole barnyard tell-all.

I ask, "Any questions?"

The fourth-graders just look at me. A girl in the second row says, "What's buggering?"

I say, ask your teacher.

Every half hour, I'm supposed to teach another herd of fourth-graders some shit nobody wants to learn, like how to start a fire. How to carve an apple-head doll. How to make ink out of black walnuts. As if this is going to get any of them into a good college.

Besides deforming the poor chickens, these fourth-graders, they all walk in here carrying some germ. It's no mystery why Denny's always wiping his nose and coughing. Head lice, pinworms, chlamydia, ringworm—for serious, these field trip kids are the pint-sized horsemen of the apocalypse.

Instead of useful Pilgrim crap, I tell them how their playground game ring-around-a-rosy is based on the bubonic plague of 1665. The Black Death gave people hard, swollen, black spots they called "plague roses," or buboes, surrounded by a pale ring. Hence "bubonic." Infected people were locked inside their houses to die. In six months, a hundred thousand people were buried in the huge mass graves.

The "pocket full of posies" was what people of London carried so they wouldn't smell the corpses.

To build a fire, all you do is pile up some sticks and dry grass. You strike a spark with a flint. You work the bellows. Don't think for a second this fire-starting routine makes their little eyes sparkle. Nobody's impressed by a spark. Kids crouch in the front row, huddling over their little video games. Kids yawn right in your face. All of them giggle and pinch, rolling their eyes at me in my breeches and dirty shirt.

Instead, I tell them how in 1672, the Black Plague hit Naples, Italy, killing some four hundred thousand people.

In 1711, in the Holy Roman Empire, the Black Plague killed five hundred thousand people. In 1781, millions died worldwide from the flu. In 1792, another plague killed eight hundred thousand people in Egypt. In 1793, mosquitoes spread yellow fever to Philadelphia, where it killed thousands.

One kid in the back whispers, "This is worse than the spinning wheel."

Other kids open their box lunches and look inside their sandwiches.

Outside the window, Denny's bent over in the stocks. This time just out of habit. The town council has announced he'll be banished right after lunch. The stocks are just where he feels most safe from himself. Nothing's locked or even closed, but he's bent over with his hands and neck where they've been for months.

On their way here from the weaver's, one kid was poking a stick in Denny's nose and then trying to poke the stick in his mouth. Other kids rub his shaved head for luck.

Starting the fire only kills about fifteen minutes, so after that I'm supposed to show each herd of kids the big cooking pots and twig brooms and bed warmers and shit.

Children always look bigger in a room with a six-foot ceiling. A kid in the back says, "They gave us fucking egg salad again."

Here in the eighteenth century, I'm sitting beside the hearth of the big open fireplace equipped with the regular torture chamber relics, the big iron pothooks, the pokers, andirons, branding irons. My big fire blazing. This is a perfect moment to take the iron pincers out of the coals and pretend to study their pitted white-hot points. All the kids step back.

And I ask them, hey kids, can anybody here tell me how people in the eighteenth century used to abuse naked little boys to death.

This always gets their attention.

No hands go up.

Still studying the pincers, I say, "Anybody?"

Still no hands.

"For real," I say and start working the hot pincers open and shut. "Your teacher must've told you about how they used to kill little boys back then."

Their teacher's outside, waiting. How it worked was, a couple hours ago, while her class was carding wool, this teacher and me wasted some sperm in the smokehouse, and for sure she thought it would turn into something romantic, but hey. Me being face deep in her wonderful rubbery butt, it's amazing what a woman will read into it if you by accident say, I love you.

Ten times out of ten, a guy means *I love this*.

You wear a foofy linen shirt, a cravat, and some breeches, and the whole world wants to sit on your face. The two of you sharing ends of your fat hot slider, you could be on the cover of some paperback bodice-ripper. I tell her, "Oh, baby, cleave thy flesh unto mine. Oh yeah, cleave for me, baby."

Eighteenth-century dirty talk.

Their teacher, her name's Amanda or Allison or Amy. Some name with a vowel in it.

Just keep asking yourself: "What would Jesus *not* do?"

Now in front of her class, with my hands good and black, I stick the pincers back into the fire, then wiggle two of my black fingers at the kids, international sign language for *come closer*.

The kids in the back push the ones in the front. The ones in the front look around, and one kid calls out, "Miss Lacey?"

A shadow in the window means Miss Lacey's watching, but the minute I look at her she ducks out of sight.

I motion to the kids, closer. The old rhyme about Georgie Porgie, I tell them, is really about England's King George the Fourth, who could just never get enough.

"Enough what?" a kid says.

And I say, "Ask your teacher."

Miss Lacey continues to lurk.

I say, "You like the fire I got here?" and nod at the flames. "Well, people need to clean the chimney all the time, only the chimneys are really small inside and they run all over the place, so people used to force little boys to climb up in them and scrape the insides."

And since this was such a tight place, I tell them, the boys would get stuck if they wore any clothes.

"So just like Santa Claus..." I say, "they climbed up the chimney..." I say, and lift a hot poker from the fire, "naked."

I spit on the red end of the poker and the spit sizzles, loud, in the quiet room.

"And you know how they died?" I say. "Anybody?"

No hands go up.

I say, "You know what a scrotum is?"

Nobody says yes or even nods, so I tell them, "Ask Miss Lacey."

Our special morning in the smokehouse, Miss Lacey was bobbing on my dog with a good mouthful of spit. Then we were sucking tongues, sweating hard and trading drool, and she pulled back for a good look at me. In the dim smoky light, those big fake plastic hams were hanging all around us. She's just swamped and riding my hand, hard, and breathing between each word. She wipes her mouth and asks me if I have any protection.

"It's cool," I tell her. "It's 1734, remember? Fifty percent of all children died at birth."

She puffs a limp strand of hair off her face and says, "That's not what I mean."

I lick her right up the middle of her chest, up her throat, and then stretch my mouth around her ear. Still jacking her with my swamped fingers, I say, "So, you have any evil afflictions I should know about?"

She's pulling me apart behind and wets a finger in her mouth, and says, "I believe in protecting myself."

And I go, "That's cool."

I say, "I could get canned for this," and roll a rubber down my dog.

She worms her wet finger up my pucker and slaps my ass with her other hand and says, "How do you think I feel?"

To keep from triggering, I'm thinking of dead rats and rotten cabbage and pit toilets, and I say, "What I mean is, latex won't be invented for another century."

With the poker, I point at the fourth-graders, and I say, "These little boys used to come out of the chimneys covered with the black soot. And the soot used to grind into their hands and knees and elbows and nobody had soap so they stayed black all the time."

This was their whole lives back then. Every day, somebody forced them up a chimney and they spent all day crawling along in the darkness with the soot getting in their mouths and noses and they never went to school and they didn't have television or video games or mango-papaya juice boxes, and they didn't have music or remote-controlled anything or shoes and every day was the same.

"These little boys," I say and wave the poker across the crowd of kids, "these were little boys just like you. They were exactly like you."

My eyes go from each kid to each kid, touching all their eyes for a moment.

"And one day, each little boy would wake up with a sore place on his private parts. And these sore places didn't heal. And then they metastasized and followed the seminal vesicles up into the abdomen of each little boy, and by then," I say, "it was too late."

Here's the flotsam and jetsam of my med school education.

And I tell how sometimes they tried to save the little boy by cutting off his scrotum, but this was before hospitals and drugs. In the eighteenth century, they still called these kind of tumors "soot warts."

"And those soot warts," I tell the kids, "were the first form of cancer ever invented."

Then I ask, does anybody know why they call it cancer?

No hands.

I say, "Don't make me call on somebody."

Back in the smokehouse, Miss Lacey was running her fingers through the clumps of her damp hair, and said, "So?" As if it's just an innocent question, she says, "You have a life outside of here?"

And wiping my armpits dry with my powdered wig, I say, "Let's not pretend, okay?"

She's bunching up her pantyhose the way women do so they can snake their legs inside, and says, "This kind of anonymous sex is a symptom of a sex addict."

I'd rather think of myself as a playboy, James Bond type of guy.

And Miss Lacey says, "Well, maybe James Bond was a sex addict."

Here, I'm supposed to tell her the truth. I admire addicts. In a world where everybody is waiting for some blind, random disaster or some sudden disease, the addict has the comfort of know-ing what will most likely wait for him down the road. He's taken some control over his ultimate fate, and his addiction keeps the cause of his death from being a total surprise.

In a way, being an addict is very proactive.

A good addiction takes the guesswork out of death. There *is* such a thing as planning your getaway.

And for serious, it's such a chick thing to think that any hu-man life should just go on and on.

See also: Dr. Paige Marshall.

See also: Ida Mancini.

The truth is, sex isn't sex unless you have a new partner every time. The first time is the only session when your head and body are both there. Even the second hour of that first time, your head can start to wander. You don't get the full anesthetic quality of good first-time anonymous sex.

What would Jesus NOT do?

But instead of all that, I just lied to Miss Lacey and said, "How can I reach you?"

I tell the fourth-graders that they call it cancer because when the cancer starts growing inside you, when it breaks through your skin, it looks like a big red crab. Then the crab breaks open and it's all bloody and white inside.

"Whatever the doctors tried," I tell the silent little kids, "every little boy would end up dirty and diseased and screaming in terrible pain. And who can tell me what happened next?"

No hands go up.

"For sure," I say, "he died, of course."

And I put the poker back into the fire.

"So," I say, "any questions?"

No hands go up, so I tell them about the fairly bogus studies where scientists shaved mice and smeared them with smegma from horses. This was supposed to prove foreskins caused cancer.

A dozen hands go up, and I tell them, "Ask your teacher."

What a frigging job that must've been, shaving those poor mice. Then finding a bunch of uncircumcised horses.

The clock on the mantel shows our half hour is almost over. Out through the window, Denny's still bent over in the stocks. He's only got until one o'clock. A stray village dog stops next to him and lifts its leg, and the stream of steaming yellow goes straight into Denny's wooden shoe.

"And what else," I say, "is George Washington kept slaves and didn't ever chop down a cherry tree, and he was really a woman."

As they push toward the door I tell them, "And don't mess with the dude in the stocks anymore." I shout, "And lay off shaking the damn chicken eggs."

Just to stir the turd, I tell them to ask the cheesemaker why his eyes are all red and dilated. Ask the blacksmith about the icky lines going up and down the insides of his arms. I call after the infectious little monsters, any moles or freckles they have, that's just cancer waiting to happen. I call after them, "Sunshine is your enemy. Stay off the sunny side of the street."

Chapter 29

After Denny's moved in, I find a block of salt-and-pepper granite in the fridge. Denny lugs home chunks of basalt, his hands stained red with iron oxide. He wraps his pink baby blanket around black granite cobbles and smooth washed river rocks and slabs of sparkling mica quartzite and brings them home on the bus.

All those babies that Denny adopts. A whole generation piling up.

Denny carts home sandstone and limestone one blocky soft pink armload at a time. In the driveway, he hoses the mud off them. Denny stacks them behind the sofa in the living room. He stacks them in the kitchen corners.

Every day, I come home from a hard day in the eighteenth century, and here's a big lava rock on the kitchen counter next to the sink. There's this little gray boulder on the second shelf down in the fridge.

"Dude," I say. "Why's there a rock in the fridge."

Denny's here in the kitchen, taking warm clean rocks out of the dishwasher and swiping them with a dish towel, and he says, "Because that's my shelf, you said so." He says, "And that's not just a rock, that's granite."

"But why in the fridge?" I go.

And Denny says, "Because the oven is already full."

The oven is full of rocks. The freezer is full. The kitchen cabinets are so full they're coming down off the wall.

The plan was only one rock a day, but Denny's got such an addictive personality. Now he has to cart home a half-dozen rocks every day just to maintain his habit. Every day the dishwasher is running and the kitchen counters are spread with my mom's good bath towels covered with rocks so they can air-dry. Round gray rocks. Square black rocks. Broken brown and streaked yellow rocks. Travertine limestone. Every new batch that Denny brings home, he loads in the dishwasher and throws the clean, dry rocks from the day before into the basement.

At first you can't see the basement floor because of all the rocks. Then the rocks are piling up around the bottom step. Then the basement's filled to halfway up the stairs. Now you open the basement door and the rocks piled inside spill out into the kitchen. Anymore, there is no basement.

"Dude, the place is filling up," I say. "It feels like we're living in the bottom half of an hourglass."

Like somehow we're running out of time.

189

Being buried alive.

Denny in his dirty clothes, his waistcoat coming apart under the arms, his cravat hanging in threads, he waits at each bus stop cradling each pink bundle against his chest. He bounces each armload when the muscles in his arms start to fall asleep. After the bus comes, Denny with dirt smeared on his cheeks snores leaned against the drumming metal inside of the bus, still holding his baby.

At breakfast I say, "Dude, you said your plan was *one* rock each day."

And Denny says, "That's all I do. Just one."

And I say, "Dude, you are such a junkie." I say, "Don't lie. I know you're doing at least ten rocks a day."

Putting a rock in the bathroom, in the medicine cabinet, Denny says, "Okay, so I'm a little ahead of schedule."

There's rocks hidden in the toilet tank, I tell him.

And I say, "Just because it's rocks doesn't mean this still isn't substance abuse."

Denny with his running nose, with his shaved head, his baby blanket wet in the rain, he waits at each bus stop, coughing. He shifts the bundle from arm to arm. With his face tucked in close, he pulls up the pink satin edge of the blanket. To better protect his baby this looks like, but really to hide the fact that it's volcanic tufa.

The rain's running off the back of his tricorner hat. Rocks tear out the inside of his pockets.

Inside his sweaty clothes, carrying all that weight, Denny keeps getting skinnier and skinnier.

Heaving around what looks like a baby, it's just a waiting game until somebody in the neighborhood gets him nailed for child abuse and neglect. People are just itching to declare somebody an unfit parent and put some kid in a foster home, hey but that's just been my experience.

Every night, I come home from a long evening of choking to death and there's Denny with some new rock. Quartz or agate or marble. Feldspar or obsidian or argillite.

Every night I come home from forging heroes out of nobodies, and the dishwasher's running. I still have to sit down and do the day's accounts, total the checks, send today's thank-you letters. A rock's sitting on my chair. My papers and stuff on the dining-room table, it's all covered with rocks.

At first, I tell Denny, no rocks in my room. He can put the rocks anywhere else. Put them in the hallways. Put them in the closets. After that I'm saying, "Just don't be putting rocks in my bed."

"But you never sleep on that side," Denny says.

I say, "That's not the point. No rocks go in my bed, that's the point."

I come home from a couple hours of group therapy with Nico or Leeza or Tanya, and there's rocks inside the microwave oven. There's rocks in the clothes dryer. Rocks inside the washing machine.

Sometimes it's three or four in the morning before Denny's in the driveway hosing off a new rock, some nights a rock so big he has to roll it inside. Then he's piling it on top the other rocks in the bathroom, in the basement, in my mom's room.

This is Denny's full-time occupation, this hustling rocks home.

Denny's last day at work, at his banishment, His Royal Colonial Governorship stood at the doors to the Customs House and read from a little leather book. His hands almost hid the little thing, but it was black leather with the pages edged with gold paint and a few ribbons dangled from the top of the spine, one black, one green, and one red ribbon.

"Like the smoke vanisheth, so shall thou drive them away and like as wax melteth at the fire," he read, "so let the ungodly perish at the presence of God."

Denny leaned closer to me and said, "The part about the smoke and the wax," Denny said, "I think he means me."

At one o'clock in the town square, His Lord High Charlie, the Colonial Governor, was reading to us, standing with his face bowed into his little book. A cold wind pulled the smoke out sideways from every chimney pot. The milkmaids were there. Cobblers were there. The blacksmith was there. All of them, their clothes and hair, their breath and wigs reeking of hash. Reeking of reefer. All of their eyes, red and wasted.

Goodwife Landson and Mistress Plain wept into their aprons, but only because mourning was in their job descriptions. A guard of men stood with muskets braced in both hands, ready to escort Denny out into the wilderness of the parking lot. The colony flag snapped, lowered to half mast at the peak of the Customs House roof. A crowd of tourists watched from behind their video cameras. They're eating popcorn out of boxes with the mutant chickens pecking crumbs at their feet. They're sucking cotton candy off their fingers.

"Instead of banishing me," Denny called out, "maybe I could just get stoned?" He said, "I mean, the rocks would make a nice going-away present."

All the wasted colonists jumped when Denny said "stoned." They looked at the colonial governor and then looked at their shoes, and it took a little bit for the red to drain out of their cheeks.

"We therefore commit his body to the earth, to be turned into corruption . . . ," the governor read as a jetliner roared low, coming in for a landing, drowning out his little speech.

The guard escorted Denny to the gates of Colonial Duns-boro, two lines of men with guns marching with Denny between them. Through the gates, through the parking lot, they marched him to a bus stop on the edge of the twenty-first century.

"So, dude," I shout from the colony gates, "now that you're dead, what are you going to do with all your free time?"

"It's what I'm *not* going to do," Denny says. "And I'm sure as hell not going to act out."

This meant hunting rocks instead of jacking off. Staying so busy, hungry, tired, and poor he won't have any energy left to hunt porno and wham the ham.

The night after he's banished, Denny shows up at my mom's house with a rock in his arms and a policeman beside him. Denny wipes his nose on his sleeve.

The cop says, "Excuse me, but do you know this man?"

Then the cop says, "Victor? Victor Mancini? Hey, Victor, how's it going? Your life, I mean." And he holds one hand up with the big flat palm facing me.

I figure the cop means for me to high-five him, so I do, but I have to jump a little, since he's so tall. Still, my hand misses his. Then I say, "Yeah, that's Denny. It's okay. He lives here."

Talking to Denny, the cop says, "Get this. I save a guy's life, and he don't even remember me."

Of course.

"That time I almost choked!" I say.

And the cop says, "You remember!"

"Well," I say, "thanks for bringing old Denny here home safe and sound." I pull Denny inside and go to close the door.

And the cop says, "You doing okay now, Victor? Is there any-thing you need?"

I go to the dining-room table and write a name on a slip of paper. I hand it to the cop and say, "Could you arrange to make this guy's life a living hell? Maybe you could pull some strings and get him in for a rectal cavity search?"

The name on the paper is His Lord High Charlie, the Colonial Governor.

What would Jesus NOT do?

And the cop smiles and says, "I'll see what's possible."

And I shut the door in his face.

Now Denny heaves the rock onto the floor, and he asks do I have a couple bucks to spare. There's a chunk of ashlar granite at a stone supply yard. Good building rock, rock with good compression strength, costs so much per ton, and Denny figures he can get this one rock for ten bucks.

"A rock is a rock," he says, "but a square rock is a blessing."

The living room looks filled up by an avalanche. First the rocks were up around the bottom of the sofa. Then the end tables were buried with just the lampshades poking up out of the rocks. Granite and sandstone. Gray and blue and black and brown rocks. In some rooms, we walk around stooped against the ceiling.

So I ask, what's he going to build?

And Denny says, "Give me the ten bucks," Denny says, "and I'll let you help."

"All these stupid rocks," I say, "what's your goal?"

"This isn't about getting something done," Denny says. "It's about the *doing*, you know, the process."

"But what are you going to do with all these rocks?"

And Denny says, "I don't know until I collect enough."

"But what's enough?" I say.

"I don't know, dude," Denny says, "I just want the days of my life to add up to something."

The way every day of your life, the way it can just disappear in front of the television, Denny says he wants a rock to show for each day. Something tangible. Just one thing. A little monument to mark the end of each day. Each day he doesn't spend jacking himself off.

"Tombstone" isn't the right word, but it's the first word that comes to mind.

"This way, maybe my life will add up to something," he says, "something that will last."

I say there needs to be a twelve-step program for rock addicts.

And Denny says, "As if that would help." He says, "When was the last time you even thought about your fourth step?"

Chapter 30

The Mommy and the stupid little shit-heel kid, they stopped at a zoo one time. This zoo was so famous it was surrounded by acres of parking lot. This was in some city you can drive to, where a line of kids and moms were waiting to get inside with their money.

This was after the false alarm at the police station, when the detectives let the kid go find the bathroom by himself, and outside parked at the curb was the Mommy saying, "You want to help liberate the animals?"

This was the fourth or fifth time she came back to claim him.

This is what the courts would later call "Reckless Abuse of City Property."

That day, the Mommy's face looked the same as those dogs where the corner of each eye turns down and too much skin makes the eyes look sleepy.

"A damn St. Bernard," she'd said with the rearview mirror pointed at herself.

She'd got a white T-shirt somewhere she'd started wearing that said *Troublemaker*. It was new but already had some nose blood on one sleeve.

The other moms and kids all just talked to each other.

The line went on for a long long time. No police were around that you could see.

While they stood, the Mommy said if you ever want to be the first person to board an airplane and if you want to travel with your pet, you can do both, easy. The airlines have to let crazy people carry their animals on their laps. The government says so.

This was more important information to live by.

Waiting in line, she gave him a few envelopes and address labels to stick together. Then she gave him some coupons and letters to fold and put inside.

"You just call the airline people," she said, "and tell them you need to bring your 'comfort animal.'"

That's really what airlines call them. It can be a dog, a monkey, a rabbit, but no way can it be a cat. The government doesn't consider a cat as comforting anybody.

The airline can't ask you to prove you're crazy, the Mommy said. It would be discrimination. You wouldn't ask a blind person to prove they were blind.

"When you're crazy," she said, "how you look or act is not your fault."

The coupons said: *Good for one free meal at the Clover Inn.*

She said crazy people and crippled people get first dibs on airline seats, so you and your monkey will be right in the front of the line no matter how many people were ahead of you. She twisted her mouth off to one side and sniffed hard through that nostril, then she twisted the other way and sniffed again. One hand was always around her nose, touching it, rubbing it. She pinched the tip. She smelled underneath her shiny new fingernails. She looked up at the sky and sniffed a drop of blood back in. Crazy people, she said, had all the power.

She gave him stamps to lick and stick on the envelopes.

The line moved a little bit at a time, and at the window, the Mommy said, "Could I get a tissue, please?" She handed the stamped envelopes into the window and said, "Would you mind mailing these for us?"

Inside the zoo were animals behind bars, behind thick plastic, across deep ditches filled with water, and the animals mostly just sprawled on the ground, pulling on themselves between their back legs.

"For crying out loud," the Mommy said, too loud. "You give a wild animal a nice clean safe place to live, you give it plenty of good healthy food," she said, "and this is how it rewards you."

The other moms leaned down to whisper to their kids, then pulled them off to go look at other animals.

In front of them, monkeys shook themselves and squirted out spurts of thick white junk. The junk ran down the inside of the plastic windows. Old white junk was already there, splashed out thin and dried to almost see-through.

"You take away their struggle to survive, and this is what you get," the Mommy said.

How porcupines get off, she said while they watched, was porcupines hump a stick of wood. The same way a witch rides a broom, porcupines rub a stick until it's stinking and gummy with their pee and juice from their glands. After it stinks enough, they'll never leave it for another stick.

Still watching the porcupine riding its stick, the Mommy said, "And such a subtle metaphor."

The little boy pictured them letting all the animals loose. The tigers and penguins, and all of them fighting. The leopards and the rhinos, biting each other. The little fuck was really hot about the idea.

"The only thing that separates us from the animals," she said, "is we have pornography." Just more symbols, she said. She wasn't sure if this made us better than the animals or worse.

Elephants, the Mommy said, can use their trunks.

Spider monkeys can use their tails.

The little boy just wanted to see something dangerous go wrong.

"Masturbation," the Mommy said, "is their only means of escape."

Until us, the boy thought.

The sad tranced-out animals, the cross-eyed bears and gorillas and otters all hunched over themselves, their glassy little eyes almost closed, almost not breathing. Their tired little paws were gummy. Their eyes all crusty.

Dolphins and whales will rub themselves against the smooth sides of their tank, the Mommy said.

Deer will rub their antlers in the grass until, she said, they orgasm.

Right in front of them, a Japanese Sun Bear tossed its little mess onto the rocks. Then the bear sprawled backward with its eyes closed. Its little puddle left to die in the sunlight.

The boy whispered, is it sad?

"Worse," the Mommy said.

She told about a famous killer whale who was in a movie and then got moved to a fancy new aquarium, but wouldn't stop messing its tank. The keepers were so embarrassed. This went on so much, now they were trying to set the whale free.

"Masturbating your way to freedom," the Mommy said. "Michel Foucault would've loved that."

She said when a boy and a girl dog copulate, the head of the boy's penis swells and the vaginal muscles of the girl constrict. Even after sex, both dogs remain locked together, helpless and miserable for a brief period of time.

The Mommy said this same scenario described most marriages.

By then, the last remaining mothers had herded their children away. When the two of them were all alone, the boy whispered, how could they get the keys to set all the animals free?

And the Mommy said, "Got them right here."

In front of the monkey cage, the Mommy reached into her purse and took out a handful of pills, little round purple pills. She threw the handful through the bars, and the pills scattered and rolled. Some monkeys crawled down to look.

For one scary moment, not whispering, the boy said, "Is it poison?"

And the Mommy laughed. "Now *that's* an idea," she said. "No, honey, we don't want to liberate the little monkeys *too* much."

The monkeys were crowding now, eating the pills.

And the Mommy said, "Relax, kiddo." She dug into her purse and brought out the white tube, the trichloroethane. "This?" she said and put one of the purple pills on her tongue. "This is just plain old garden-variety LSD."

Then she pushed the tube of trichloroethane up one side of her nose. Or maybe she didn't. Maybe it wasn't this way at all.

200

Chapter 31

Denny's already sitting ringside in the dark, sketching on the yellow pad in his lap, three and a half empty beer bottles on the table next to him. He doesn't look up at the dancer, a brunette with straight black hair, on her hands and knees. She snaps her head from side to side to whip the stage with her hair, her hair looking purple in the red light. With her hands, she smooths the hair back off her face and crawls to the edge of the stage.

The music is loud dance techno mixed with samples of dogs barking, car alarms, Hitler youth rallies. You hear sounds of breaking glass and gunshots. You hear women screaming and fire engine sirens in the music.

"Hey Picasso," the dancer says, and she dangles her foot in front of Denny.

Without looking up from his pad, Denny takes a buck out of his pants pocket and slips it between her toes. On the seat next to him is another rock wrapped in his pink blanket.

For serious, the world is gone wrong when we dance to fire alarms. Fire alarms don't mean fires anymore.

If there were a real fire, they'd just have somebody with a nice voice announce, "Buick station wagon, license number BRK 773, your lights are on." In the event of a real nuclear attack, they'd just shout, "Phone call at the bar for Austin Letterman. Phone call for Austin Letterman."

The world won't end with a whimper or a bang, but with a discreet, tasteful announcement: "Bill Rivervale, phone call holding, line two." Then, nothing.

With one hand, the dancer takes Denny's money from between her toes. She lies on her front, her elbows propped on the edge of the stage, squashing her breasts together, and says, "Let's see how it turned out."

Denny makes a couple fast lines and turns the pad for her to see.

And she says, "That's supposed to be me?"

"No," Denny says, and turns the pad to study it himself. "It's supposed to be a composite order column the way the Romans made. See here," he says, and points to something with his smudged finger, "see how the Romans combined the volutes of the Ionic order with the Corinthian acanthus leaves but still kept all the proportions the same."

The dancer, she's Cherry Daiquiri from our last visit here

202

only now her blond hair's dyed black. On the inside of one thigh is a little round bandage.

By now I've walked up to look over Denny's shoulder, and I say, "Dude."

And Denny says, "Dude."

And I say, "It sounds like you've been at the library again."

To Cherry, I say, "It's good you took care of that mole."

Cherry Daiquiri swings her hair in a fan around her head. She bows, then throws her long black hair back over her shoulders. "And I tinted my hair," she says. With one hand, she reaches back for a few strands and holds them out near me, rubbing them between two fingers.

"It's black now," she says.

"I figured it's safer," she says, "since you told me blondes have the highest amount of skin cancer."

Me, I'm shaking each beer bottle, trying to find the one with any beer left to drink, and I look at Denny.

Denny's drawing, not listening, not even here.

Corinthian Tuscan composite architraves of the entablature . . . They should let some people into the library by prescription only. For serious, books about architecture are Denny's pornography. Yeah, first it's a few rocks. Then it's fan-tracery vaulting. My point is, this is America. You start out with hand jobs and progress to orgies. You smoke some dope and then, the big H. This is our whole culture of bigger, better, stronger, faster. The key word is progress.

In America, if your addiction isn't always new and improved, you're a failure.

To Cherry, I tap my head. Then I point my finger at her. I wink and say, "Smart girl."

She's trying to bend one foot behind her head and says, "You can't be too careful." Her bush is still shaved, her skin still freckled pink. Her toenails are silver. The music changes to a blast of machine-gun fire, then the whistle of falling bombs, and Cherry says, "Break time." She finds the slit in the curtain and she's gone backstage.

"Look at us, dude," I say. I find the last bottle of beer and it's warm. I say, "All women have to do is get naked, and we give them all our money. I mean, why are we such slaves?"

Denny flips over the page on his pad and starts something new.

I move his rock to the floor and sit down.

I'm just tired, I tell him. It seems women are always bossing me around. First my mom, and now Dr. Marshall. In between, there's Nico and Leeza and Tanya to keep happy. Gwen, who wouldn't even let me rape her. They're all just in it for themselves. They all think men are obsolete. Useless. As if we're just some sexual appendix.

Just the life support system for an erection. Or a wallet.

From now on, I say, I'm not giving any more ground.

I'm going on strike.

From now on, women can open their own doors.

They can pick up the check for their own dinners.

I'm not moving anybody's big heavy sofas, not anymore.

No more opening stuck jar lids, either.

And never again am I ever going to put down another toilet seat.

Hell, from now on I'm peeing on every seat.

With two fingers, I give the waitress the international sign language for two. Two more beers, please.

I say, "Let's just see women try and get along without me. Let's just watch their little female world grind to a halt."

204

The warm beer tastes from Denny's mouth, his teeth and Chapstick, that's how bad I need to drink right now.

"And for real," I say, "if I'm on a sinking ship, I'm getting in the lifeboat first."

We don't need women. There are plenty other things in the world to have sex with, just go to a sexaholics meeting and take notes. There's microwaved watermelons. There's the vibrating handles of lawn mowers right at crotch level. There's vacuum cleaners and beanbag chairs. Internet sites. All those old chat room sex hounds pretending to be sixteen-year-old girls. For serious, old FBI guys make the sexiest cyberbabes.

Please, just show me one thing in this world that is what you'd think.

To Denny I say, this is me talking, I say, "Women don't want equal rights. They have more power being *oppressed*. They *need* men to be the vast enemy conspiracy. Their whole identity is based on it."

And Denny turns just his head, owl-style, to look at me, his eyes bunched under his eyebrows, and he says, "Dude, you are spiraling out of control."

"No, I mean it," I say.

I say I could just kill the guy who invented the dildo. I really could.

The music changes to an air raid siren. Then a new dancer struts out, glowing pink inside some sheer baby doll lingerie, her bush and breasts so almost there.

She drops one strap off her shoulder. She sucks on her index finger. Her other shoulder strap drops, and it's only her breasts that keep her lingerie from falling to her feet.

Denny and me both watching her, the lingerie drops.

Chapter 32

When a tow truck from the auto club gets here, the front desk girl needs to go out to meet it, so I tell her, sure, I'll watch her desk.

For serious, but when the bus dropped me off at St. Anthony's today I noticed two of her tires were flat. Both rear wheels are resting right on the rims, I told her, and forced myself to make eye contact the whole time.

The security monitor shows the dining room, where old women are eating different shades of gray mashed food for lunch.

The intercom dial is set on number one, and you can hear elevator music and water running somewhere.

The monitor cycles through the crafts room, empty. Ten seconds pass. Then the dayroom, where the television is dark. Then ten seconds later, the library, where Paige is pushing my mom in her wheelchair past the shelves of battered old books.

With the intercom control, I dial-switch around until I hear them on number six.

"I wish I had the courage not to fight and doubt everything," my mom says. She reaches out and touches the spine of a book, saying, "I wish, just once, I could say, '*This*. This is good enough. Just because I *choose* it.'"

She takes the book out, sees the cover, and shoves the book back on the shelf, shaking her head.

And from the speaker, scratchy and muffled, my mom's voice says, "How did you decide to become a doctor?"

Paige shrugs. "You have to trade your youth for something. . . ."

The monitor cycles to a view of the empty loading dock behind St. Anthony's.

Now in voice-over, my mom's voice says, "But how did you make the commitment?"

And Paige's voice-over says, "I don't know. One day, I just wanted to be a doctor . . . ," and fades into some other room.

The monitor cycles to a view of the front parking lot, where a tow truck is parked and the driver is kneeling next to a blue car. The front desk girl stands off to one side with her arms folded.

I dial-switch from number to number, listening.

The monitor cycles to show me sitting with my ear to the intercom speaker.

There's the clatter of somebody typing on number five. On

eight, there's the whir of a blow-dryer. On two, I hear my mom's voice saying, "You know the old phrase 'Those who don't remember the past are condemned to repeat it'? Well, I think those who *remember* their past are even worse off."

In voice-over, Paige says, "Those who remember the past tend to get the story really screwed up."

The monitor cycles to show them going down a corridor, a book open in my mom's lap. Even in black-and-white, you can tell it's her diary. And she's reading it, smiling.

She looks up, twisting to see Paige behind the wheelchair, and says, "In my opinion, those who remember the past are paralyzed by it."

And Paige pushes her along, saying, "How about: 'Those who can forget the past are way ahead of the rest of us'?"

And their voices fade out again.

There's somebody snoring on number three. On number ten, there's the creak of a rocking chair.

The monitor cycles to show the front parking lot, where the girl is signing something on a clipboard.

Before I can find Paige again, the front desk girl will be back, saying her tires are fine. She'll be looking at me sideways, again.

What Would Jesus NOT Do?

As it turns out, some asshole just let the air out of them.

Chapter 33

Wednesdays mean Nico.

Fridays mean Tanya.

Sundays mean Leeza, and I catch her in the parking lot at the community center. Two doors down from the sexaholics meeting, we waste some sperm in a janitor's closet with a mop next to us, left standing in a bucket of gray water. There's cases of toilet tissue for Leeza to lean over, and I'm splitting her ass so hard that with my every drive, she head-butts a shelf of folded rags. I'm licking the sweat off her back for a nicotine buzz.

This is life on earth as I knew it. The kind of rough, messy sex where you first want to spread some newspapers. This is me trying to put things back the way they were before Paige Marshall. Period revival. Me trying to reconstruct how my life worked until just a few weeks ago. How my dysfunction used to function so beautifully.

Asking the back of Leeza's scrubby hair, I say, "You'd tell me if I was getting too sweet, wouldn't you?"

Pulling her hips back against me, I say, "Tell the truth."

I'm ramming at a regular steady pace, asking, "You don't think I'm getting soft, do you?"

To keep from triggering, I picture airplane crash sites and stepping in crap.

My dog burning hard, I imagine police photos of car wrecks and point-blank shotgun damage. To keep from feeling anything, I just keep stuffing it.

Stuffing dick, stuffing feelings. When you're a sexaholic, it's for sure the same thing.

Plugged in deep, I reach around her. Forced in tight, I reach under her to twist a hard pointed nipple in each hand.

And sweating her dark brown shadow into the light brown case of toilet paper, Leeza says, "Ease up." She says, "Just what are you trying to prove?"

That I'm an unfeeling jerk.

That I really don't care.

What would Jesus NOT do?

Leeza, Leeza with her three-hour release form, she grips the case of toilet paper and hacks and coughs, and with my hands I feel her abs spasm rock-hard and rippling between my fingers. The muscles of her pelvic floor, the pubococcygeus muscles, called the PC muscles for short, they spasm and the clenched drag on my dog is incredible.

See also: Gräfenberg Spot.

See also: Goddess Spot.

See also: Tantric Sacred Spot.

See also: Taoist Black Pearl.

Leeza spreads her hands open against the wall and shoves herself back at me.

All these names for the same place, all these symbols for the real thing. The Federation of Feminist Health Care Centers calls it the urethral sponge. The seventeenth-century Dutch anatomist Regnier de Graaf called this same mass of erectile tissue, nerves, and glands the female prostate. All these names for the two inches of urethra you can feel through the front wall of the vagina. The anterior wall of the vagina. What some people call the bladder neck.

All of this just the same bean-shaped territory everybody wants to name.

To stake with their own flag. Their symbol.

To keep from triggering, I picture first-year anatomy and dissecting out the two legs of the clitoris, the crura, each about as long as your index finger. Picture dissecting out the corpus cavernosa, the two cylinders of erectile tissue in the penis. We cut out the ovaries. We removed the testes. You learn to cut out all the nerves and lay them off to one side. The cadavers stinking with Formalin, formaldehyde. That new-car smell.

With this cadaver stuff in mind, you can ride for hours without getting anywhere.

You can kill a lifetime without feeling anything but skin. That's the magic of these sexaholic chicks.

When you're an addict, you can go without feeling anything except drunk or stoned or hungry. Still, when you compare this to other feelings, to sadness, anger, fear, worry, despair, and depression, well, an addiction no longer looks so bad. It looks like a very viable option.

Monday, I stay home after work and sort through my mom's old tapes from therapy sessions. Here are two thousand years of women on one shelf. Here's my mother's voice, steady and deep the way it was when I was a little shit.

The bordello of the subconscious.

Bedtime stories.

Imagine a heavy weight pressing your body, settling your head and arms, deeper and deeper into the cushions of the couch. The tape playing in headphones, remember to fall asleep on a towel.

Here's the name Mary Todd Lincoln on one taped session.

No way. Too ugly.

See also: The Wallis Simpson session.

See also: The Martha Ray session.

Here's the three Brontë sisters. Not real women, but symbols, just their names as empty shells you can project into, you can fill with antique stereotypes and clichés, milk-white skin and bustles, button shoes and hoop skirts. Naked except for whalebone corsets and crochet snoods, here are Emily and Charlotte and Anne Brontë lying around naked and bored on horsehair settees one fetid hot afternoon in the parlor. Sex symbols. You fill in the rest, the props and positions, the rolltop desk, the pump organ. Insert yourself as Heathcliff or Mr. Rochester. Just put in the tape and relax.

As if we can ever imagine the past. The past, the future, life on other planets, everything is such an extension, such a projection of life as we know it.

Me locked in my room, Denny comes and goes.

As if it's just some innocent accident, I catch myself thumbing through the Marshalls in the phone book. She's not listed. After work some nights, I take the bus that goes past St. Anthony's. She's never in any of the windows. Riding past, you can't guess which is her car in the parking lot. I don't get off.

Whether I'd slash her tires or leave a love note, I don't know.

Denny comes and goes, and every day there's fewer rocks in the house. And if you don't see somebody every day, you see them change. Me watching from an upstairs window, Denny comes and goes pushing bigger and bigger rocks in a shopping cart, and every day, Denny looks a little bigger inside his old plaid shirt. His face gets tan, his chest and shoulders get big enough to spread the plaid out so it doesn't hang in folds. He's not huge, but he's bigger, big for Denny.

Watching Denny from the window, I am a rock. I am an island.

I call down, does he need any help?

On the sidewalk, Denny looks around, his arms hugging a rock to his chest.

"Up here," I say. "Do you need me to help you?"

Denny heaves the rock into his shopping cart and shrugs. He shakes his head and looks up at me, one hand shading his eyes. "I don't need help," he says, "but you can help if you want."

Never mind.

What I want is to be needed.

What I need is to be indispensable to somebody. Who I need is somebody that will eat up all my free time, my ego, my attention. Somebody addicted to me. A mutual addiction.

See also: Paige Marshall.

It's the same way a drug can be something good and something bad.

You don't eat. You don't sleep. Eating Leeza isn't really eating. Sleeping with Sarah Bernhardt, you're not really asleep.

The magic of sexual addiction is you don't ever feel hungry or tired or bored or lonely.

On the dining-room table, all the new cards pile up. All the checks and best wishes from a lot of strangers who want to believe they're somebody's hero. Who think they're needed. Some woman writes about how she's started a prayer chain for me. A spiritual pyramid scheme. As if you can gang up on God. Bully Him around.

The fine line between praying and nagging.

Tuesday evening, a voice on the answering machine is asking for my permission to move my mom up to the third floor at St. Anthony's, the floor where you go to die. What I hear first is this isn't Dr. Marshall's voice.

Yelling back at the answering machine, I say, sure. Move the crazy bitch upstairs. Make her comfortable, but I'm not paying for any heroic measures. Feeding tubes. Respirators. The way I react could be nicer, but the soft way the administrator talks to me, the hush in her voice. The way she assumes that I'm a nice person.

I tell her soft little recorded voice not to call me again until Mrs. Mancini is good and dead.

Unless I'm scamming for money, I'd rather people hate me than feel sorry for me.

Hearing this, I'm not angry. I'm not sad. All I feel anymore is horny.

And Wednesdays mean Nico.

In the women's room, the padded fist of her pubic bone punching me in the nose, Nico wipes and smears herself up and down my face. For two hours, Nico laces her fingers together across the back of my head and pulls my face into her until I'm choking down pubic hair.

Tonguing inside her labia minora, I'm tonguing the folds of Dr. Marshall's ear. Breathing through my nose, I'm stretching my tongue toward salvation.

Thursday is Virginia Woolf, first. Then it's Anaïs Nin. Then there's just enough time for a session with Sacajawea before it's morning, and I have to go to work in 1734.

In between, I write down my past in my notebook. This is doing my fourth step, my fearless and complete moral inventory.

Fridays mean Tanya.

By Friday, there are no more rocks in my mom's house.

Tanya comes by the house, and Tanya means anal.

The magic of getting butt is she's as tight as a virgin every time. And Tanya brings toys. Beads and rods and probes, these all smell like bleach, and she smuggles them around in a black leather bag she keeps in the trunk of her car. Tanya works my dog with one hand and her mouth while she presses the first ball on a long string full of greasy red rubber balls against my trapdoor.

My eyes closed, I'm trying to relax enough.

Breathe in. Then out.

Think of the monkey and the chestnuts.

Slow and even, in and then out.

Tanya twisting the first ball against me, I say, "You'd tell me if I sounded too needy, wouldn't you?"

And the first ball pops inside.

"Why don't people believe me," I say, "when I tell them I just don't care?"

And the second ball pops in.

"I really really can't give a shit about anything," I say.

Another ball pops in.

"I'm not going to get hurt, again," I say.

Something else pops inside me.

Tanya still throating my dog, she makes a fist around the dangling string and yanks.

Imagine a woman yanking your guts out.

See also: My dying mother.

See also: Dr. Paige Marshall.

Tanya yanks again, and my dog triggers, the white soldiers gobbing against the bedroom wallpaper beside her face. She yanks again, and my dog's coughing dry and still coughing.

And still triggering dry, I say, "Damn. For serious, I felt *that*." *What would Jesus NOT do?*

Leaning forward with both my hands spread against the wall, my knees folding a little, I say, "Easy does it." I tell Tanya, "You're not starting a lawn mower."

And Tanya kneeling under me, still looking at the greasy, stinking balls on the floor, says, "Oh boy." She lifts the string of red rubber balls for me to see, and she says, "There are supposed to be ten."

There's only eight and what looks like a lot of empty string.

My ass hurts so much, I finger around back there and then check my fingers for blood. As much as I hurt right now, you'd be amazed there's not blood everywhere.

And gritting my teeth, I say, "That was fun, don't you think?"

And Tanya says, "I need you to sign my release form so I can get back to jail." She's dangling the string of balls into her black bag and says, "You're going to want to stop by an emergency room."

See also: Impacted colon.

See also: Bowel blockage.

See also: Cramping, fever, septic shock, heart failure.

It's been five days since I remember feeling hungry enough to eat. I haven't been tired. Or worried or angry or afraid or thirsty. If the air in here smells bad, I can't tell. I only know this is Friday because Tanya is here.

Paige and her dental floss. Tanya and her toys. Gwen with her safe word. All these women are yanking me around on a string.

"No, really," I tell Tanya. I sign the form, under *sponsor*, and say, "Really, nothing's wrong. I don't feel anything left inside."

And Tanya takes the form and says, "I can't believe that."

What's funny is, I'm still not sure I believe it either.

Chapter 34

Without insurance or even a driver's license, I call a cab to come jump-start my mom's old car. On the radio, they talk about where to find traffic, a two-car accident on the bypass, a stalled tractor-trailer on the airport freeway. After I fill the gas tank, I just find an accident and get in line. Just to feel like I'm part of something.

Sitting in traffic, my heart would beat at regular speed. I'm not alone. Trapped there, I could just be a normal person headed home to a wife, kids, a house. I could pretend that my life was more than just waiting for the next disaster. That I knew how to function. The way other kids would "play house," I could play commuter.

After work, I go visit Denny on the empty block where he's laid out his rocks, the old Menningtown Country Townhouses block where he's pasting row on top of row with mortar until he's already got a wall, and I say, "Hey."

And Denny says, "Dude."

Denny says, "How's your mom?"

And I say I don't care.

Denny trowels a layer of gritty gray mud on top of the last row of stones. With the pointed steel end of the trowel, he fusses with the mortar until it's even. With a stick, he smoothes the joints between rocks he's already laid.

A girl's sitting under an apple tree close enough you can see she's Cherry Daiquiri from the strip club. A blanket is spread out under her, and she's lifting white cartons of take-out food from a brown grocery bag and opening each carton.

Denny starts bedding stones into the new mortar.

I say, "What are you building?"

Denny shrugs. He twists a square brown rock deeper into the mortar. With the trowel, he chinks mortar between two stones. Assembling his whole generation of babies into something huge.

Doesn't he need to build it on paper, first? I say, don't you need a plan? There's permits and inspections you have to get. You have to pay fees. There's building codes you have to know.

And Denny says, "How come?"

He rolls around rocks with his foot, then finds the best one and fits it in place. You don't need a permit to paint a picture, he says. You don't need to file a plan to write a book. There're books that do more damage than he ever could. You don't need your poem inspected. There's such a thing as freedom of expression.

Denny says, "You don't need a permit to have a baby. So why do you need to buy permission to build a house?"

And I say, "But what if you build a dangerous, ugly house?"

And Denny says, "Well, what if you raise a dangerous, ass-holey kid?"

And I hold my fist up between us and say, "You better not mean *me*, dude."

Denny looks over at Cherry Daiquiri sitting in the grass and says, "Her name's Beth."

"Don't think for a minute that the city is going to buy your First Amendment logic," I say.

And I say, "She's not really as attractive as you think."

With the bottom of his shirt, Denny wipes the sweat off his face. You can see his abs are rippled armor, and he says, "You need to go see her."

I can see her from here.

"Your mom, I mean," he says.

She doesn't know me anymore. She won't miss me.

"Not for her," Denny says. "You need to go complete this for you."

Denny, his arms flicker with shadows where his muscles flex. Denny, now his arms stretch the sleeves of his sour T-shirt. His skinny arms look big around. His pinched shoulders spread wide. With every row, he's having to lift the stones a little higher. With every row, he's having to be stronger. Denny says, "You want to stay for Chinese food?" He says, "You look a little wasted."

I ask, is he living with this Beth girl now?

I ask if he's got her pregnant or anything.

And Denny lugging a big gray rock with both hands at his waist, he shrugs. A month ago, this was a rock the two of us could hardly lift together.

If he needs it, I tell him I got my mom's old car running.

"Go see how your mom is," Denny says. "Then come and help."

Everybody at Colonial Dunsboro says to say hello, I tell him.

And Denny says, "Don't lie to me, dude. I'm not the one who needs cheering up."

Chapter 35

Fast-forwarding through the messages on my mom's answering machine, there's the same soft voice, hushed and understanding, saying, "Condition is deteriorating . . ." Saying, "Critical . . ." Saying, "Mother . . ." Saying, "Intervene . . ."

I just keep hitting the fast-forward button.

Still on the shelf for tonight, there's Colleen Moore, whoever she was. There's Constance Lloyd, whoever that is. There's Judy Garland. There's Eva Braun. What's left is definitely the second string.

The voice on the message machine stops and starts.

"... been calling some of the fertility clinics listed in his mother's diary ..." it says.

It's Paige Marshall.

I rewind.

"Hello, this is Dr. Marshall," she says. "I need to talk to Victor Mancini. Please tell Mr. Mancini that I've been calling some of the fertility clinics listed in his mother's diary, and they all seem to be legitimate. Even the doctors are real." She says, "The oddest part is that they get very upset when I ask them about Ida Mancini."

She says, "This is looking like something more than just Mrs. Mancini's fantasy."

A voice in the background says, "Paige?"

A man's voice.

"Listen," she says. "My husband's here, so would Victor Mancini please visit me at St. Anthony's Care Center as soon as possible."

The man's voice says, "Paige? What are you up to? Why are you whispering—"

And the line goes dead.

Chapter 36

So Saturday means visiting my mom.

In the lobby of St. Anthony's, talking to the front desk girl, I tell her I'm Victor Mancini and I'm here to see my mom, Ida Mancini.

I say, "Unless, I mean, unless she's dead."

The front desk girl gives me that look, the one where you tuck your chin down and look at the person you feel so, so sorry for. You tilt your face down so your eyes have to look up at the person. That look of submission. Lift your eyebrows into your hairline as you look up. It's that look of infinite pity. Squash your mouth down into a frowny face, and you'll know the exact way the front desk girl is looking at me.

And she says, "Of course your mother is still with us."

And I say, "Don't take this the wrong way, but I kind of wish she wasn't."

Her face forgets for a second how sorry she is, and her lips pull back to show her teeth. The way to make most women break eye contact is to run your tongue around your lips. The ones who don't look away, for serious, bingo.

Just go back, she tells me. Mrs. Mancini is still on the first floor.

It's Miss Mancini, I tell her. My mom's not married, unless you count me in that creepy Oedipal way.

I ask if Paige Marshall is here.

"Of course she is," the front desk girl says, now with her face turned a little away from me, looking at me out the corner of her eye. The look of distrust.

Beyond the security doors, all the crazy old Irmas and Lavernes, the Violets and Olives start their slow migration of walkers and wheelchairs coming my way. All the chronic undressers. All the dumped grannies and squirrels with their pockets full of chewed food, the ones who forget how to swallow, their lungs full of food and drink.

All of them, smiling at me. Beaming. They're all wearing those plastic bracelets that keep the doors locked, but they still look better than I feel.

In the dayroom, the smell of roses and lemons and pine. The loud little world begging for attention from inside the television. The shattered jigsaw puzzles. Nobody's moved my mom up to the third floor yet, the death floor, and in her room Paige Marshall's sitting in a tweed recliner, reading her clipboard with her glasses on, and when she sees me says, "Look at you." She says, "Your mother isn't the only one who could use a stomach tube."

I say I got her message.

My mom is. She's just in bed. She's just asleep is all, her stomach just a bloated little mound under the covers. Her bones are the only thing left in her arms and hands. Her head sunk in her pillow, she squeezes her eyes shut. The corners of her jaw swell as her teeth clench for a moment, and she brings her whole face together to swallow.

Her eyes fall open, and she stretches her green-gray fingers at me, in a creepy underwater way, a slow-motion swimming stroke, trembling the way light does at the bottom of a swimming pool, when you're little and staying overnight in some motel just off some highway. The plastic bracelet hangs around her wrist, and she says, "Fred."

She swallows again, her whole face bunching with the effort, and says, "Fred Hastings." Her eyes roll to one side and she smiles at Paige. "Tammy," she says. "Fred and Tammy Hastings."

Her old defense attorney and his wife.

All my notes for being Fred Hastings are at home. If I drive a Ford or a Dodge, I can't remember. How many kids I'm supposed to have. What color did we finally paint the dining room. I can't remember a single detail about how I'm supposed to live my life.

Paige still sitting in the recliner, I step close to her and put a hand on her lab coat shoulder and say, "How are you feeling, Mrs. Mancini?"

Her terrible green-gray hand comes up level and rocks from side to side, the universal sign language for so-so. With her eyes closed, she smiles and says, "I was hoping you'd be Victor."

Paige shrugs my hand off her shoulder.

And I say, "I thought you liked me better."

I say, "Nobody likes Victor very much."

My mother stretches her fingers toward Paige and says, "Do you love him?"

Paige looks at me.

"Fred, here," my mom says, "do you love him?"

Paige starts clicking and unclicking her ballpoint pen, fast. Not looking at me, looking at the clipboard in her lap, she says, "I do."

And my mom smiles. And stretching her fingers toward me, she says, "And do you love her?"

Maybe the way a porcupine thinks about its stinking stick, if you'd call that love.

Maybe the way a dolphin loves the smooth sides of its pool.

And I say, "I guess."

My mom tucks her chin into her neck sideways, eyeballing me, and says, "Fred."

And I say, "Okay, yes." I say, "I love her."

She brings her terrible green-gray fingers back to rest on her mounded belly and says, "You two are so lucky." She closes her eyes and says, "Victor isn't very good at loving people."

She says, "What I'm most afraid of is, after I'm gone, there will be no one left in the entire world who'll love Victor."

These frigging old people. These human ruins.

Love is bullshit. Emotion is bullshit. I am a rock. A jerk. I'm an uncaring asshole and proud of it.

What would Jesus NOT do?

If it comes down to a choice between being unloved and being vulnerable and sensitive and emotional, then you can just keep your love.

If what I just said about loving Paige was a lie or a vow, I don't know. But it was a trick. This is just heaps more chick bullshit. There is no human soul, and I am absolutely for sure seriously not going to fucking cry.

227

My mom, her eyes stay closed, and her chest inflates and deflates in long, deep cycles.

Breathe in. Breathe out. Imagine a heavy weight pressing your body, settling your head and arms, deeper and deeper.

And she's asleep.

Paige stands up from the recliner and nods her head toward the door, and I follow her out into the hallway.

She looks around and says, "You want to go to the chapel?"

I'm not really in the mood.

"To talk," she says.

I say, okay. Walking with her, I say, "Thanks for back there. For lying, I mean."

And Paige says, "Who says I was lying?"

Does that mean she loves me? That's impossible.

"Okay," she says. "Maybe I fibbed a little. I like you. Some."

Breathe in. Breathe out.

In the chapel, Paige shuts the door behind us and says, "Feel," and takes my hand to hold it against her flat stomach. "I checked my temperature. It's not my time anymore."

With the load already building up behind whatever in my guts, I tell her, "Yeah?" I say, "Well, I may have beat you to it."

Tanya and her rubber butt toys.

Paige turns and walks away from me, slow, and still turned away she says, "I don't know how to talk to you about this."

The sun through the stained-glass window, a whole wall in a hundred shades of gold. The blond wood cross. Symbols. The altar and the Communion rail, it's all here. Paige goes to sit on one of the benches, a pew, and she sighs. Her one hand grips the top of her clipboard, and her other lifts some clipped papers to show something red underneath them.

My mom's diary.

She hands the diary to me and says, "You can check the facts yourself. In fact, I recommend you do so. If only for your own peace of mind."

I take the book, and it's still gibberish inside. Okay, Italian gibberish.

And Paige says, "The only good thing is there's no absolute assurance that the genetic material they used was from the actual historic figure."

Everything else checks out, she says. The dates, the clinics, the specialists. Even the church people she talked to have insisted the material stolen, the tissue the clinic cultured, was the only authenticated foreskin. She says this has opened a giant political can of worms in Rome.

"The only other good thing," she says, "is I didn't tell anybody who you were."

Jesus Christ, I say.

"No, I mean who you are *now*," she says.

And I say, "No, I was just swearing."

How this feels is like I just got back the results on a bad biopsy. I say, "So what does this mean?"

Paige shrugs. "When you think about it, nothing," she says. She nods toward the diary in my hand and says, "Unless you want to ruin your life, I'd recommend you burn that."

I ask, how does this affect us, her and me?

"We shouldn't see each other anymore," she says, "if that's what you mean."

I ask, she doesn't believe this junk, does she?

And Paige says, "I've seen you with the patients here, the way they're all at peace after they talk to you." Sitting there, she leans forward with her elbows on her knees and her chin in her hands, and she says, "I just can't take the chance that your mother is right. Not everybody I talked to in Italy could be delusional. I mean, what if you're really the beautiful and divine son of God?"

229

The blessed and perfect mortal manifestation of God.

A belch rumbles up from my blockage, and the taste in my mouth is acid.

"Morning sickness" isn't the right term, but it's the first term that comes to mind.

"So what you're saying is you only sleep with mortals?" I say.

And Paige leaning forward, she gives me that pity look, the one the front desk girl does so well with her chin tucked to her chest, her eyebrows lifted into her hairline, and she says, "I'm so sorry I butted in. I promise you, I won't tell a soul."

And what about my mom?

Paige sighs and shrugs. "That's easy. She's delusional. Nobody would believe her."

No, I meant, will she die soon?

"Probably," Paige says, "unless there's a miracle."

Chapter 37

Ursula stops to catch her breath and looks up at me. She shakes the fingers of her one hand and squeezes the wrist with her other hand and says, "If you were a churn, we'd have butter a half hour ago."

I go, sorry.

She spits in her hand and makes a fist around my dog and says, "This sure isn't like you."

Anymore, I won't even pretend to know what I'm like.

For sure this is just another slow day in 1734, so we're flopped in a pile of hay in the stable. Me with my arms crossed behind my head, Ursula is curled up against me. We don't move very much or the dry hay pokes us through our clothes. We both look up into the rafters, the wood beams and woven underside of the thatched roof. Spiders dangle down on their strands of web.

Ursula starts yanking and says, "You see Denny on television?"

When?

"Last night."

What for?

Ursula shakes her head, "Building something. People are complaining. People think it's some kind of church, and he won't say what kind."

It's pathetic how we can't live with the things we can't understand. How we need everything labeled and explained and deconstructed. Even if it's for sure unexplainable. Even God.

"Defused" isn't the right word, but it's the first word that comes to mind.

It's not a church, I say. I throw my cravat back over one shoulder and pull the front of my shirt out of my pants.

And Ursula says, "They think it's a church on TV."

With the fingertips of one hand, I press around my navel, the umbilicus, but digital palpation is inconclusive. I tap and listen for changes in sound that might indicate a solid mass, but precussing is inconclusive.

The big trapdoor muscle that keeps the shit inside you, doctors call that the *rectal shelf,* and after you shove something above that shelf, no way is it coming out without a lot of help. In hospital emergency rooms, they call this kind of help *colorectal foreign bodies management.*

To Ursula, I say, could she put her ear against my bare stomach and tell me if she hears anything.

"Denny never was very together," she says, and leans in to press her warm ear against my belly button. Navel. Umbilicus, doctors would call it.

A typical patient presenting colorectal foreign bodies is a male in his forties or fifties. The foreign body is almost always what the doctors call *self-administered*.

And Ursula says, "What am I listening for?"

Positive bowel sounds.

"Gurgles, squeaks, rumbles, anything," I say. Anything that indicates I'll have a bowel movement someday, and the stool isn't just packing up behind some obstruction.

As a clinical entity, the occurrence of colorectal foreign bodies rises dramatically every year. There are reports of foreign bodies that stayed in place for years without perforating the bowel or causing significant health complications. Even if Ursula hears something, it won't be conclusive. Really this would take an abdominal roentgenogram and proctosigmoidoscopy.

Picture yourself on the examining table with your knees pulled to your chest in what they call the jackknife position. Your buttocks would be separated and held apart with adhesive tape. Somebody would apply periabdominal pressure while somebody else would insert two tissue forceps and attempt to transanally manipulate and extract the foreign body. Of course, this is all done with regional anesthesia. Of course, nobody is giggling and taking pictures, but still.

Still. This is me I'm talking about.

Picture the sigmoidoscope view on a television screen, a bright light pushing along a clenched tunnel of mucosal tissue, wet and pink, pushing into the puckered darkness until it's there on TV for everybody to see: the dead hamster.

See also: The Barbie doll head.

See also: The red rubber butt ball.

Ursula's hand has stopped its up-and-down jumping, and she says, "I can hear your heart beat." She says, "You sound pretty scared."

No. No way, I tell her, I'm having a swell time.

"You don't feel like it," she says, her breath hot on my periabdominal region. She says, "I'm getting carpal tunnels."

"You mean *carpal tunnel syndrome*," I say. "And you can't because it won't be invented until the Industrial Revolution."

To keep the foreign body from moving higher into the colon, you can provide traction by using a Foley catheter and inserting a balloon into the colon above the body. Then inflate the balloon. More common is a vacuum above the foreign body; this is usually the case with self-administered wine or beer bottles.

Her ear still against my belly, Ursula says, "Do you know whose it is?"

And I say, that's not funny.

With bottles self-administered open end first, you have to insert a Robinson catheter around the bottle and allow air to flow past it and break the vacuum. With bottles self-administered closed end first, insert a retractor into the open end of the bottle, then fill the bottle with plaster. After the plaster sets around the retractor, pull it to remove the bottle.

Using enemas is another method, but less reliable.

Here with Ursula in the stables, you can hear it start to rain outside. The rain pattering on the thatch, the water running in the street. The light in the windows is dimmer, dark gray, and there's the quick repeating splash of somebody running for cover. The deformed black-and-white chickens squeeze in through a broken board in the walls and fluff their feathers to shake off the water.

And I say, "What else does the TV say about Denny?"

Denny and Beth.

I say, "Do you think Jesus automatically knew he was Jesus from the start, or did his mom or somebody tell him and he grew into it?"

A soft rumble comes up from my lap, but not from inside me.

Ursula breathes out, then snores again. Her hand goes limp around me. Limp me. Her hair spills across my legs. Her warm soft ear is sunk into my stomach.

The hay itches up through the back of my shirt.

The chickens scratch in the dust and hay. The spiders spin.

Chapter 38

How to make an ear candle is you take a piece of regular paper and roll it into a thin tube. There's no real miracle to it. Still, you have to start with the stuff you already know.

This is just more flotsam and jetsam left over from medical school, something I teach now to the field trip kids at Colonial Dunsboro.

Maybe you have to work your way up to the real bona fide miracles.

Denny comes to me after stacking rock outdoors in the rain all day and says he's got earwax so bad he can't hear. He sits in a chair in my mom's kitchen with Beth there, standing by the back door, leaning back a little with her butt against the edge of the kitchen counter. Denny sits with the chair pulled sideways to the kitchen table and one of his arms resting on the table.

And I tell him to hold still.

Rolling the paper into a tight tube, I say, "Just supposing," I say, "Jesus Christ had to practice being the Son of God to get any good at it."

I tell Beth to turn off the kitchen lights, and I twist one end of the thin paper tube into the tight dark tunnel of Denny's ear. His hair's grown out some, but we're talking less of a fire hazard than most people have. Not too deep, I twist the tube into his ear only far enough so it stays in place when I let go.

To concentrate, I try and not think of Paige Marshall's ear.

"What if Jesus spent all his growing up getting things wrong," I say, "before he ever got a single miracle right?"

Denny sitting in the chair, in the dark, the white paper tube juts out his ear.

"How is it we don't read about Jesus' failed first attempts," I say, "or how he didn't really crank out the big miracles until he was over thirty?"

Beth pushes out the crotch of her tight jeans at me, and I use her zipper to light a kitchen match and carry the little flame across the room to Denny's head. Using the match, I light the end of the paper tube.

From striking the match, the room smells full of sulfur.

Smoke unwinds from the burning end of the tube, and Denny says, "You're not going to let it hurt me, are you?"

The flame creeps in closer to his head. The burned end of the tube curls open and comes apart. Black paper edged with worming orange sparks, these hot bits of paper drift toward the ceiling. Some bits of black paper curl and fall.

That's really what this is called. An ear candle.

And I say, "How about if Jesus got started by just doing nice things for people, you know, helping old ladies cross the street or telling people when they'd left their headlights on?" I say, "Well, not that *exactly*, but you get the idea."

Watching the fire curl closer and closer to Denny's ear, I say, "How about if Jesus spent years working up to the big loaves-and-the-fishes thing? I mean, that Lazarus deal is probably something he'd have to build up to, right?"

And Denny's eyes are twisted over to try and see how close the fire is, and he says, "Beth, is it about to burn me?"

And Beth looks at me and says, "Victor?"

And I say, "It's okay."

Leaning back even harder against the kitchen counter, Beth twists her face not to see and says, "It looks like some kind of weird torture."

"Maybe," I say, "maybe even Jesus didn't believe in himself at first."

And I lean into Denny's face, and with one puff, blow out the flame. With one hand cupped under Denny's jaw, to keep him still, I slip the last of the paper tube out of his ear. When I show it to him, the paper is gummy and dark with the earwax the fire wicked out.

Beth turns on the kitchen light.

Denny shows the burned little tube to her, and Beth smells it and says, "Stinky."

I say, "Maybe miracles are like a talent, and you have to start with the small stuff."

Denny puts a hand over his clean ear and then uncovers it. He covers and uncovers it again, and says, "Definitely better."

"I don't mean like Jesus did card tricks," I say, "but just not hurting people would be a good start."

Beth comes around, and she holds her hair back with one hand so she can bend and look into Denny's ear. She squints and gets her head around to see in from different angles.

Rolling another sheet of paper into a thin tube, I say, "You were on TV the other day, I hear."

I say, "I'm sorry." Just twisting the paper tube tighter and tighter in my hands, I say, "That was my fault."

Beth stands straight and looks at me. She shakes her hair back. Denny sticks a finger in his clean ear and digs around, then he smells the finger.

And just holding the paper tube, I say, "From now on, I want to try and be a better person."

Choking in restaurants, fooling people, I'm not going to do that kind of shit anymore. Sleeping around, casual sex, that kind of shit.

I say, "I called the city and complained about you. I called the TV station and told them a bunch of stuff."

My stomach hurts, but if it's guilt or impacted stool, I can't tell.

Either way, I'm so full of shit.

For a second it's easier to look at the dark kitchen window above the sink, the night outside it. Reflected in the window, there's me looking as wasted and thin as my mom. The new righteous, maybe-divine Saint Me. There's Beth looking at me with her arms folded. There's Denny sitting beside the kitchen table, digging in his dirty ear with his fingernail. Then he peers under the nail.

"The thing is, I just wanted you to need my help," I say. "I wanted you to have to ask me for it."

Beth and Denny look at me for real, and I look at all three of us reflected in the window.

"Sure, yeah," Denny says. "I need your help." To Beth he says, "What's this about us being on TV?"

And Beth shrugs and says, "It was Tuesday, I think." She says, "No, wait, what is today?"

And I say, "So you need me?"

And Denny still sitting in the chair, he nods at the paper tube I've got ready. He lifts his dirty ear to me and says, "Dude, do it again. It's cool. Clean out my other ear."

Chapter 39

It's dark and starting to rain when I get to the church, and Nico's waiting for me in the parking lot. She's struggling around inside her coat, and for a moment one sleeve hangs empty, then she snakes her arm back inside it. Nico reaches her fingers inside the cuff of her other sleeve and pulls out something lacy and white.

"Hold on to this for me," she says and hands me a warm fistful of lace and elastic.

It's her bra.

"Just for a couple hours," she says. "I'm not wearing any

pockets." She's smiling with one corner of her mouth, her top teeth biting a little on her bottom lip. Her eyes sparkle with rain and streetlight.

Not taking her stuff, I tell her, I can't. Not anymore.

Nico shrugs, and tucks the bra back inside the sleeve of her coat. All the sexaholics have gone inside already, to Room 234. The hallways are empty with shiny waxed linoleum and bulletin boards on the walls. Church news and kids' art projects posted everywhere. Finger-painting pictures of Jesus and the apostles. Jesus and Mary Magdalen.

Heading for Room 234, I'm a step ahead of Nico when she grabs the back of my belt and pulls me over against a bulletin board.

The way my gut aches, the bloating and cramps, when she pulls on my belt, the pain makes me belch acid up the back of my throat. My back against the wall, she slips her leg between mine and lifts her arms around my head. Her breasts wedged warm and soft between us, Nico's mouth fits over mine, and we're both breathing her perfume. Her tongue's more in my mouth than in hers. Her leg's rubbing not my erection, but my impacted bowel.

The cramping could mean colorectal cancer. It could mean acute appendicitis. Hyperparathyroidism. Adrenal insufficiency.

See also: Intestinal obstruction.

See also: Colorectal foreign bodies.

Cigarette smoking. Fingernail biting. It used to be my cure for everything was sex, but with Nico swimming against me, I just can't.

Nico says, "Okay, we'll find a different place."

She steps back, and I bend double with the ache in my guts and stumble down to Room 234 with Nico hissing behind me.

"No," she's hissing.

Inside Room 234, the group leader's saying, "We're going to work on the fourth step tonight."

"Not in there," Nico's saying until we're standing in the open doorway being looked at by the crowd of people sitting around a big, low table stained with paint and lumpy with dried paste. The chairs are little plastic scoops so low everybody's knees jut up in front of them. These people just stare at us. These men and women. Urban legends. These sexaholics.

The group leader says, "Is there anybody here still working on their fourth step?"

Nico slides against me and whispers into my ear, she whispers, "If you go in there, in with all those losers," Nico says, "I'm never getting with you again."

See also: Leeza.

See also: Tanya.

And I come around the table to drop myself into a plastic chair.

With everybody watching, I say, "Hello. I'm Victor."

Looking into Nico's eyes, I say, "My name is Victor Mancini, and I'm a sexaholic."

And I say how I've been stuck on my fourth step for what seems like forever.

The feeling is less like an ending than just another starting point.

And still leaning in the doorway, not just eye juice but tears, rolling black mascara tears, burst out of Nico's eyes, and she smears them away with her hand. Nico says, she shouts, "Well, I'm not!" And out of the sleeve of her coat, her bra drops on the floor.

Nodding at her, I say, "And this is Nico."

And Nico says, "You people can all get fucked." She snatches up her bra and she's gone.

It's then everybody says, Hello Victor.

And the group leader says, "Okay."

He says, "As I was saying, the best place to find insight is to remember where you lost your virginity. . . ."

Chapter 40

Somewhere north-northeast above Los Angeles, I was getting sore, so I asked Tracy if she'd let up for a minute. This is another lifetime ago.

With a big hank of white spit looped between my knob and her lower lip, her whole face hot and flushed from choking, still holding my sore dog in her fist, Tracy settles back on her heels and says how in the Kama Sutra, it tells you to make your lips really red by wiping them with sweat from the testicles of a white stallion.

"For real," she says.

Now there's a weird taste in my mouth, and I look hard at her lips, her lips and my dog the same big purple color. I say, "You don't do that stuff, do you?"

The doorknob rattles and we both look, fast, to make sure it's locked.

This is that first time, what every addiction is about getting back to. That first time that no subsequent time is ever as good as.

Nothing's worse than when a little kid opens the door. What's next worst is when some man throws open the door and doesn't understand. Even if you're still alone, when a kid opens the door you have to, fast, cross your legs. Pretend it's all an accident. An adult guy might slam the door, might yell, "Lock it next time, ya moron," but he's still the only one blushing.

After that, what's worse, Tracy says, is being a woman the Kama Sutra would call an elephant woman. Especially if you're with what they call a hare man.

This animal thing refers to genital size.

Then she says, "I didn't mean that to sound the way it did."

The wrong person opens the door, and you're in their nightmares all week.

Your best defense is unless somebody is on the make, no matter who opens the door and sees you sitting there, they always assume it's their mistake. Their fault.

I always did. I used to walk in on women or men riding the toilet on airplanes on trains or Greyhound buses or in those little single-seat either/or unisex restaurant bathrooms, I'd open the door to see some stranger sitting there, some blonde all blue eyes and teeth with a ring through her navel and wearing high heels, with her g-string stretched down between her knees and the rest of her clothes and bra folded on the little counter next to the sink. Every time this happened I'd always wonder, *why the hell don't people bother to lock the door?*

As if this ever happens by accident.

Nothing on the circuit happens by accident.

It could be, on the train somewhere between home and work, you'll open a bathroom door to find some brunette, with her hair pinned up and only her long earrings trembling down alongside her smooth white neck, and she's just sitting inside with the bottom half of her clothes on the floor. Her blouse open with nothing inside but her hands cupped under each breast, her fingernails, her lips, her nipples all the same cross between brown and red. Her legs as smooth white as her neck, smooth as a car you could drive two hundred miles an hour, and her hair the same brunette all over, and she licks her lips.

You slam the door and say, "Sorry."

And from somewhere deep inside, she says, "Don't be."

And she still doesn't lock the door. The little sign still saying: Vacant.

How this happens is I used to fly round-trip from the East Coast to Los Angeles when I was still in the medical program at USC. During breaks in the school year. Six times I opened the door on the same yoga redhead naked from the waist down with her skinny legs pulled up cross-legged on the toilet seat, filing her nails with the scratch pad of a matchbook, as if she's trying to catch herself on fire, wearing just a silky blouse knotted over her breasts, and six times she looks down at her freckled pink self with the road crew orange rug around it, then her eyes the same gray as tin metal look up at me, slow, and every time says, "If you don't mind," she says, "I'm in here."

Six times, I slam the door in her face.

All I can think to say is, "Don't you speak English?"

Six times.

This all takes less than a minute. There isn't time to think.

But it happens more and more often.

Some other trip, maybe cruising altitude between Los Angeles and Seattle, you'll open the door on some surfer blond with both tanned hands wrapped around the big purple dog between his legs, and Mr. Kewl shakes the stringy hair off his eyes, points his dog, squeezed shiny wet inside a glossy rubber, he points this straight at you and says, "Hey, man, make the time. . . ."

It gets to be, every time you go to the bathroom, the little sign says vacant, but it's always somebody.

Another woman, two knuckles deep and disappearing into herself.

A different man, his four inches dancing between his thumb and forefinger, primed and ready to cough up the little white soldiers.

You begin to wonder, just what do they mean by *vacant*.

Even in an empty bathroom, you find the smell of spermicidal foam. The paper towels are always used up. You'll see the print of a bare foot on the bathroom mirror, six feet up, near the top of the mirror, the little arched print of a woman's foot, the five round spots left by her toes, and you'd wonder, *what happened here?*

Like with coded public announcements, "The Blue Danube Waltz" or Nurse Flamingo, you wonder, *what's going on?*

You wonder, *what aren't they telling us?*

You'll see a smear of lipstick on the wall, down almost to the floor, and you can only imagine what was going on. There's the dried white stripes from the last pull-out moment when somebody's dog tossed his white soldiers against the plastic wall.

Some flights the walls will still be wet to the touch, the mirror fogged. The carpet sticky. The sink drain is sucked full, choked with every color of little curled hair. On the bathroom counter, next to the sink, is the perfect round outline in jelly, contraceptive jelly and mucus, of where somebody set her diaphragm. Some flights, there's two or three different sizes of perfect round outlines.

These are the domestic leg of longer flights, transpacific or flights over the pole. Ten-to-sixteen-hour flights. Direct flights, Los Angeles to Paris. Or from anywhere to Sydney.

My Los Angeles trip number seven, the yoga redhead whips her skirt off the floor and hurries out after me. Still zipping herself up in the back, she trails me all the way to my seat and sits next to me, saying, "If your goal is to hurt my feelings, you could give lessons."

She's got this shining soap opera kind of hairdo, only now her blouse is buttoned with a big floppy bow in the front and everything, pinned down with a big jewelry brooch.

You say it again, "Sorry."

This is westbound, somewhere north-northwest above Atlanta.

"Listen," she says, "I work just too hard to take this kind of shit. You hear me?"

You say, "I'm sorry."

"I'm on the road three weeks out of every month," she says. "I'm paying for a house I never see . . . soccer camp for my kids . . . just the cost of my dad's nursing home is incredible. Don't I deserve something? I'm not bad-looking. The least you can do is not shut the door in my face."

This is really what she says.

She ducks down to put her face between me and the magazine I'm pretending to read. "Don't make like you don't know," she says. "It's not like sex is anything secret."

And I say, "Sex?"

And she puts a hand over her mouth and sits back.

She says, "Oh, gosh, I'm so sorry. I just thought . . ." and reaches up to push the little red stewardess button.

A flight attendant comes past, and the redhead orders two double bourbons.

I say, "I hope you're planning to drink them both."

And she says, "Actually, they're both for you."

This would be my first time. That first time that no subsequent time is ever as good as.

"Don't let's fight," she says and gives me her cool white hand. "I'm Tracy."

A better place this could've happened is a Lockheed TriStar 500 with its strip mall of five large bathrooms isolated in the rear of the tourist-class cabin. Spacious. Soundproof. Behind everybody's back where they can't see who comes and goes.

Compared to that, you have to wonder what kind of animal designed the Boeing 747–400, where it seems every bathroom opens onto a seat. For any real discretion, you have to trek back to the toilets in the back of the rear tourist cabin. Forget the single lower-level sidewall bathroom in business class unless you want everybody to know what you've got going.

It's simple.

If you're a guy, how it works is you sit in the bathroom with your Uncle Charlie whipped out, you know, the big red panda, and you work him up to parade attention, you know, the full upright position, and then you just wait in your little plastic room and hope for the best.

Think of it as fishing.

If you're Catholic, it's the same feeling as sitting in a confessional. The waiting, the release, the redemption.

Think of it as catch-and-release fishing. What people call "sport fishing."

The other way how it works is you just open doors until you find something you like. It's the same as the old game show where whatever door you choose, that's the prize you take home. It's the same as the lady and the tiger.

Behind some doors, it's somebody expensive back from first class for some slumming, a little cabin-class rough trade. Less chance she'll meet anybody she knows. Behind other doors, you'll get some aged beef with his brown tie thrown back over one shoulder, his hairy knees spread against the wall on each side, petting his leathery dead snake and then he says, "Sorry bud, nothing personal."

Those times, you'll be too grossed even to say, "As if."

Or, "In *your* dreams, buddy."

Still, the reward rate is just great enough to keep you pushing your luck.

The tiny space, the toilet, two hundred strangers just a few inches away, it's so exciting. The lack of room to maneuver, it helps if you're double-jointed. Use your imagination. Some creativity and a few simple stretching exercises and you can be knock, knock, knockin' on heaven's door. You'll be amazed how fast the time flies.

Half the thrill is the challenge. The danger and risk.

So, it's not the Great American West or the race to the South Pole or being the first man to walk on the moon.

It's a different kind of space exploration.

You're mapping a different kind of wilderness. Your own vast interior landscape.

It's the last frontier to conquer, other people, strangers, the jungle of their arms and legs, hair and skin, the smells and moans that is everybody you haven't done. The great unknowns. The last forest to devastate. Here's everything you've only imagined.

You're Chris Columbus sailing over the horizon.

You're the first caveman to risk eating an oyster. Maybe this *particular* oyster isn't new, but it's new to you.

Suspended in the nowhere, in the halfway fourteen hours between Heathrow and Jo-burg, you can have ten true-life adventures. Twelve if the movie's bad. More if the flight's full, less if there's turbulence. More if you don't mind a guy's mouth doing the job, less if you return to your seat during meal service.

What's not so great about that first time is, when I'm drunk and first getting bounced on by the redhead, by Tracy, what happens is we hit an air pocket. Me gripping the toilet seat, I drop with the plane, but Tracy's blasted off, champagne popping off me with the rubber still inside, hitting the plastic ceiling with her hair. My trigger goes the same instant, and my gob's suspended in the air, weightless hanging white soldiers in the midway between her still against the ceiling and me still on the can. Then slam, we come back together, her and the rubber, me and my gob, planted back down on me, reassembled pop-beads-style, all one-hundred-plus pounds of her.

After those kind of good times, it's a wonder I'm not wearing a truss.

And Tracy laughs and says, "I love it when that happens!"

After that, just normal turbulence bounces her hair in my face, her nipples against my mouth. Bounces the pearls around her neck. The gold chain around my neck. Juggles my dice in their sack, pulled up tight over the empty bowl.

Here and there, you pick up little tips to improve your performance. Those old French Super Caravelles for example, with their triangular windows and real curtains, they have no first-class toilet, only two in the back of tourist, so you'd best not try anything fancy. Your basic Indian tantric position works okay. Both

252

of you standing face to face, the woman lifts one leg along the side of your thigh. You go at it the same as in "splitting the reed" or the classic flanquette. Write your own Kama Sutra. Make stuff up.

Go ahead. You know you want to.

This is assuming the two of you are anywhere close to the same height. Otherwise, I can't be blamed for what happens.

And don't expect to get spoon-fed here. I'm assuming some basic knowledge on your part.

Even if you're stuck on a Boeing 757–200, even in the tiny forward toilet, you can still manage a modified Chinese position where you're sitting on the toilet and the woman settles onto you facing away.

Somewhere north-northeast above Little Rock, Tracy tells me, "*Pompoir* would make this a snap. It's when Albanian women just milk you with their constrictor vaginae muscles."

They jerk you off with just their insides?

Tracy says, "Yeah."

Albanian women?

"Yeah."

I say, "Do they have an airline?"

Something else you learn is when a flight attendant comes knocking, you can wrap things up fast with the Florentine Method, where the woman grips the man around the base and pulls his skin back, tight, to make it more sensitive. This speeds up the process considerably.

To slow things down, press hard on the underside at the base of the man. Even if this doesn't stop the event, the whole mess will back up into his bladder and save you both a lot of cleanup. Experts call this "Saxonus."

The redhead and me, in the big rear bathroom of a McDonnell Douglas DC-10 Series 30CF, she shows me the negresse position, where she gets her knees up on either side of the sink and I press my open hands on the back of her pale shoulders.

Her breath fogging the mirror, her face red from being crouched down, Tracy says, "It's in the Kama Sutra that if a man massages himself with juice from pomegranate, pumpkin, and cucumber seeds, he'll swell up and stay huge for six months."

This advice has a kind of Cinderella deadline to it.

She sees the look on my face in the mirror and says, "Cripes, don't take everything so personally."

Somewhere due north above Dallas, I'm trying to work up more spit while she tells me the way to make a woman never leave you is to cover her head with nettle thorns and monkey dung.

And I'm, like, no kidding?

And if you bathe your wife in buffalo milk and cow bile, any man who uses her will become impotent.

I say, I wouldn't be surprised.

If a woman soaks a camel bone in marigold juice and puts the liquid on her eyelashes, any man she looks at will become bewitched. In a pinch, you can use peacock, falcon, or vulture bones.

"Look it up," she says. "It's all in the big book."

Somewhere south-southeast above Albuquerque, my face coated thick as egg white from licking her, my cheeks rug-burned from her hair, Tracy says how ram's testicles boiled in sugared milk will restore your virility.

Then she says, "I didn't mean that the way it sounded."

And I thought I was doing pretty good. Considering two double bourbons, and I've been on my feet for three hours at this point.

Somewhere south-southwest above Las Vegas, both of us our

tired legs flu-shaky, she shows me what the Kama Sutra calls "browsing." Then "sucking the mango." Then "devouring."

Struggling together in our tight little wipe-clean plastic room, suspended in a time and place where anything goes, this isn't bondage, but it's close.

Gone are the golden old Lockheed Super Constellations where each port and starboard bathroom was a two-room suite: a dressing room with a separate toilet room behind a door.

The sweat running down the smooth muscles of her. The two of us bucking together, two perfect machines doing a job we're designed for. Some minutes we're touching with just the sliding part of me and the little edges of her getting raw and pulled out, my shoulders leaning back squared against the plastic wall, the rest of me bucking forward from the waist down. From standing on the floor, Tracy gets one foot up on the edge of the sink and leans on her raised knee.

It's easier to see ourselves in the mirror, flat and behind glass, a movie, a download, a magazine picture, somebody else, not us, somebody beautiful without a life or a future outside this moment.

Your best bet on a Boeing 767 is the large center toilet in the rear of the tourist-class cabin. You're just plum out of luck on the Concorde, where the toilet compartments are minuscule, but that's just my opinion. If all you're doing is peeing or doing your contact lenses or tooth brushing, I'm sure they're roomy enough.

But if you have any ambition to manage what the Kama Sutra calls "the crow" or "cuissade" or anything where you'll need more than two inches of back-and-forth motion, you'd better hope you get a European Airbus 300/310 with its party-sized rear tourist-class toilets. For the same kind of countertop space and legroom, you can't do better than the two rear toilets in a British Aerospace One-Eleven for plush.

Somewhere north-northeast above Los Angeles, I'm getting sore, so I ask Tracy to let up.

And I say, "Why do you do this?"

And she says, "What?"

This.

And Tracy smiles.

The people you meet behind unlocked doors are tired of talking about the weather. These are people tired of safety. These people have remodeled too many houses. These are tanned people who've given up smoking and white sugar and salt, fat, and beef. They're people who've watched their parents and grandparents study and work for a lifetime only to end up losing it all. Spending everything just to stay alive on a feeding tube. Forgetting even how to chew and swallow.

"My father was a doctor," Tracy says. "The place where he's at now, he can't even remember his own name."

These men and women sitting behind unlocked doors know a bigger house is not the answer. Neither is a better spouse, more money, tighter skin.

"Anything you can acquire," she says, "is only another thing you'll lose."

The answer is there is no answer.

For real, this is a way heavy moment.

"No," I say and run a finger between her thighs. "I meant *this*. Why do you shave your bush?"

"Oh, that," she says and rolls her eyes, smiling. "It's so I can wear g-string panties."

While I settle on the toilet, Tracy's examining the mirror, not seeing herself as much as checking what's left of her makeup, and with one wet finger she wipes away the smudged edge of her lipstick. With her fingers, she rubs away the little bite marks around her nipples. What the Kama Sutra would call Scattered Clouds.

Talking to the mirror, she says, "The reason I do the circuit is because, when you think about it, there's no good reason to do anything,"

There is no point.

These are people who don't want an orgasm as much as they just want to forget. Everything. For just two minutes, ten minutes, twenty, a half hour.

Or maybe when people are treated like cattle, that's how they act. Or maybe that's just an excuse. Maybe they're just bored. It could be that nobody's made to sit all day in a cramped packing crate full of other people without moving a muscle.

"We're healthy, young, awake and alive people," Tracy says. "When you look at it, which act is more unnatural?"

She's putting back on her blouse, rolling her pantyhose back up.

"Why do I do anything?" she says. "I'm educated enough to talk myself out of any plan. To deconstruct any fantasy. Explain away any goal. I'm so smart I can negate any dream."

Me still sitting here naked and tired, the flight crew announces our descent, our approach into the greater Los Angeles area, then the current time and temperature, then information about connecting flights.

And for a moment, this woman and I just stand and listen, looking up at nothing.

"I do this, *this,* because it feels good," she says and buttons her blouse. "Maybe I don't really know why I do it. In a way, this is why they execute killers. Because once you've crossed some lines, you just keep crossing them."

Both hands behind her back, zipping up her skirt, she says, "The truth is I don't really *want* to know why I do casual sex. I just keep doing," she says, "because the minute you give yourself a good reason, you'll start chipping away at it."

She steps back into her shoes and pats her hair on the sides and says, "Please don't think this was anything special."

Unlocking the door, she says, "Relax." She says, "Someday, everything we just did will look like small potatoes to you."

Edging out into the passenger cabin, she says, "Today is just the first time you've crossed this particular line." Leaving me naked and alone, she says, "Don't forget to lock the door behind me." Then she laughs and says, "That's if you want it locked anymore."

Chapter 41

The front desk girl doesn't want any coffee.

She doesn't want to go check on her car in the parking lot.

She says, "If anything happens to my car, I'll know who to blame."

And I tell her, shhhhhhhhh.

I tell her I hear something important, a gas leak or a baby crying somewhere.

It's my mom's voice, muffled and tired, coming over the intercom speaker from some unknown room.

Standing at the desk in the lobby of St. Anthony's, we listen, and my mom says, "The slogan for America is 'Not Good Enough.' Nothing's ever fast enough. Nothing's big enough. We're never satisfied. We're always improving . . ."

The front desk girl says, "I don't hear any gas leak."

The faint, tired voice says, "I spent my life attacking everything because I was too afraid to risk creating anything . . ."

And the front desk girl cuts it off. She presses the microphone and says, "Nurse Remington to the front desk. Nurse Remington to the front desk, immediately."

The fat security guard with his chest pocket full of pens.

But when she lets go of the microphone, the intercom voice comes on again, faint and whispery.

"Nothing was ever good enough," my mom says, "so here at the end of my life, I'm left with nothing . . ."

And her voice fades away.

There's nothing left. Only white noise. Static.

And now she's going to die.

Unless there's a miracle.

The guard blows through the security doors, looking at the front desk girl, asking, "So? What's the situation here?"

And on the monitor, in grainy black-and-white, she points at me bent double with the ache in my guts, me carrying my swollen gut around in both hands, and she says, "Him."

She says, "This man needs to be restricted from the property, starting right now."

Chapter 42

How it showed up on the news last night was just me shouting, waving my arms in front of the camera, with Denny a little ways behind me, working to set a rock in a wall, and Beth just a little behind him, hammering a boulder into dust, trying to carve a statue.

On TV, I'm jaundiced yellow, hunchbacked from the swell and weight of my guts coming apart on the inside. Bent over, I'm lifting my face to look into the camera, my neck looping from my head down into my collar. My neck as thin as an arm, my

Adam's apple sticks out as big as an elbow. This is yesterday right after work, so I'm still wearing my Colonial Dunsboro blousey linen shirt and my britches. With the buckle shoes and the cravat, this doesn't help.

"Dude," Denny says, sitting next to Beth at Beth's apartment while we watch ourselves on TV. He says, "You don't look so hot."

I look like that dumpy Tarzan from my fourth step, the one bent over with the monkey and the roasted chestnuts. The tubby savior with his beatific smile. The hero with nothing left to hide.

On TV, all I was trying to do was explain to everybody that there was no controversy. I was trying to convince people that I'd started the mess by calling the city and saying I lived nearby and some nutcase was building without a permit, I didn't know what. And the worksite posed a hazard to area children. And the guy doing the work didn't look too savory. And it was no doubt a Satanic church.

Then I'd called them at the TV station and said the same stuff.

And that's how this all started.

The part about how I did all this just to make Denny need me, well, I didn't explain that part. Not on television.

For real, all my explanation got left on the cutting-room floor because on TV, I'm just this sweaty bloated maniac trying to put my hand over the camera lens, yelling at the reporter to go away and swatting my other hand at the microphone boom that swings through the shot.

"Dude," Denny says.

Beth videotaped my little fossilized moment, and we watch it over and over.

Denny says, "Dude, you look possessed by the devil or something."

Really, I'm possessed by a whole different deity. This is me trying to make good. I'm trying to work some little miracles so I can build up to the big stuff.

Sitting here with a thermometer in my mouth, I check and it says 101 degrees. The sweat keeps juicing out of me, and to Beth I say, "I'm sorry about your sofa."

Beth takes the thermometer for a look, then puts her cool hand on my forehead.

And I say, "I'm sorry I used to think you were a stupid airhead bimbo."

Being Jesus means being honest.

And Beth says, "That's okay." She says, "I never cared what you thought. Only Denny." She shakes the thermometer and slips it back under my tongue.

Denny rewinds the tape, and there I am, again.

Tonight, my arms ache and my hands are soft and raw from working with the lime in the mortar. To Denny, I say, so how does it feel to be famous?

Behind me on television, the walls of rock rise and swell round into the base for a tower. Other walls rise around gaps for windows. Through a wide doorway, you can see a wide flight of stairs rising inside. Other walls trail off to suggest the foundations for other wings, other towers, other cloisters, colonnades, raised pools, sunken courtyards.

The voice of the reporter is asking, "This structure you're building, is it a house?"

And I say we don't know.

"Is it a church of some kind?"

We don't know.

The reporter leans into the shot, a man with brown hair combed into one fixed swell above his forehead. He tilts his hand-held microphone toward my mouth, asking, "What are you building, then?"

We won't know until the very last rock is set.

"But when will that be?"

We don't know.

After so long living alone, it feels good to say "we."

Watching me say this, Denny points at the TV and says, "Perfect."

Denny says, the longer we can keep building, the longer we can keep creating, the more will be possible. The longer we can tolerate being incomplete. Delay gratification.

Consider the idea of Tantric Architecture.

On TV, I tell the reporter, "This is about a process. This isn't about getting something done."

What's funny is I really think I'm helping Denny.

Every rock is a day Denny doesn't waste. Smooth river granite. Blocky dark basalt. Every rock is a little tombstone, a little monument to each day where the work most people do just evaporates or expires or becomes instantly outdated the moment it's done. I don't mention this stuff to the reporter, or ask him what happens to his work the moment after it goes out on the air. Airs. Is broadcast. Evaporates. Gets erased. In a world where we work on paper, where we exercise on machines, where time and effort and money passes from us with so little to show for it, Denny gluing rocks together seems normal.

I don't tell the reporter all that.

There I am, just waving and saying we need more rocks. If people will bring us rocks, we'd appreciate it. If people want to help, that would be great. My hair stiff and dark with sweat, my belly bloated over the front of my pants, I'm saying the only thing we don't know is how this will turn out. And what's more is we don't want to know.

Beth goes into the kitchenette to pop popcorn.

I'm starving but I don't dare eat.

On TV is the final shot of the walls, the bases for a long loggia of columns that will rise to a roof, someday. Pedestals for statues. Someday. Basins for fountains. The walls rise to suggest buttresses, gables, spires, domes. Arches rise to support vaults someday. Turrets. Someday. The bushes and trees are already growing in to hide and bury some of it. Branches grow in through the windows. The grass and weeds grow waist-high in some rooms. All of this spreading away from the camera, here's just a foundation we may none of us see completed in our lifetime.

I don't tell the reporter that.

From outside the shot, you can hear the cameraman shout, "Hey, Victor! Remember me? From the Chez Buffet? That time you almost choked . . ."

The telephone rings and Beth goes to get it.

"Dude," Denny says, and rewinds the tape again. "What you just told them, that's just going to drive some people crazy."

And Beth says, "Victor, it's your mom's hospital. They've been trying to find you."

I yell back, "In a minute."

I tell Denny to run the tape again. I'm almost ready to deal with my mom.

Chapter 43

For my next miracle, I buy pudding. This is chocolate pudding, vanilla and pistachio pudding, butterscotch pudding, all of it loaded with fat and sugar and preservatives and sealed inside little plastic tubs. You just peel off the paper top and spoon it up.

Preservatives is what she needs. The more preservatives, I figure, the better.

A whole shopping bag full of puddings in my arms, I go to St. Anthony's.

It's so early the girl isn't at her desk in the lobby.

Sunk in her bed, my mom looks up from inside her eyes and says, "Who?"

It's me, I say.

And she says, "Victor? Is it you?"

And I say, "Yeah, I think so."

Paige isn't around. Nobody's around, it's so early on a Saturday morning. The sun's just coming in through the blinds. Even the television in the dayroom is quiet. Mom's roommate, Mrs. Novak the undresser, is curled on her side in the next bed, asleep, so I whisper.

I peel the top off the first chocolate pudding and find a plastic spoon in the shopping bag. With a chair pulled up beside her bed, I lift the first spoonful of pudding and tell her, "I'm here to save you."

I tell her I finally know the truth about myself. That I was born a good person. A manifestation of perfect love. That I can be good, again, but I have to start small. The spoon slips between her lips and leaves the first fifty calories inside.

With the next spoonful, I tell her, "I know what you had to do to get me."

The pudding just sits there, brown and glistening on her tongue. Her eyes blink, fast, and her tongue sweeps the pudding into her cheeks so she can say, "Oh, Victor, you know?"

Spooning the next fifty calories into her mouth, I say, "Don't be embarrassed. Just swallow."

Through the muck of chocolate, she says, "I can't stop thinking what I did is terrible."

"You gave me life," I say.

And turning her head away from the next spoonful, away from me, she says, "I needed United States citizenship."

The stolen foreskin. The relic.

I say that doesn't matter.

267

Reaching around, I spoon more into her mouth.

What Denny says is that maybe the second coming of Christ isn't something God will decide. Maybe God left it up to people to develop the ability to bring back Christ into their lives. Maybe God wanted us to invent our own savior when we were ready. When we need it most. Denny says maybe it's up to us to create our own messiah.

To save ourselves.

Another fifty calories go into her mouth.

Maybe with every little effort, we can work up to performing miracles.

Another spoonful of brown goes into her mouth.

She turns back to me, her wrinkles squeezing her eyes narrow. Her tongue sweeps pudding into her cheeks. Chocolate pudding wells out the corners of her mouth. And she says, "What the hell are you talking about?"

And I say, "I know that I'm Jesus Christ."

Her eyes fall open wide, and I spoon in more pudding.

"I know you came from Italy already impregnated with the sacred foreskin."

More pudding into her mouth.

"I know you wrote this all in Italian in your diary so I wouldn't read it."

More pudding into her mouth.

And I say, "Now I know my true nature. That I'm a loving caring person."

More pudding goes into her mouth.

"And I know I can save you," I say.

My mom, she just looks at me. Her eyes filled with total infinite understanding and compassion, she says, "What the fuck are you getting at?"

She says, "I stole you out of a stroller in Waterloo, Iowa. I wanted to save you from the kind of life you'd get."

Parenthood being the opiate of the masses.

See also: Denny with his baby stroller full of stolen sandstone.

She says, "I kidnapped you."

The poor deluded, demented thing, she doesn't know what she's saying.

I spoon in another fifty calories.

"It's okay," I tell her. "Dr. Marshall read your diary and told me the truth."

I spoon in more brown pudding.

Her mouth stretches open to speak, and I spoon in more pudding.

Her eyes bulge and tears slide down the sides of her face.

"It's okay. I forgive you," I tell her. "I love you, and I'm here to save you."

With another spoonful halfway to her mouth, I say, "All you have to do is swallow this."

Her chest heaves, and brown pudding bubbles out her nose. Her eyes roll back. Her skin, it's getting bluish. Her chest heaves again.

And I say, "Mom?"

Her hands and arms tremble, and her head arches back deeper into her pillow. Her chest heaves, and the mouthful of brown muck sucks back into her throat.

Her face and hands are more blue. Her eyes rolled over white. Everything smells like chocolate.

I press the nurse call button.

I tell her, "Don't panic."

I tell her, *"I'm sorry. I'm sorry. I'm sorry. I'm sorry . . ."*

Heaving and flopping, her hands clawing at her throat. This is how I must look choking in public.

Then Dr. Marshall's standing on the other side of her bed, with one hand tilting my mom's head back. With her other hand, she scoops pudding out of her mouth. To me, Paige says, "What's happened?"

I was trying to save her. She was delusional. She doesn't remember I'm the messiah. I'm here to save her.

Paige leans over and breathes into my mom. She stands again. She breathes into my mom's mouth again, and each time she stands there's more brown pudding smeared around Paige's mouth. More chocolate. The smell is everything we breathe.

Still holding a cup of pudding in one hand and the spoon in the other, I say, "It's okay. I can do this. Just like with Lazarus," I say. "I've done this before."

And I spread my hands open against her heaving chest.

I say, "Ida Mancini. I command you to live."

Paige looks up at me between breaths, her face smeared with brown. She says, "There's been a little misunderstanding."

And I say, "Ida Mancini, you are whole and well."

Paige leans over the bed and spreads her hands next to mine. She presses with all her strength, again and again and again. Heart massage.

And I say, "That's really not necessary." I say, "I *am* the Christ."

And Paige whispers, "Breathe! Breathe, damn it!"

And from somewhere higher up on Paige's forearm, somewhere tucked high up her sleeve, a plastic patient bracelet falls down to around Paige's hand.

It's then all the heaving, the flopping, the clawing and gasping, everything, it's right then when everything stops.

"Widower" isn't the right word, but it's the first word that comes to mind.

Chapter 44

My mother's dead. My mom's dead, and Paige Marshall is a lunatic. Everything she told me she made up. Including the idea that I'm, oh I can't even say it: Him. Including that she loves me.

Okay, likes me.

Including that I'm a natural-born nice person. I'm not.

And if motherhood is the new God, the only thing sacred we have left, then I've killed God.

It's jamais vu. The French opposite of déjà vu where everybody is a stranger no matter how well you think you know them.

Me, all I can do is go to work and stagger around Colonial Dunsboro, reliving the past again and again in my mind. Smelling the chocolate pudding smeared on my fingers. I'm stuck in the moment when my mom's heart stopped heaving and the sealed plastic bracelet proved Paige was an inmate. Paige, not my mom, was the deluded one.

I was the deluded one.

At that moment, Paige looked up from the chocolate mess smeared all over the bed. She looked at me and said, "Run. Go. Just get out."

See also: "The Blue Danube Waltz."

Staring at her bracelet was everything I could do.

Paige came around the bed to grab my arm and said, "Let them think I did this." She dragged me to the doorway, saying, "Let them think she did it to herself." She looked up and down the hallway and said, "I'll wipe your prints off the spoon and put it in her hand. I'll tell people you left the pudding with her yesterday."

As we pass doors, they all snap locked. It's from her bracelet.

Paige points me to an outside door and says she can't go any closer or it won't open for me.

She says, "You were not here today. Got it?"

She said a lot of other stuff, but none of it counts.

I'm not loved. I'm not a beautiful soul. I'm not a good-natured, giving person. I'm not anybody's savior.

All of that's bogus now that she's insane.

"I just murdered her," I say.

The woman who just died, who I just smothered in chocolate, she wasn't even my mother.

"It was an accident," Paige says.

And I say, "How can I be sure of that?"

Behind me, as I stepped outside, somebody must have found

272

the body, because they kept announcing, "Nurse Remington to Room 158. Nurse Remington, please come immediately to Room 158."

I'm not even Italian.

I'm an orphan.

I stagger around Colonial Dunsboro with the birth-deformed chickens, the drug-addicted citizens, and the field-trip kids who think this mess has anything to do with the real past. There's no way you can get the past right. You can pretend. You can delude yourself, but you can't re-create what's over.

The stocks in the middle of the town square are empty. Ursula leads a milk cow past me, both of them smelling like dope smoke. Even the cow's eyes are dilated and bloodshot.

Here, it's always the same day, every day, and there should be some comfort in that. The same as those television shows where the same people are trapped on the same desert island for season after season and never age or get rescued, they just wear more makeup.

This is the rest of your life.

A herd of fourth-graders run by, screaming. Behind them's a man and a woman. The man's holding a yellow notebook, and he says, "Are you Victor Mancini?"

The woman says, "That's him."

And the man holds the notebook up and says, "Is this yours?"

It's my fourth step from the sexaholics group, my complete and ruthless moral inventory of myself. The diary of my sex life. All my sins accounted for.

And the woman says, "So?" To the man with the notebook, she says, "Arrest him, already."

The man says, "Do you know a resident of the St. Anthony's Constant Care Center named Eva Muehler?"

Eva the squirrel. She must've seen me this morning, and she's told them what I did. I killed my mom. Okay, not my mom. That old woman.

The man says, "Victor Mancini, you're under arrest for suspicion of rape."

The girl with the fantasy. It must be she filed charges. The girl with the pink silk bed I ruined. Gwen.

"Hey," I say. "She wanted me to rape her. It was her idea."

And the woman says, "He's lying. That's my mother he's bad-mouthing."

The man starts reciting the Miranda deal. My rights.

And I say, "Gwen's your *mother?*"

Just by her skin, you can tell this woman's older than Gwen by ten years.

Today, the whole world must be deluded.

And the woman shouts, "*Eva Muehler* is my mother! And she says you held her down and told her it was a secret game."

That's it. "Oh, her," I say. I say, "I thought you meant this *other* rape."

The man stops in the middle of his Miranda deal and says, "Are you even listening to your rights, here?"

It's all in the yellow notebook, I tell them. What I did. It was just me accepting responsibility for every sin in the world. "You see," I say, "for a while, I really did think I was Jesus Christ."

From behind his back, the man snaps out a pair of handcuffs.

The woman says, "Any man who would rape a ninety-year-old woman has to be crazy."

I make a nasty face and tell her, "No kidding."

And she says, "Oh, so now you're saying my mother's not attractive?"

And the man snaps the cuffs around one of my hands. He turns me around and snaps my hands together behind my back

274

and says, "How about we go somewhere and straighten this all out?"

In front of all the losers of Colonial Dunsboro, in front of the druggies and the crippled chickens and the kids who think they're getting an education and His Lord High Charlie the Colonial Governor, I'm arrested. It's the same as Denny in the stocks, but for real.

And in another sense, I want to tell them all not to think they're any different.

Around here, everybody's arrested.

Chapter 45

The minute before I left St. Anthony's for the last time, the minute before I was out the door and running, Paige tried to explain.

Yes, she was a doctor. Talking in a rush, her words crowded together. Yes, she was a patient committed here. Clicking and unclicking her ballpoint pen, fast. She was really a doctor of genetics, and she was only a patient here because she'd told the truth. She wasn't trying to hurt me. Pudding still smeared around her mouth. She was just trying to do her job.

In the hallway, during our last moment together, Paige pulled my sleeve so I'd have to look at her, and she said, "You have to believe this."

Her eyes were bulging so the whites showed all around the iris, and the little black brain of her hair was coming loose.

She was a doctor, she said, a specialist in genetics. From the year 2556. And she'd traveled back in time to become impregnated by a typical male of this period in history. So she could preserve and document a genetic sampling, she said. They needed the sample to help cure a plague. In the year 2556. This wasn't a cheap and easy trip. Traveling in time was the equivalent of what space travel is for humans now, she said. It was a chancy, expensive gamble, and unless she came back impregnated with an intact fetus, any future missions would be canceled.

Here in my 1734 costume, bent double with my impacted bowels, I'm still stuck on her idea of a *typical male*.

"I'm only locked in here because I told people the truth about myself," she says. "You were the only available reproductive male."

Oh, I say, that makes this all *lots* better. Now everything makes perfect sense.

She just wanted me to know that, tonight, she was to be recalled to the year 2556. This would be the last time we'd ever see each other, and she just wanted me to know that she was grateful.

"I'm profoundly grateful," she said. "And I do love you."

And standing there in the hallway, in the strong light from the sun rising outside the windows, I took a black felt-tipped pen from the chest pocket of her lab coat.

The way she stood with her shadow falling on the wall behind her for the last time, I started to trace her outline.

And Paige Marshall said, "What's that for?"

It's how art was invented.

And I said, "Just in case. It's just in case you're not crazy."

Chapter 46

In most twelve-step recovery programs, the fourth step makes you write a complete and relentless story of your life as an addict. Every lame, suck-ass moment of your life, you have to get a notebook and write it down. A complete inventory of your crimes. That way it's always in your head. Then you have to fix it all. This goes for alcoholics, drug abusers, and overeaters as well as sex addicts.

This way you can go back and review the worst of your life anytime you want.

Still, those who remember the past aren't necessarily any better off.

My yellow notebook, in here is everything about me, seized with a search warrant. About Paige and Denny and Beth. Nico and Leeza and Tanya. The detectives read through it, sitting across a big wood table from me in a locked soundproof room. One wall is a mirror, for sure with a video camera behind it.

And the detectives ask me, what was I hoping to accomplish by admitting to other people's crimes?

They ask me, what was I trying to do?

To complete the past, I tell them.

All night, they read my inventory and ask me, what does all this mean?

Nurse Flamingo. Dr. Blaze. "The Blue Danube Waltz."

What we say when we can't tell the truth. What anything means anymore, I don't know.

The police detectives ask if I know the whereabouts of a patient named Paige Marshall. She's wanted for questioning about the apparent smothering death of a patient named Ida Mancini. My apparent mother.

Miss Marshall disappeared last night from a locked ward. There's no visible signs of forced escape. No witnesses. Nothing. She's just vanished.

The staff at St. Anthony's were humoring her in the delusion, the police tell me, that she was a real doctor. They let her wear an old lab coat. It made her more cooperative.

The staff say she and I were pretty chummy.

"Not really," I say. "I mean, I saw her around, but I didn't really know anything about her."

The detectives tell me I don't have a lot of friends among the nursing staff.

See also: Clare, RN.

See also: Pearl, CNA.

See also: Colonial Dunsboro.

See also: The sexaholics.

I don't ask if they've bothered checking for Paige Marshall in the year 2556.

Digging in my pocket, I find a dime. I swallow it, and it goes down.

In my pocket, I find a paper clip. But it goes down, too.

While the detectives look through my mom's red diary, I look around for anything larger. Something too large to swallow.

I've been choking to death for years. By now this should be easy.

After a knock on the door, they bring in a dinner tray. A hamburger on a plate. A napkin. A bottle of ketchup. The backup in my guts, the swelling and pain, make it so I'm starving, but I can't eat.

They ask me, "What's all this in the diary?"

I open the hamburger. I open the bottle of ketchup. I need to eat to survive, but I'm so full of my own shit.

It's Italian, I tell them.

Still reading, the detectives ask, "What's this stuff that looks like maps? All these pages of drawings?"

It's funny, but I'd forgot all that. Those are maps. Maps I did when I was a little boy, a stupid, gullible little shit. You see, my mom told me that I could reinvent the whole world. That I had that kind of power. That I didn't have to accept the world the way it stood, all property-lined and micromanaged. I could make it anything I wanted.

That's how crazy she was.

And I believed her.

And I slip the cap from the bottle of ketchup into my mouth. And I swallow.

In the next instant, my legs snap straight so fast my chair flies over behind me. My hands go to gripping around my throat. I'm on my feet and gaping at the painted ceiling, my eyes rolled back. My chin stretches out away from my face.

Already the detectives are half out of their seats.

From not breathing, the veins in my neck swell. My face gets red, gets hot. Sweat springs up on my forehead. Sweat blots through the back of my shirt. With my hands, I hold tight around my neck.

Because I can't save anybody, not as a doctor, not as a son. And because I can't save anybody, I can't save myself.

Because now I'm an orphan. I'm unemployed and unloved. Because my guts hurt, and I'm dying anyway, from the inside out.

Because you have to plan your getaway.

Because after you've crossed some lines, you just keep crossing them.

And there's no escaping from constant escape. Distracting ourselves. Avoiding confrontation. Getting past the moment. Jacking off. Television. Denial.

The detectives look up from the diary, and one says, "Don't panic. It's like it says in the yellow notebook. He's just faking it."

They stand and watch me.

My hands around my throat, I can't draw any air. The stupid little boy who cried wolf.

Like that woman with her throat full of chocolate. The woman not his mommy.

For the first time in longer than I can remember, I feel peaceful. Not happy. Not sad. Not anxious. Not horny. Just all the higher parts of my brain closing up shop. The cerebral cortex. The cerebellum. That's where my problem is.

I'm simplifying myself.

Somewhere balanced in the perfect middle between happiness and sadness.

Because sponges never have a bad day.

Chapter 47

One morning the school bus pulled up to the curb, and while his foster mother stood waving, the stupid little boy got on. He was the only passenger, and the bus blew past the school at sixty miles per hour. The bus driver was the Mommy.

This was the last time that she came back to claim him.

Sitting behind the huge steering wheel and looking up at him in the visor mirror, she said, "You'd be amazed how easy it is to rent one of these."

She turned into an on-ramp for the freeway and said, "This

gives us a good six hours head start before the bus company reports this crate stolen."

The bus rolled down onto the freeway, and the city rolled by outside, and after there wasn't a house every second, the Mommy told him to come sit up next to her. She took a red diary from a bag of stuff and took out a map, all folded.

With one hand, the Mommy shook the map open across the steering wheel, and with her other hand she unrolled her window. She worked the steering wheel with her knees. With just her eyes, she looked back and forth between the road and the map.

Then she crumpled the map and fed it out the window.

The whole time, the stupid boy just sat there.

She said to get the red diary.

When he tried to give it, she said, "No. Open it to the next page." She said to find a pen in the glove compartment and fast, because there was a river coming up.

The road cut through everything, all the houses and farms and trees, and in a moment they were on a bridge going across a river that went off forever on both sides of the bus.

"Quick," the Mommy said. "Draw the river."

As if he'd just discovered this river, as if he'd just discovered the whole world, she said to draw a new map, a map of the world just for himself. His own personal world.

"I don't want you to just accept the world as it's given," she said.

She said, "I want you to invent it. I want you to have that skill. To create your own reality. Your own set of laws. I want to try and teach you that."

The boy had a pen now, and she said to draw the river in the book. Draw the river, and draw the mountains up ahead. And name them, she said. Not with words he already knew, but to make up new words that didn't already mean a bunch of other stuff.

To create his own symbols.

The little boy thought with the pen in his mouth and the book open in his lap, and after a little, he drew it all.

And what's stupid is, the little boy forgot all this. It wasn't until years later that the police detectives found this map. That he remembered he did this. That he could do this. He had this power.

And the Mommy looked at his map in the rearview mirror and said, "Perfect." She looked at her watch, and her foot pressed down, and they went faster, and she said, "Now write it in the book. Draw the river on our new map. And get ready, there's lots more stuff that needs a name coming up."

She said, "Because the only frontier left is the world of intangibles, ideas, stories, music, art."

She said, "Because nothing is as perfect as you can imagine it."

She said, "Because I won't always be around to nag you."

But the truth is, the kid didn't want to be responsible for himself, for his world. The truth is, the stupid little shit was already planning to make a scene in the next restaurant, to get the Mommy arrested and out of his life forever. Because he was tired of adventure, and he thought his precious, boring, stupid life would just go on and on forever.

He was already choosing between safety, security, contentment, and her.

Driving the bus with her knees, the Mommy reached over and squeezed his shoulder and said, "What do you want for lunch?"

And as if it was just an innocent answer, the little boy said, "Corn dogs."

Chapter 48

In another minute, the arms come around me from behind. Some police detective is hugging me tight, double-fisting me under the rib cage, breathing into my ear, "Breathe! Breathe, damn it!"

Breathing into my ear, "You're okay."

Two arms hug me, lift me off my feet, and a stranger whispers, "You're going to be fine."

Periabdominal pressure.

Somebody pounds me on the back the way a doctor pounds a newborn baby, and I let fly with the bottle cap. My bowels burst loose down my pant leg with the two rubber balls and all the shit piled up behind them.

My entire private life made public.

Nothing left to hide.

The monkey and the chestnuts.

In the next second, I'm collapsed on the floor. I'm sobbing while someone tells me how everything is all right. I'm alive. They saved me. I almost died. They hold my head to their chest and rock me, saying, "Just relax."

They put a glass of water to my lips and say, "Hush."

They say it's all over.

Chapter 49

Mobbed around Denny's castle are a thousand people I can't re-member, but who will never forget me.

It's almost midnight. Stinking and orphaned and unem-ployed and unloved, I pick my way through the crowd until I get to Denny, standing in the middle, and I say, "Dude."

And Denny goes, "Dude." Watching the mob of people hold-ing rocks.

He says, "You should definitely not be here right now."

After we were on TV, all day Denny says, all these smiling

people keep turning up with rocks. Beautiful rocks. Rocks like you won't believe. Quarried granite and ashlar basalt. Dressed blocks of sandstone and limestone. They come one by one, bringing mortar and shovels and trowels.

They all ask, each of them, "Where's Victor?"

This is so many people they filled the block so nobody could get any work done. They all wanted to give me their stone in person. All these men and women, they've all been asking Denny and Beth if I'm doing okay.

They say I looked really terrible on television.

All it will take is one person to brag about being a hero. Being a savior, and how he'd saved Victor's life in a restaurant.

Saved *my* life.

The term "powder keg" pretty much nails it.

Out on the edge of things, some hero's got everybody talking. Even in the dark, you can see the revelation ripple through the crowd. It's the invisible line between the people still smiling and the people not.

Between everybody who's still a hero and the people who know the truth.

And everybody stripped of their proudest moment, they start looking around. All these people reduced from saviors to fools in an instant, they're going a little nuts.

"You need to scram, dude," Denny says.

The crowd is so thick you can't see Denny's work, the columns and walls, the statues and stairways. And somebody shouts, "Where's Victor?"

And someone else shouts, "Give us Victor Mancini!"

And for sure, I deserve this. A firing squad. My whole overextended family.

Someone turns on the headlights of some car, and I'm spotlighted against a wall.

My shadow looming horrible over all of us.

Me, the deluded little rube who thought you could ever earn enough, know enough, own enough, run fast enough, hide well enough. Fuck enough.

Between me and the headlights are the outlines of a thousand faceless people. All the people who thought they loved me. Who thought they'd given me back my life. The legend of their lives, evaporated. Then one hand comes up with a rock, and I close my eyes.

From not breathing, the veins in my neck swell. My face gets red, gets hot.

Something thuds at my feet. A rock. Another rock thuds. A dozen more. A hundred more thuds. Rocks crash and the ground shakes. Rocks crumble together around me and everyone's shouting.

It's the martyrdom of Saint Me.

My eyes closed and watering, the headlights shine red through my eyelids, through my own flesh and blood. My eye juice.

More thuds against the ground. The ground quakes and people scream with effort. More shaking and crashing. More swearing. And then everything gets quiet.

To Denny I say, "Dude."

Still with my eyes closed, I sniff and say, "Tell me what's happening."

And something soft and cotton and not very clean-smelling closes around my nose, and Denny says, "Blow, dude."

And then everybody's gone. Almost everybody.

Denny's castle, the walls are pulled down, the rocks busted and rolled away from how hard they fell. The columns are toppled. The colonnades. The pedestals thrown over. The statues, smashed. Busted rock and mortar, rubble fills the courtyards, fills the fountains. Even the trees are splintered and flattened down under the fallen rock. The battered stairways lead to nowhere.

Beth sits on a rock, looking at a busted statue that Denny made of her. Not how she looked for real, but how she looked to him. As beautiful as he thinks. Perfect. Busted, now.

I ask, earthquake?

And Denny says, "You're close, but this was some other kind of act of God."

There wasn't one stone on top of another.

Denny sniffs and says, "You smell like crap, dude."

I'm not supposed to leave town until further notice, I tell him. The police asked me.

Outlined in the headlights is just one last person. Just a hunched black silhouette until the headlights veer off, the parked car drives away.

In the moonlight, we look, Denny and Beth and I, to see who's still here.

It's Paige Marshall. Her white lab coat smudged and the sleeves rolled up. The plastic bracelet around her wrist. Her deck shoes are wet and squishing.

Denny steps forward and tells her, "I'm sorry, but there's been a gross misunderstanding."

And I tell him, no, it's cool. It's not what he thinks.

Paige steps closer and says, "Well, I'm still here." Her black hair is all undone, the little black brain of her bun. Her eyes all swollen and red all around them, she sniffs and shrugs and says. "I guess that means I'm insane."

We all look down at the scattered rocks, just rocks, just some brown lumps of nothing special.

One leg of my pants is wet with shit and still sticking to my leg on the inside, and I say, "Well." I say, "I guess I'm not saving anybody."

"Yeah, well." Paige holds up her hand and says, "You think you can get this bracelet off me?"

I say, yeah. We can try.

Denny is kicking through the fallen rock, rolling rocks with his foot until he stoops to pick one up. Then Beth goes to help him.

Paige and I just look at each other, at who each other is for real. For the first time.

We can spend our lives letting the world tell us who we are. Sane or insane. Saints or sex addicts. Heros or victims. Letting history tell us how good or bad we are.

Letting our past decide our future.

Or we can decide for ourselves.

And maybe it's our job to invent something better.

In the trees, a mourning dove calls. It must be midnight.

And Denny says, "Hey, we could use some help here."

Paige goes, and I go. The four of us dig with our hands under the edge of the rock. In the dark, the feeling is rough and cold and takes forever, and all of us together, we struggle to just put one rock on top of another.

"You know that ancient Greek girl?" Paige says.

Who drew the outline of her lost lover? I say, yeah.

And she says, "You know that eventually she just forgot him and invented wallpaper."

It's creepy, but here we are, the Pilgrims, the crackpots of our time, trying to establish our own alternate reality. To build a world out of rocks and chaos.

What it's going to be, I don't know.

Even after all that rushing around, where we've ended up is the middle of nowhere in the middle of the night.

And maybe knowing isn't the point.

Where we're standing right now, in the ruins in the dark, what we build could be anything.